D0711254

ALSO BY BRYONY PEARCE

Angel's Fury

BRYONY PEARCE

The WEIGHT of SOULS

STRANGE
CHEMISTRY

STRANGE CHEMISTRY
An Angry Robot imprint
and a member of the Osprey Group

Lace Market House
54-56 High Pavement
Nottingham NG1 1HW
UK

www.strangechemistrybooks.com
Strange Chemistry #14

A Strange Chemistry paperback original 2013
1

A catalogue record for this book is available
from the British Library.

ISBN: 978 1 90884 463 7
eBook ISBN: 978 1 90884 465 1

Cover art by Steven Wood

For my not so ugly sisters,
Claire McCarthy, Ros Taylor and Gill Fourie

By hook or by crook you'll be first in this book

"*Deep into that darkness peering, long I stood there wondering, fearing,*
Doubting, dreaming dreams no mortal ever dared to dream before."

Edgar Allen Poe, The Raven

1

It's coming to take you away

Dead men take me to the nicest places.

I pulled my hood further over my eyes and glowered at the block of flats. Stained net curtains billowed from otherwise bare windows and, on half the balconies, shirts and greying underwear were hanging out to dry. My bones thrummed with a deep bass that seemed to boom through the tarmac itself; the music actually came through an open window on the ground floor.

It was twilight but the streetlights hadn't yet lit. Most of them were smashed. On my way through the estate I'd walked through shards of glass like crackling bird bones. The car park was lit by a burning trash can and acrid smoke stung tears from my eyes. I shifted further from the drifting ash without taking my eyes from the third floor flat I was staking out.

The wall in front of me was daubed with graffiti: slogans, gang signs and a portrait of a dark-eyed boy with a date beneath his shoulders. But I wasn't here for

9

Cayden's killers; human justice had taken care of them and Cayden ought to be at rest.

I turned my eyes back to the flat I was watching and clenched my fist around the Mark the dead man had pressed onto my hand. It wouldn't be long now before I could pass it on to his killers. Evening had fallen and, like a pack of wolves, the gang members would be drawn outside by the gibbous moon, ready for my own form of retribution.

"Jesus loves you. It's not too late to change. Repent." The wild-haired white man with the sandwich-board was standing on the corner at the other side of the lot. His cries had been providing an urgent counterpoint to the gangsta rap that rattled the concrete slabs of the flats.

"Repent, ye sinners." He shouted one last time and shook his fist as the door to the flats banged open.

Then he clutched his sandwich board around himself and ran.

As he disappeared round the corner I returned my gaze to the emerging gang.

"You packing, Shawn?" The voice carried across the lot.

"Course, Jay. You said we got *plans* tonight." A whip-thin gang member opened his jacket to flash a Magnum and I swallowed. This was going to be harder than I'd thought.

I wondered if I had time to wait till tomorrow and do the job in the daylight, but I'd been wearing the dead man's Mark for nearly two weeks already. Mum's voice blew through my head like the wind.

"If the touch of a ghost leaves a stain on your skin, you must avenge their death. Track down their killer and transfer the Mark to them, but do it quickly because the Mark is a beacon for the Darkness and if you wear it too long, it may come for you."

The gang were here now and I didn't have time to wait. I straightened and started forwards.

The smallest member of the gang spotted me. Suggestively he adjusted the crotch of his baggy jeans. "Hey, look, it's Lucy Liu, innit? Come for some real man, Lucy Liu?"

He couldn't have been much older than I was and I had to suppress an explosion of laughter that would probably have killed me.

Heart pounding, I stopped. My toes were inches from the trainers of the oldest gang member, who didn't look far into his twenties. Jay, they'd called him.

His friends closed around me.

"It's them. The one who killed me has a scar through his right eyebrow."

The dead man who had been shadowing me drifted forward. I tilted my head meaningfully. Every member of the gang was sporting the double whammy of cap and hood pulled low over their eyes. I couldn't tell who I was looking for. On a few occasions I'd seen the Darkness actually come for the killers I'd Marked, and I had no intention of sending it after an innocent.

"It was him. The biggest one." The dead man was murmuring under his breath, as though they'd be able to hear him.

I realised I had been holding my breath and exhaled. Then I held out my hand hoping the gang leader would shake; it was the easiest way of transferring the Mark and most of my victims really did fall for it.

Jay snorted. "Where d'you think you are? Buckingham Palace?"

His crew nudged each other and instead of shaking my hand Jay raised my palm to his lips and kissed it. "There you go, princess."

The boys to my left whistled and the skinny one to my right massaged his crotch again. I smiled tightly as Jay lifted his head and revealed the black stain that now covered his lips; the Mark that had just doomed him to the Darkness.

I snatched my hand away and stole a glance at the palm. It was clean.

"You need to get out of here."

I suppressed a groan. Dead men, masters of the obvious.

"So, Lucy Liu, what d'you want with the Streatham Crew?" Jay smiled with his blackened mouth and I shuddered. As the night continued to bleach the world of colour he looked more and more like a wolf who had just lifted its head from a deer's gut.

I brought up one of my stock tales. "I'm looking for a guy named Dan Brown."

"Dan Brown." The one called Shawn squared up. "You think we know someone called," he raised his voice two or three social classes, "Dan Brown."

I took a step backwards trying to make it looked natural. "He's a friend. He ran away from home.

Someone said he might have been seen around here and I was told you guys knew everyone, so–"

"Hold up, Shawn." Jay pushed his cap up to reveal a scar. A weight lifted from my chest. I had Marked the right guy. "We ain't seen no 'Dan Brown'. But why don't you leave your number? If we hear something I can call you."

I cleared my throat. Leaving my phone number wasn't a great idea. On the other hand if I didn't...

"Sure." I forced my voice into an eager tone, grateful for his help. "Should I programme it into your phone?" I held out my hand and Jay leaned in so close his breath coated my face. My nose filled with the smell of too much aftershave and my eyes went to the Mark that pulsed across his lips. For a moment the gang held its breath then Jay laughed and pulled an iPhone from his pocket.

"Here then, girlie – gimme your number."

With fingers that felt like sticks I fumbled with the unfamiliar operating system then pinned on a semi-flirtatious smile as I handed the phone back. "I've put it under 'Lucy'."

Jay nodded and, with his eyes on mine, flicked through his contacts. "Got your number," he said in a tone that crackled with menace.

"Yeah." I took a backwards step and a dog howled in the distance. "I'd better go. Thanks." The crew watched me retreat until I reached a rusted Toyota Corolla boosted up on some bricks. I was steeling myself to turn my back on the pack when quiet dropped like a guillotine and cut the howling dog off mid-note.

I clapped my hands over my ears as the air pressure built. When it came the Darkness brought not only the absence of light, but also of sound. It was as though its deadly arrival bent the rules of our world.

"Something ain't right, Jay." Shawn's voice carried through the quiet as he fiddled with his baseball cap. Suddenly the shadows cast by the smoking trash can started to grow.

Jay spotted the moving Darkness and jumped back but, with startling suddenness, it rose into a looming column and he stumbled.

Like a coward I squeezed my eyes shut, unable to watch, as screams rent the air. They were oddly muffled as if they came from a distant television rather than the five gang members.

Then three loud bangs penetrated the blanket of silence. The one called Shawn was using his gun. I ducked quickly behind the car and left the dead man standing in the centre of the car park, avidly scrutinising the action. Jay started running, inadvertently drawing the Darkness away from his posse.

It seeped across the derelict space like an ink spill, blotting out everything it covered, and its advance was unhurried as though it knew its prey couldn't escape.

Then my heart thudded. Jay was running towards *me*.

"Did you do this?" he screamed.

I leaped to my feet, but he caught me in a second. He grabbed my upper arms and swung me round.

"What is it?"

Like acid eating away the world and revealing nothing beneath, the monstrous Darkness inched forwards. I'd never seen it this close before; never taken the risk. "It's the Darkness," I whispered. "It's coming to take you away."

"Take me where, bitch?"

"I don't know. I've never seen what happens after."

"Make it stop."

I shook my head. "I can't."

"What d'you mean *can't*?" he snarled. "Crazy bitch. Call. It. Off."

"I don't know how," I whispered.

The Darkness reached us and I was trapped. Then, as if I was standing on a rock, the tide split in two and flowed around my feet. Hypnotised, I turned my head.

Against my back the rise and fall of Jay's chest halted; he was holding his breath. The Darkness seemed to withdraw for a second, and then it struck. Jay's nails scrabbled at the fine skin of my throat and I cried out as, with a terrifying jerky speed, Jay was sucked into the Darkness as if he'd never been.

Fear-sweat stuck my hair to my head and my heart hammered so hard I thought my ribs would break. Trembling, I stared into the void.

The Darkness appeared to pulsate, forming a hole from our universe into another, blacker plane. The harder I stared, the less I could see. Inside, lights seemed to flash, but it was just the nerves firing in my straining eyes. There was no sign of Jay, no sign of anything at all. Not for the first time, I wondered what happened to those I'd Marked.

After an age of staring the adrenaline washed out of my limbs and I started to sway. The Darkness hadn't advanced so I tried a backwards step. When it did not follow I turned and ran.

"Thank you." The lawyer who'd dragged me into this was behind me once more. When I stopped he leaned under the single working streetlamp. He cast no shadow.

"You're satisfied? Justice has been done?"

He nodded and his lined face sagged. "I'm sorry I had to involve you. I didn't realise you'd be so young. I'd have left you alone, but it was hard to track you down and I didn't know if I'd be able to find someone else with your gift."

"Whatever. You got your justice. You can go now, can't you?"

"I can."

"So go."

The street light shone between his open fingers and, as I watched, it penetrated the flesh. Gradually the lawyer faded like a photograph left in the sun until there was nothing left but the night breeze.

2

The gang's all here

Outside the train station two rowdy groups were passing drinks around and getting ready to party. Their noise made me stop in the light puddling beneath a neon sign.

Maybe I should go for the night bus instead.

I grimaced at the bus stop. Streatham Common to Shepherds Bush was three changes and it would take me almost an hour and a half. Shivering, I pulled my jacket closer. It wasn't that cold, but my sweat was drying in the cool air and my skin was prickling. The idea of slumping into a seat on the over-ground and switching off till Clapham Junction was appealing.

I started towards the station but two steps out of the light I stopped with the shadows pressing against me. She was standing on the edge of the largest group of girls, trying to look like she fitted in.

She almost made it.

The group were dressed for clubbing and, all around her, bare legs protruded from short skirts. The girl's skirt

17

was short but it was pastel pink, her blouse had little flowers on it and she had a blue cardigan round her waist. She was dressed for a summer picnic, not a night out.

The girl was pretty and she looked sweet; a bit like Hannah. I wanted to believe that she was tagging along with a group that weren't quite her friends, that there was a good reason she'd got the dress code so wrong.

I took a step towards a BT phone box, leaned against the grey curve of plastic and kept my eyes on her. She leaned towards whoever was speaking and laughed in all the right places. But the other girls together made a single organism, constantly touching or hugging, shoving one another, patting a friend's hair back into place, adjusting a neckline or shirt. *She* was careful not to come into contact with any of the others and she did no touching of her own.

A final partygoer ran along the street, laughing breathlessly. "I'm late, I'm late, I'm sorry."

The group milled for one more moment then they all reached in their bags for their Oyster cards and moved into the station, boys and girls merging as they went.

This girl had no bag. That clinched it for me.

I took a step backwards but the dead girl offered no sign that she was aware of my presence and continued to drift with the laughing group towards the turnstiles. It was possible she didn't know I was there. Sometimes I saw the newly dead… but what she was wearing told me she hadn't died that recently. Maybe she was hanging around a particular person, a sister or best friend, watching over them or something.

I didn't take my eyes off her.

The last of the group disappeared through the turnstiles. If she was waiting for me she wouldn't follow them in.

The girl's shoulders twitched and she hesitated. It was as if she was conflicted about walking through the gate without paying. Then she straightened, stepped away from the turnstile and turned to face me.

Our gazes clashed for a moment. Her face was pathetically full of hope.

I ran.

I knew she was after me. I could hear her light sandals clacking on the pavement.

I pounded past the bus stop, but where was I running to? Hastily I palmed my Oyster card. If I could circle back to the station, I might be able to jump on a train before she caught up.

Each breath already had a sharp edge to it and I had to press a fist into my side as I sprinted for the corner. Ghosts didn't have to breathe; on foot she'd outlast me.

"You alright, love?" A middle aged man held his arm out, but I barged past.

"Sorry," I gasped.

Then the growl and hiss of a labouring engine made me raise my head. A double-decker lumbered round the corner glowing like Christmas and it was a Routemaster with an open rear.

A whoop whistled out of me and I hurled myself towards the road. As the bus passed, I reached for the pole, leaped and swung myself on board.

Immediately I turned. The dead girl was only two steps behind. Quickly I lifted my hand out of her reach, but kept contact with the metal pole. She grinned and reached out, already jumping towards me.

As her hand went straight through the metal her eyes widened. So, she was new enough not to have known about that. Or maybe she was just stupid.

She hit the floor with her chest, her feet dragged on the road and she scrabbled desperately, trying to get the rest of her body onto the bus.

I crouched just out of her reach and looked at her in silence.

"Please," she begged. "I know you can help me." She stretched out her hand, as though I'd take it.

I watched her without moving until she lost her grip.

"That was dangerous, young lady."

I turned with my heart in my throat.

It wasn't another ghost but the bus conductor, glaring at me with rancid disapproval.

"You don't know the half of it." I showed him my card and he gestured to an empty seat.

"You should wait at a bus stop, like everyone else. If you'd been run over who'd be blamed?"

I nodded and mumbled apologies as I made my way down the aisle. A quick glance in the mirror at the bottom of the stairs revealed three passengers on the top deck. I wondered about going up to check that they too were among the living, but the conductor frowned at me.

"Sit down, or I'll have to ask you to get off at the next stop."

I sighed and compromised by choosing one of the seats in the disabled area, so I couldn't be pinned in place. Then I slumped onto the chair, crossed my arms, pulled my hood over my hair and leaned my head on the window.

Ten minutes towards Brixton the bus pulled into a crowded stop. My shoulders tensed and I prepared to jump for the exit if I had to.

"Oh Gawd, look who it is."

The familiar drawl penetrated my eardrums like a dental drill. It was Tamsin Harper, she of the faux US accent, the fake blonde hair and the fluffy angora jumpers.

I blinked. *What was* she *doing on the night bus in this part of town?*

She wasn't alone.

Great. The gang's all here. Tamsin, Justin, James, Harley and Pete. Lions and tigers, bitches and bears, oh my.

Tamsin leaned into her boyfriend's chest, giving him a primo view down the front of her gaping trench coat. His eyes glazed for a moment, then flickered up to meet mine.

For a moment there seemed to be something deeper than the usual disdain in the rich brown of them, and I pictured him as I always secretly saw him, a Victorian poet dumped into the wrong era. Justin was almost, but not quite, too thin; his uniform always clean and pressed, but not like a dork, more like he was too cool to bother to mess with it. Even when he was quietly directing the rest of the gang, he had a sprawling air. He always looked as if he was leaning on something, even if he wasn't.

For a moment he looked almost pleased to see me. Then his mouth assumed its familiar curl and his long fingers brushed Tamsin's wrist. "So who picked the 118?" he laughed. "Did you know she'd be here, Petey? You trying to tell us something?" And there it was, tacit permission given to his cronies. I was fair game.

"She who?" Pete's newly bald head bobbed from the centre of the pack. He'd been laughing with Harley but now he stopped and stared. "What're you doing here?"

I grit my teeth. "Minding my own business, *Petey*."

"Whatever." Pete gave Justin a nudge. "C'mon, man, pick a seat, I gotta take a load off."

As Justin steered Tamsin towards the stairs, I relaxed. Then Tamsin glanced back and pursed her lips like an evil kiss. She pulled Justin to a stop. "Actually, I want to sit down here." She led the way to the back of the bottom deck, watching me over her shoulder; a cat anticipating a cream-filled mouse. She hadn't finished with me yet.

Harley's voice tore my eyes away from her. "Awright, Chickety China." He leered at me from beneath his heavily gelled ringlets, shoved past Pete and loped after the loved-up couple.

But when Pete tried to follow him a thick forearm barred the way: James.

Justin led the group and Tamsin was nastiest but James was the most dangerous. I'd fought with him since I caught him pulling the legs off crane flies when we were nine years old. For some reason though, the teachers loved him. With his blond hair and blue eyes, I suppose he appeared to be a good guy.

I exhaled with deliberate calm as my eyes raked the fine hairs on his exposed wrist and stopped on the edge of a tattoo. Despite myself I tilted my head trying to see the whole thing. It looked like a letter "V".

"New tattoo? You still trying to be cool, Jimbo?" My voice shook slightly, betraying my nerves only to Pete who knew me almost better than anyone else. His eyes widened in a silent warning to back down and take whatever James was planning to dish out. It was the single concession he'd give me. Whatever James did, Pete would fall in line, it was one of the reasons we were no longer close.

But James seemed to ignore my comment. He shifted to address Pete, even as his eyes continued to burn into mine.

"You should stay here with your girlfriend, *Petey*."

I glared into James' dead orbs. His hair caught the orange light, setting his head on fire as he gave Pete a shove. "Why don't you give her a kiss?"

Pete cannoned into my arm and I jerked as if burned. Pete jumped back just as violently. "Cut it out," he growled and he rubbed his arm where it had touched me. James just grinned and planted himself in the aisle.

"You're not getting past till you give her a kiss, Petrol Pete."

A giggle from the back of the bus caught my attention. Tamsin was leaning forward, red lips parted in an excited exclamation. Justin was trying to regain her attention, but to her, it seemed, he no longer existed.

Trapped by my seat Pete avoided my eyes. Invisible red ants crawled over me as I played my part and forced myself to pretend he wasn't standing there and that we'd never meant anything to each other.

Finally the bus lurched into motion.

"Do it, Pete, I dare you." Tamsin was laughing out loud now.

"Kiss, kiss," Harley was chanting. Pete's mahogany skin glowed with mortification.

James sneered. Then I jerked as he caught my hood and yanked it back. One big hand curled around the back of my neck and forced my face up to the light. I tried to reach back and dislodge him, but the seat was in the way. I squirmed, but he started to squeeze and I stopped moving. Beneath James' jock facade simmering violence bubbled and I was in too vulnerable a position to knock off his veneer. So I held myself still, trying not to feel like a pinned bug.

He examined me as I glared, turning my face with pressure on my carotid and in the sensitive dip above my collar bone.

"She's pig ugly, Pete," James leered. "But I have seen worse. Don't worry, we won't tell anyone at school." Involuntarily I shuddered and he grinned. He forced me to lift off my seat, pulled my head back and slanted it towards Pete. I clenched my fists, refusing to look at my former friend with anything like pleading.

Dog-like pants moistened my forehead as James leaned in, excited. He narrowed his eyes at Pete. "Do it," he snapped.

Pete shuffled and glowered downwards as if the situation was my fault. "C'mon, man, let's just sit down."

"Not till you give her a proper snog." James shook me. "Loosen her up a bit."

"It's not going to happen. Let it go." I spoke through gritted teeth.

Pete tried to edge past again, but James planted his feet and blocked the aisle. "Maybe I should do it, then, what d'you reckon?" He inspected me more closely, moving his face towards mine with slow deliberation.

"Anything that goes near my mouth gets bitten." I showed my teeth hoping, pointlessly, that Pete would step in before things went too far.

Then James' grip loosened and he looked up. I followed his gaze.

"I think you kids should sit down." The conductor was fiddling nervously with his belt, but his jaw was set in a firm line.

Immediately James released me and started to slide into the seat behind mine.

"Not there." The conductor looked at me, then back at my tormentor. "You can sit at the back with the kids you got on with."

James gave his adults-only smile and reached to pat my shoulder. "Hey, no worries, mate. We're friends from school. Aren't we, China?" His nails dug into my collar bone.

"Actually," I turned, wide-eyed, "I've never seen them before."

"Right." The conductor exhaled. "Look, I'm not having trouble on this bus. Either you move to the back, son, or you get off." He leaned on the seat opposite. "And I'll be staying right here until the young lady reaches her stop."

James moved his hand from my seat and leaned back. He stared the conductor out for an uncomfortable minute.

"James, what's taking so long?" Justin's arm was around Tamsin's shoulder and he was stretched out on the back seat, apparently relaxed, but his eyes were steady on us. "We've got stuff to discuss. You're holding us up, man."

Finally James sucked air between his teeth, a long hiss of displeasure, then he stood. With a final smirk at the conductor he trailed his fingers along the back of my seat. "See you at school, China." Then he bent to put his mouth against my ear. "You'd have liked it," he whispered.

The conductor jerked his head and James held his hands up and loped up the bus. Tamsin giggled excitedly as he sat next to her.

Pete followed, with relief in the set of his spine.

The conductor watched until they were settled, then he sat down himself.

"Thanks," I muttered and he nodded.

Gratefully I huddled into my hoodie, counting down the minutes until I could change buses.

When the Routemaster reached my stop, the conductor waved me off. My shoulder blades itched as the vehicle drew away and I turned. James was standing at the back, watching me. As the bus drew away the streetlights set his eyes on fire. The otherworldly glow pursued me until Justin appeared behind him and tugged him back down.

I shivered and pulled my hoodie close. I couldn't waste any more time on James. I was still an hour from home and there was a city full of the dead to avoid.

3

They aren't ghosts, they're hallucinations

As I dragged myself round the corner of our road, my limbs felt like china, fragile with fatigue. The only thing that kept me moving was the knowledge that I would soon be in bed.

But halfway down the street I realised the lights in our flat were on. *No way.* I checked my watch. If Dad was waiting up, it was because he wanted to talk to me.

I sighed so deeply my chest hurt and moved into the light cast by the living room window. Movement inside told me that Dad had seen my approach. I glanced at his chair-lift, considered it briefly then climbed the stairs slowly as an old woman.

"Where've you been?"

"You know where." I kept my back to him as I peeled off my hoodie and hung it by the door. There was a small rip in the arm. I didn't even remember doing it. His silence pricked at me. I shook my hair out till it brushed my shoulders, then turned round. I held up my hands to show him the unblemished palms.

"No black mark. So you're well at the moment. No hallucinations?"

"They're not–" I stopped and shook my head. "I'm fine."

He held up a syringe. "I need another sample."

"Why now?" I wrapped suddenly aching arms around myself.

"Cameron suggested your blood may change when you're ill. I need to take a sample now and when the blackness next appears so I can compare them."

"You've got loads of samples."

"I don't know which are from when the illness has hold of you." He frowned and rolled forward in his wheelchair. "Don't be difficult, Taylor."

I took a step backwards. "Can't we do this in the morning?"

"You don't know when the stain will next appear."

"The ghosts can't come into the house, Mum made sure of that. I'll be fine in the morning."

"There's no such thing as ghosts." He stopped his advance and I stared down at his greying hair and bloodshot eyes. He looked as tired as I felt. "You know how I feel about you going out after so-called killers. The only reason I've let you up till now, is that you don't seem to be doing anything dangerous and after you've done it you feel better for a while. But I'm beginning to think this thing you do is feeding your illness, not improving it."

I stared at his serious frown. "What are you saying?"

"I don't think you should go out like this any more."

My cheeks went cold. "You remember what happened last time you kept me in? How dark the Mark got?"

"Yes, and I know your mother told you this *Darkness* would come for you, but this story she fed you – it's only a *story*."

"It isn't."

"Maybe you need to *let* the Darkness come. Cameron says it could be a psychological symptom of the cure that you don't really want."

"*Dad*. You met this guy in a chat room."

He set his jaw. "I don't want you doing this any more."

I licked my lips. "How are you going to stop me?" My voice was so quiet he had to roll nearer to hear.

When he worked out what I'd said, his wheelchair wobbled. Then his face reddened and stubble stood out on his cheeks like shadows. "As long as you live under my roof, you'll do as I say."

I shook my head. "I do as you say. I give you sample after sample." I pulled my sleeves up until he could see the livid bruises inside my elbows. "I don't dare get changed with the others for games in case they think these are track marks."

Dad closed his eyes briefly and his fist tightened around the syringe in his hand.

"I took those anti-psychotic medications you found on the Internet." I shuddered and choked into silence as the memories slid up, blurred as if Vaselined, vague and full of holes. Memories of being so dazed that I could barely identify the ghosts that Marked me.

"I know *that* prescription made you worse–"

"*No*, Dad. I'm not taking anything else. I'm not giving up the only thing that makes it better. I'm not going to let you do this to me." He opened his mouth but I bulldozed over him. "I know you're trying to find a cure but you can't stop me avenging the dead."

"You enjoy it," he spat. "Cameron's right, you want this illness. It makes you feel close to your mother."

I gasped and for a moment we gaped at each other.

"You believe that?" I whispered.

"I… I don't know." His hands dropped to his lap.

"You think I *enjoy* this?" Suddenly tiredness stole my voice. I couldn't fight any more.

Pete's face floated in front of mine, his expression a match of the one from earlier, revealing his disgust at my touch. Swiftly I closed my eyes, banishing the cruel reminder of our lost friendship. We'd been close once, before Mum had died. Back then I was top of my class at school and I had a life. Now what was I? A soon-to-be drop out. A social leper who spent more time with the dead than the living. A freakish embarrassment to the people who had once cared about me.

I had one friend left, Hannah, and I had no idea how long it would be before she tired of my strangeness. One day I'd lose everything. I had no future and it hurt to think about my past. What was the point of talking about how much I hated my life?

I held out my arm. "Take your sample. I'm going to bed."

Dad shook his head. "Not here. In the study."

He turned his wheelchair awkwardly in the narrow hallway and rolled swiftly ahead of me, as if afraid I'd suddenly change my mind.

Dad pushed open the door and gestured me past him. Inside, the room looked more like a lab than ever. The only thing of Mum's I could see was the book that I secretly called *The Tale of Oh-Fa*. She had first read it to me when I'd started seeing ghosts, then every night after that for two years. It was the diary of one of my ancestors, a recount of his experiences on a doomed archaeological dig in Egypt, translated into English by his granddaughter. A true account of where our curse came from.

Dad had taken it away from me after the accident, but by then I had it memorised anyway, just as, I suppose, Mum had intended. Initially the story had squatted like a toad in the back of my mind, but now I was grateful for every twisted word. Through them I could hear Mum's voice and feel her hand over mine.

Sit me in front of an exam paper and my mind can go blank, yet *The Tale of Oh-Fa*, unseen for three years, clung to my memory with an unshakable grip.

I barely had to think about it and the words were there, describing the moment my ancestor sold our family out. The pages were always ready to appear in front of me, every word etched in the sound of her voice:

"*Greatest of the Lords of Death, forgive me.*"

In tones like rolling thunder a voice, unsuited to its jackal's muzzle, spoke. "*Last of the grave robbers.*"

I gabbled a desperate apology as the Lord's tongue flicked his canines. "*Your aura carries death. Your baby is trying to be born, but your wife can push no longer.*"

"*Can you save them?*" *I could hardly believe I was asking a boon of the beast.*

"*I will send aid to your wife and child, but you will serve me. The child birthing as we speak will serve me. Her children will serve me. Their children will be mine.*"

Visions of my newborn daughter filled my head. Perhaps I could trade my own soul, but not that of my child. "*Yours, Lord?*"

"*I will gift you with the power to see those in need of justice. You will track down the unrighteous and send them into the Darkness – to me.*"

A hole opened a hand's span from my outstretched arm. In it my eyes perceived the glimmer of gold. To my shame I could not drag my gaze away. "*Yours if you pledge yourself to me.*"

Of course he made the pledge. The promise of treasure was enough to push him towards the decision he secretly wanted to make. Facing a monster, who would really choose to die in order to save a bunch of children that hadn't even been born?

And so he doomed us all. My mother, my grandmother, great grandmother, endless cousins and second cousins, the list went on. If I had children of my own, they would likely suffer the same fate, driven to insanity and early death.

Now the book was open; Dad must have been reading it for some reason. I couldn't see which page he had been looking at so I glanced away from the memories it brought. It hurt to think of Mum and her ancestor's legacy of death.

"You've got new equipment." I nodded dully at the large microscope that stood at the back of the room.

"I know you hate this, Taylor." Dad rolled closer. "I know you think things would be different if your mother was still here. But this thing you have, it's a genetic condition and if I can't cure you, maybe I can make it so you can have kids without passing that particular gene on."

I stared at him. "You think I want kids?"

His eyes widened. "Don't you?"

Laughter bubbled up, until I vibrated like the chandelier in the hallway. "Who'd have kids with *me*?"

Dad looked sadly at his wasted legs. "You're a beautiful girl, one day you'll fall in love."

I snorted. "Yeah, then maybe the guy will ask me out, I'll run out on him because there's a ghost he can't see and that'll be the end of it. Give it up, Dad. I'm not falling in love with some guy who thinks I'm crazy, not like Mum did."

The words spilled out before I could stop them, and as soon as they tainted the air, I wished I could take them back. Dad's face whitened.

"What did you say?"

"Dad, I–"

"You know nothing about your mum and me."

I straightened. "You think I don't remember? You tried to make her go into a hospital because you thought she was a nut-job. You tried to stop her teaching me how to deal with this." I waved my newly empty palms. "You never believed her, not for one minute. I don't know why she never left you."

Dad's fists gripped the arms of his chair so tightly I could hear the creak of metal.

"She'd never have left–"

"That's true, if she left, she'd have lost me, you'd have made sure of that. Any court would have sided with you and had her locked up for her own safety."

"You think that's the only reason she stayed?"

"I can't think of any other," I growled.

Dad wheeled himself backwards, his arms shaking. His eyes when he looked at me had no recognition in them. Then he reached blindly out to the desk beside him. His hand groped until it knocked the ever-present picture on its side and he picked it up, cradled it to his chest, then tilted it back and stared into the flat emulsion of my mother's eyes. I wondered what he saw behind the glass.

"It's true, your mum and I fought about the fact she wouldn't seek treatment for her illness. But that isn't the whole story, how could it be? She used to say I was the great love she had been promised." His voice hoarsened. "She was certainly mine." He stroked her picture. "When the Mark was on her she said I kept her sane, that looking after us helped her life make sense." He sighed. "I think that without us, her hallucinations would have taken her over completely." His fingers continued to move restlessly over the image of her face.

"I never told you how we met." He spoke without looking at me, still I shook my head.

"I had just finished university. I was doing rounds of interviews, trying to get a position in a reputable lab, but there weren't that many places out there. I'd just had a really bad time with an old goat who hated me from the moment I opened my mouth." Strangely this made him smile. "It had been one of the worst hours of my life." He shook his head. "I was drowning my sorrows in the nearest pub when this vision walked in." His eyes clouded with memory. "God, she was incredible. She wore her hair loose in those days and it just seemed to float around her like a…" he paused, then smiled. "Like a fairy cloak, black as night. She was wearing this elegant dress thing and high heels like she'd just come from a party. But she walked into this rough pub like she had every reason to be there, no hesitation, just total confidence. She looked around for a moment then walked up to this enormous bloke at the bar. She stood next to him then offered to buy him a drink. As soon as the pint was poured she shook his hand and turned to walk out of the pub, like that was it." He shook his head again. "The bloke got all bolshy, trying to make her stay, thinking he had a right to something because she'd bought him a beer." He grinned. "I was about to stand up, to try and help her out, but I got my feet tangled in my briefcase. It didn't matter though. She leaned into the idiot and whispered something in his ear. Then she did some fancy martial arts thing on him and dumped him on the floor.

"She was walking out and my heart was just tearing out of my chest, trying to go with her when she stopped at my table and looked at me with these eyes like pools of still water." He sighed. "She just stared at me, long and steady, for a moment then she took my hand." He tightened his hand on her picture. "She said something odd, I'll never forget it. She said 'I was wondering when you'd be along'. Then she led me out of the pub and into a wine bar down the road. That was it for me. I never loved anyone like I loved her. I never knew why she was in that bar."

"Yes, you do." I edged towards him. "She was Marking a murderer."

Dad ground his teeth. "I loved your mum so desperately I was willing to ignore her hallucinations. I didn't think they were a problem for us, not until I realised they could affect you. That's when I started pushing her to get treated."

"Dad–" I bit off my insulting comment, not wanting to inflict so much pain again. "Look, even if I met this mythical guy who'd put up with me, I wouldn't risk inflicting this *condition* on a child." My voice was hoarse. "I'm surprised Mum did."

Dad stared up at me, finally meeting my eyes. "Taylor, me and your mum, we talked it through. We looked at her family records before she got pregnant. The condition runs in her family, but there was a fifty-fifty chance you'd be fine. We thought it was worth the risk. She loved you from before you were even conceived. She wanted you. *We* wanted you."

I shook my head. "No. You wanted the kid who *didn't* get the curse. Not me."

Dad gaped as if I'd punched him in the chest. "How could you think that?" He rolled towards me swiftly, dropping Mum's photo in his lap so that he could grab my hand. "I love you."

"But you're trying to change me, just like you tried to change her. You'd love me more if I was normal."

He shook his head and his fingers gripped mine more tightly. "I couldn't love you more. I couldn't have loved your mum more." He was actually crying.

My eyes widened and I felt cold all over. I'd made Dad cry. He hadn't even cried at the funeral.

"I can't believe you'd think that. That I've made you think that."

I couldn't stop myself, even seeing his tears I couldn't choke the words away. "Then why try to force her to a doctor if you loved her so much? If you love me."

"It was an illness, Taylor. You don't love someone less because they aren't well." His chest heaved. "You try to help them." He realised he was crushing my hand and released his grip. I rubbed the life back into my fingers without looking away from his face.

"I wanted her to go to a doctor, because I thought if we found some drugs that helped her, then you wouldn't have to suffer at all, you could go on the same prescription from the very beginning."

"But she wouldn't go."

Dad half-smiled. "She was so stubborn – like somebody else I know." He groaned and rubbed his hand through his hair. "It upset me, her refusal. I couldn't understand why she wouldn't want to help you, especially when you got sick too."

"If you're so sure I'm crazy, why don't you send me away? Get me locked up and cured like you wanted to do to her."

He looked at his wasted legs where they lay unmoving on the chair. He swallowed.

"Dad?"

"It was her last wish." He heaved a sobbing breath. "The last thing she said to me as we lay trapped in that wreck was, 'Don't send Taylor away'. I'd made her worry about it so much that she used her last breath to get that assurance. Not to tell me she loved us, but to make me swear. And that's why I have to work so hard to find a cure myself, because I had to make that promise."

I was crying myself now, silent howls that hurt my chest. I had to make this stop. I blinked furiously to hold back the tears and thrust out my arm. "Just do it."

Dad gaped owlishly at my bare wrist then hung his head to stare once more at my mother's picture. "Maybe we should do this in the morning."

I pulled my sleeve back down and backed out of the room, glancing once more at *The Tale of Oh-Fa* as I left.

What I wouldn't give for Dad to be right, for there to be a cure.

But Mum had always said it when she fought with Dad – you can't cure a curse.

4

Crash and burn

Hannah's hair was orange today. It bobbed opposite me like a neon dandelion. I was focusing my blurring eyes on the way the sun glowed off the fluffy ends, mainly because last night's hunt had stopped me from revising for yet another test.

Hannah glanced up at me with her *X-Files* pen in her mouth. She narrowed her eyes in concern when she saw my lack of activity.

I shrugged helplessly and watched her agonise, trying to work out a way to get her answers over to me. I shook my head, telling her not to worry. She cut her eyes to the clock, to the teacher and back to my empty page. Her hand twitched as if she was going to slide hers across. I shook my head more vigorously and Miss Carroll's whipped up.

"Heads down," she snapped.

Hannah's head plunged as if she'd been dunked. I ducked more slowly and as I turned my eyes back to the set of unanswerable questions I caught sight of Justin to my right. He was failing to hide his amusement at my obvious crash and burn. I noted with grim dismay that his sheet was filled with cramped handwriting.

Surreptitiously I looked around the room. Pete was frowning over his work, his dark eyes flicking from the questions to the page with the intense focus that was such a part of everything he did. James was next to him, glaring at the question paper as if it had offended him. I straightened a little. Maybe I wasn't the only one due for a fail this week. Then he stabbed his pencil on the paper and started to write, pushing so hard I could hear the scratching of his answers over the rustling and quiet sighs that otherwise filled the air.

I sighed. Maybe I could attempt question five. Maybe. I picked up my pencil just as the bell rang.

Figures.

"What happened? You were fine with this stuff when we did it in class." Hannah looked tragic.

"It's OK, Han, I just forgot to revise." I avoided her eyes and packed up my bag.

"But you didn't answer *anything*."

I shrugged. "My mind went blank."

"Like it's ever been anything else," Tamsin sneered as she elbowed past. "But then I suppose you've got your career mapped out already. You'll be working at the takeaway, bagging the prawn crackers. Don't need good grades for that." She tossed her hair and shouldered Hannah aside, knocking my bag onto the floor in the process. Books and pens flew and I grabbed for it quickly, but not quickly enough. The box of Lillets I carried burst and sellophaned cotton sticks rolled around the floor, slippery as crayons. One rolled to a halt in front of Justin and I burned crimson as he nudged it with his toe, eyebrows climbing into his hairline.

"What's the matter, Hargreaves, never seen a tampon before?" I snapped. But it was hard to seem unconcerned while scrabbling on the floor to pick them up. Hannah bent to help me, swiping them into the box, but they wouldn't go in any which way and we had to spend time organising them as the back of my neck set on fire.

"Maybe your *girlfriend* doesn't need them yet." I spoke to Justin, but glared at Tamsin.

She shook her head at me coolly. "Some of us don't share these things with everyone." She hoisted her bag higher on her shoulder. "*Some* of us have class." She flicked her hair again and posed, waiting for Justin to take her arm. He actually stepped over me to get to her.

Pete was behind him as always. Shame and disgust warred on his face as he edged by. Hannah didn't even raise her head and my heart hurt as I realised she wasn't even trying with him any more. There was a time when the two of them had been close, but that hadn't been true for a while.

I hunched my shoulders over the last of the offending items and shoved the box back in my bag, making sure to put them in the zipped compartment.

Finally I stood and came face to face with James.

He stood far too close, crowding my space. He was so tall my nose was inches from his collar bone and I could smell his stale deodorant, which had obviously been over-taxed by the test. I was forced to look up at him.

Once he saw me raise my eyes, his mouth curved into a cool smile and my chest tightened. That smile had nothing friendly in it whatsoever. My forearms prickled as goosebumps pebbled the skin. Automatically I tried to step back, but the table was in the way.

"Come on, James." It was Pete. He was leaning on the doorjamb. He deliberately avoided looking at me, but I just knew he was finally staging a rescue.

I couldn't take it. Not from him.

My spine straightened, even as the splinters on the edge of the table pricked my thighs. "Yes, go on, Jimbo, Daddy's waiting."

My words made James' lip twitch and he leaned further forward. Some part of me expected him to reveal fangs. The classroom faded away until there was only James with his huge body and stinking breath.

Then I heard Hannah squeak and Miss Carroll's voice brought the room back into being. "Don't you have another class to go to?"

I swallowed as James waited an insolent few seconds then stepped back. "Yes, Miss, on my way."

Hannah grabbed my arm. Her shirt shivered with the thumping of her heart. "Are you alright?" she whispered.

"Of course." I squeezed her elbow. "He's a Neanderthal, you know that. Does whatever Justin wants."

And that was the problem wasn't it? Because Justin Hargreaves said so, I was fair game and no one had the guts to do anything about it.

●●●●

It hadn't always been this way. I'd once been part of a trio: Pete, Hannah and myself. All three of us were just a little bit different. Pete was the only black guy in the year, I was the only oriental and then there was Hannah. She was a pale-skinned Scot who wanted to be Willow from *Buffy the Vampire Slayer*. Her hair changed its hue two or three times a term in line with her mum's boyfriends. We weren't in any of the popular cliques, but we weren't at the bottom of the pecking order either. We hovered somewhere in the middle, nobody bothered about us. We were just normal. And then... we weren't. Or at least, I wasn't.

I glanced out of the window, remembering. The clown had stood right *there* on the day my life had changed. The balloons that no other child could see had tangled just there, around the netball posts. I still heard the *flap-slap* of his shoes in my nightmares. I clenched my fist around the ghost of my first ever Mark, the one the dead joker had left when he had touched me. I had thought it was just black greasepaint until I realised that there was no washing it off. The clown had been the ghost to start it all.

Rage threatened to boil and I pushed the memory down, "parked it" as the counsellor I saw after the accident was fond of saying. I visualised the garage, the space where the images would sit waiting for their next outing.

Then I walked with Hannah out of the classroom.

"I don't want to do this. Can't you pick something else?"

The whine came from the common room. I tightened my grip on Hannah's arm. "We shouldn't get involved."

"I know. Heads down." Hannah dropped her eyes and we walked forward, prepared to ignore whatever was happening.

The group was clustered around a plastic table. *What a surprise…* Justin, Tamsin, James and Harley. Only Pete was missing.

Justin leaned nonchalantly against the table in the centre of the room. The rest of them had a boy from the year below pinned against a chairback. The kid looked terrified.

"You wanted in." James jabbed him in the chest with a stiffened finger and I saw red.

"Taylor," Hannah squeaked and tried to grab me, but I was already moving. I shoved my bag back at her.

"Leave him alone, you penis extension."

Tamsin turned, already laughing. "*You* want *us* to leave him alone?" She stroked a red nail across the boy's cheek and I shuddered. "What do you want us to do, Alan? You want us to leave you alone?"

"I-I…" The boy's collar moved with the bobbing of his Adam's apple.

"You know what'll happen, Alan." James leaned in, menacing.

"He's younger than you. Have some self-respect!" I clenched my fists.

Tamsin took a slow pace towards me. "You want to take his place, Godzilla?"

"Hey, no!" Alan grabbed her arm. "I'm in, I told you. I'll do it, whatever you want." He avoided my eyes. "She's not taking my place."

"That's nice of you kid, but–"

"Go away, alright? Just go away." Red spots decorated Alan's cheeks as if he'd been slapped. Around the redness he was pale and scared.

"I can tell a teacher," I murmured.

He shook his head violently. "I'm OK, don't do anything."

I raised my eyebrows. "You want these arseholes to harass you? Fine." I spun on my heel and saw Justin's supercilious grin. "You are such a tool," I snapped at him.

Hannah was right behind me, ready to back me up like always. I grabbed my bag from her clenched fists, swung it over my shoulder and stalked towards the corridor. "Come on, Hannah, we're late for science."

Behind me I heard a sound like a growl. It was almost inhuman. I stopped and turned. Once more James was glowering at me, head lowered so his eyes were shadowed by his jutting brow. "Neanderthal," I muttered, but I increased my pace.

"That class sucked." Hannah shoved her hair out of her eyes and shuddered. She was sweating through her shirt. "I hate physics. I loathe it. Seriously, how can you stand it?"

I snorted while I quickly checked the courtyard for anyone out of place.

"Honestly, I thought my brain was going to explode." Hannah pressed her hands on either side of her head, little orange tufts of hair sticking out between her fingers. "I have a headache. I need to go to the office."

"You mean because it's a double lesson and we've got it again after lunch?"

"I'd forgotten. I'll die. I'll literally drop dead from an aneurysm."

I burst out laughing. She looked so wretched. Hannah in drama mode was always funny. Not that she saw it that way.

"Come on, Han," I sighed. "If it makes you feel better I'm going to fail that class too."

"Stop laughing, you cow. It doesn't make me feel better. You and exams are a disaster. You break my heart. I'm going to get drugs, lots of drugs."

"Good luck with that." I shoved her gently in the direction of the office. "I'll see you later. Usual spot?"

Hannah nodded carefully as if she really was worried that a sudden movement would topple her head from her shoulders. I watched her totter away, smiled and swung my bag higher on my shoulder. The sun was trying to burn through the clouds; I'd eat outside and get in our "spot" early. Way better than running the gauntlet of the common room and eating alone in a room full of cliques.

I was sitting with my legs in the weak sunshine, enjoying the feel of the rays on my shins. My sandwich had gone soggy in my lunchbox, but I was picking the filling out and eating it between crisps. The wall of the art room was warming my back and I had a clear view of the courtyard. Hannah wasn't keeping me company, but my hands were clean of dead men's Marks, there was no sign of anything out of the ordinary and I was feeling relatively alright with the world.

I looked down to pick some more cucumber from my sandwich and a shadow fell over me.

I caught my breath; had I missed a ghost?

No. I forced my shoulders to relax, ghosts don't cast shadows.

I glanced up. It was the boy from earlier: Alan.

"Hey," I grunted, but he said nothing and didn't move. "What's up?"

He took a deep breath and crouched next to me. "Sorry about this," he whispered.

"Huh?" I had time to get my legs half under me, but that just had me off balance when he shoved me, hard. I teetered for a second then fell on my side, dropping my lunch into the dust and twisting my wrist under my hip. Shock froze me for a moment, long enough for him to grab my bag and run for it.

"What just happened?" I shouted; then I leaped up and sprinted after him.

My feet flew across the concrete and my skirt flipped up to my thighs. I could run, so the stupid kid didn't stand a chance. Despite my confusion I was almost enjoying the chase. Alan cut across the grass, heading for the athletics track. My bag bumped against his back, shedding pens and books like Hansel in the forest. I'd pick them up later. Right now I wanted my hands on the little toad.

All my attention was on the fleeing junior; the redness on his neck, the hammer of his trainers on the hard-packed earth. Around us our classmates were stopping what they were doing and pointing, starting to laugh. I didn't care.

I was almost caught up with him when I passed the storage shed next to the long jump pit.

My foot caught on something that hadn't been there when Alan scampered past. I careered forward, my arms spinning as I tried to keep my balance. Then a brutal shove caught me from behind and I literally flew off my feet.

I smashed face first into the sandpit.

I didn't even have time to cry out. The grains abraded my face like sandpaper and crammed my mouth and nose. They stung my chest like carpet burn, and padded out my shirt. My already-twisted wrist shrieked with pain and I lay there stunned and unable to move, wondering what had happened.

Then something hit my back and I pushed myself up, spitting grit. Alan stood above me, shaking my bag upside down to empty it. Once more the Lillets spilled out, this time pattering onto my bare legs.

Rage almost blinded me and my ears rang, but still I could hear the laughter. I turned and there they were, James and Harley, holding onto each other so they weren't floored by their own hilarity. Over by the track Justin and Tamsin stood holding hands and grinning like idiots.

I flashed to Alan in the common room with Justin's gang trying to get him to do something.

That did it.

I flew out of the sandpit, shedding fine grains like a rattlesnake. I covered the ground in seconds and threw myself at Justin, wrapping my hands around his throat.

I still had sand in my mouth, so I spat it at him while cursing and trying to throttle the superior look off his face.

Distantly I heard Tamsin shrieking and hands closed around my upper arms, pulling me free.

"You think this is funny?" I yelled. "You still think it's funny?"

Everything had gone red. I kicked and fought against whoever had me in his grip.

"Calm down, Tay." It was Pete's voice in my ear with the name he hadn't used in years. Where had he come from? I drooped in his hold and looked around. The whole school had to be watching.

My scratched skin started to throb and my cheeks burned.

"Can't control herself." Tamsin's delighted voice blowtorched through my daze. "Typical foreigner. Just attacked us for no reason."

I was about to blow sky high when I heard Miss Carroll. "No reason, Tamsin? Then why are her things all over the sandpit? Justin, obviously she blames you and I'm sure she has good cause. I'm getting sick of having to do this, but both of you come with me to see Mr Barnes. Again."

5

A lot of opportunities

The corridor outside Mr Barnes' office smelled of Dettol and vomit. I hunched on the hard chair with my bag between my legs. A trail of sand had followed me in and now poured from the flap and pooled at my feet. I'd shaken out as much as I could before coming inside, but it was everywhere. My bra itched like crazy.

Way more annoyingly, Justin wasn't the slightest bit rumpled. I hadn't even managed to mess up his tie. It remained in its usual loosened knot, an inch below his top button. Along with everything about Justin it was a little too relaxed, but remained just the right side of messy. Everywhere Justin went he looked at home.

I ground my teeth. His legs were stretched out in front of him, his ankles crossed just as they had been on the bus. His arms were loosely folded and he was leaning his head against the artwork behind his chair. His hair too, was just the right side of messy, a touch too long, it was starting to curl at the ends and he had to push it aside to glance over at me, brown eyes sparkling with amusement.

"So, what're you going to say?" He smirked. "That I was watching some year nine stuff you in the sandpit, so you decided I needed a beat down?"

"Don't even!" My fists had curled already and he'd only needed a single sentence. "I know you put him up to it. I heard you all."

"You saw us talking to Alan, but that was it." He checked his fingernails as if he was about to go for a manicure.

"Then why did he apologise before he pushed me over? I'm not stupid. I don't know what hold you have over him, but there must be something."

Justin shrugged. "When Mr Barnes brings him in, I'm sure he'll mention it if I, as you say, 'have something' on him." His fingers made air quotes and I wanted to break them off and stuff them down his throat.

I sat on my hands.

"You're a dick," I muttered.

"Yeah?" Justin actually looked away, flicking a grain of sand from his blazer. "I didn't do anything to you, Taylor."

"You don't have to," I snarled. "You just point the dogs in the right direction. It's always been that way. Why me? That's what I want to know. Are you a racist? Is that what I should tell Mr Barnes?"

Justin's cool eyes widened for a moment and he snorted. Then he leaned back in his chair. "You really don't remember, do you?"

"Remember what?"

"My first day in this dump. You don't remember what you did."

"What *I* did?"

His first day at school was the day I met the clown; the end of my normal life. I thought I remembered everything about those terrifying hours, but my memories of Justin were vague. On that day he was just the new boy.

With a bitter little smile Justin shook his head. He resumed leaning on the mural and ignored me.

"Come on then, what did I do to you?"

He shrugged. "It obviously isn't that important, not if you don't even remember."

"It obviously *is* that important."

"Leave it, Oh."

I was groping about for a way to make him tell me what I'd done when the memory clarified.

I headed for my usual seat but someone was already there – a new boy. He sat with his back to the room, looking out of my window, so all I could see was his neatly clipped hair, almost as dark as mine, and his thin brown fingers playing restlessly with a pencil.

"Hey." The boy turned and our eyes met. My first feeling was disappointment. He wasn't black like Pete, or even half-and-half, like me; he was just a boy with a deep tan. His eyes were brown, like mine, but they flickered nervously, taking in my clenched fists and the sight of Pete and Hannah standing behind me. I narrowed my eyes. "That's my seat."

He bit his lip and said nothing. I glanced at the teacher. Mr Barnes wasn't looking at us so I squared my shoulders.

"You're new, so you don't know. But that's my seat. Harley's not here today, why don't you go and sit next to James?"

In his place across the classroom James heard his name, and leaned back to study us until my hackles rose. Finally he used one toe to push the empty seat back: a silent invitation to the new boy.

But the new boy gripped the table. He wasn't going anywhere.

I pressed my lips together. "Look, today's my birthday and I'd really like to sit in my own seat near my mates." I tried a smile.

The boy licked his lips. "It's your birthday?"

"I'm ten."

He looked out the window a final time then sighed and raised his voice loud enough for the rest of the class to hear. "Well seeing as it's your birthday." When he moved past the three of us he looked as if he really was doing me a favour.

At the end of the lesson I was right behind Pete when the necklace Hannah had given me slithered into my vest.

I fixed the loose clasp as the classroom emptied around me.

When I had it refastened I stood, then paused with the strangest feeling that someone was watching me. My eyes went to the corner of the playground.

I leaned closer to the window and saw something bright moving in the shadows. As I stared, a single crimson balloon appeared from the back of the building.

It hung for a moment in a breath of still air then danced across the playground. No one looked up to watch it fly. Not one single child.

I walked quickly down the corridor. This was the third balloon I'd seen since the clown had appeared at the end of my street. I assumed he was some sort of naff birthday treat from Mum and Dad but his eerie silence had creeped me out and I had been grateful to jump on the bus and leave him behind. Now I was beginning to loathe the sight of balloons. Did it mean he had followed me to school?

I flung the double doors open and almost crashed into the new boy. James had him half pinned against the wall.

"Come on – truth or dare? You've got to choose."

Justin's face was pale under his tan and he was clutching his bag like a lifebelt.

"Just go with dare," I muttered. "How bad can it be?"

Justin looked grateful as I sped past but I wasn't thinking about him any more, I was thinking about the balloons I had been seeing all day. Balloons the colour of blood.

Was that what he was upset about? That I hadn't helped him when James had him pinned.

I lowered my brows, trying to place him more firmly in my recollection of that day.

Mrs Pickard cleared her throat meaningfully and I glowered at the paper in front of me. We were meant to be writing a poem called *Myself*. I picked up my pen.

"Today is my birthday," I wrote. "I am ten."

Something made me look up. Justin was sitting bolt upright, pen clenched in his fist. "What's up with the new boy?" I whispered.

Pete shrugged and Hannah turned in her chair.

Justin stood slowly. He looked anxiously at James who nodded.

"What's the matter, Justin?" Mrs Pickard looked concerned.

Justin swallowed audibly. "I-I want to change seats, please."

"Change seats? What on earth for?" Mrs Pickard peered at his chair.

Justin shuffled his feet. "I-it's the smell," he muttered.

"Smell?" Mrs Pickard wrinkled her nose. "I can't smell anything."

"It's your smell." Despite his harsh words, Justin looked miserable. "I can't stand the stink and I need to move." He swallowed again. "Have you tried deodorant?"

Mrs Pickard's mouth fell open and she immediately gathered her cardigan around herself.

"Shut up, Pete." I hissed as the class began to snigger. James was laughing so hard he could barely keep his seat.

Justin looked wretched as Mrs Pickard fled from the room with tears in her eyes.

"Nice one!" James called. "You win."

Justin turned and glared at me but I ignored him; there was a red balloon sliding along the window.

••••

It was true that I had told Justin to take the dare, which probably got him in a great deal of trouble, but James was the one who had forced him to do it. Why was he mad at me? I opened my mouth to ask him and the office door opened.

"Miss Oh and Mr Hargreaves. Do come in. Again."

"This is getting old, Miss Oh." Mr Barnes shuffled papers on his desk and glared at me over his glasses. Did he think that made him look intelligent, intimidating? It just made me think he needed bifocals. The twit.

"I know that you have suffered a *significant* loss." He paused respectfully. "But that was three years ago now and you have been given enough leeway." He dropped the papers and slapped the desk with his palms. "*Enough*, do you understand?"

"Wait a minute," I gasped as if the air in the room was thin. "How is this *my* fault? I was attacked. Look at me." I gave a little kick and sand spattered the carpet.

"That's as may be, Miss Oh, and I will be talking to the perpetrator afterwards. However, Mr Hargreaves was *not* your attacker, was he? I have witnesses who say you launched yourself at him with no provocation whatsoever."

"He put him up to it. I heard."

Mr Barnes raised his bushy eyebrows. "You specifically heard Mr Hargreaves tell Mr Fisher to steal your bag and push you in the sandpit?"

"I..."

"I didn't think so."

Mr Barnes shook his head. "Now, I don't know what's gone on between you two. A lovers' spat, perhaps?" I choked, coughing sand out of my throat that I hadn't even realised was there. Justin remained in his semi-slouch, only a twitch of his fingertips showing his own reaction. Mr Barnes ignored me and continued. "I won't have this bullying behaviour in my school." Unbelievably he was looking at me.

"I–"

"I know you were also attacked, Miss Oh, but not by Mr Hargreaves. Apologise to him. Mr Fisher will be doing the same to you later on."

Air huffed in and out of my nose, as if it was too offended to enter the lips that would have to betray me. I pressed my mouth closed and shook my head. "Miss Oh, for every three seconds you do not apologise, you will receive one day of detention."

Justin looked at me and tilted his head, insolently waiting for my apology.

"One… two… three."

I said nothing.

Mr Barnes shook his head and made a mark on his notebook. "One day of detention, Miss Oh. And again, one… two…"

I couldn't risk it, the more time I spent in school, the more time the ghosts had to find me. My eyes traced movement on the courtyard, a man in a suit. Was he meant to be there?

Only my house was safe.

Then there was Hannah. She'd go spare if she had to sit on her own at break and lunch.

"I'm sorry," I spat. The words were like poison on my tongue.

"Sorry for what?" Mr Barnes prompted.

My cheeks burned as if someone was holding a brand to my face. "I'm sorry that I attacked you, Justin."

"That's right." Mr Barnes sat back with his hands across his stomach. "You know, I feel privileged to be at the helm of this school. Can you guess why?"

I shook my head, still burning and itching and hating him with every heartbeat. "This school has opportunities, Miss Oh. It isn't like other institutions, where there is a single popular 'gang' in each year with everyone else excluded. I've seen people from different year groups 'run together', I've seen the unpopular suddenly become accepted, even admired. There are opportunities, Miss Oh, for the daring. For those brave enough to grasp them with both hands."

Justin made his first noise, a cross between a hiccup and a gasp and I frowned at him. Mr Barnes was off on one of his aimless rants. Why was Justin bothered?

Mr Barnes removed his glasses and stared off into space. "This school has history, Miss Oh." He leaned forward one more time, his eyes suddenly sharp. This time he was looking at Justin. "*Qui audet vincit*. Who dares wins. Isn't that right, Mr Hargreaves?"

Justin swallowed, audibly. "That's right, Mr Barnes."

Mr Barnes nodded and put his glasses back on. "And there is nothing new under the sun, Miss Oh." He tapped his paper. "Another detention for you. I'll also be writing a letter to your father. I'll expect his reply by return."

••••

"Taylor, I–" Justin's voice contained some sort of apology and I wasn't having that from him, no way.

"Leave me alone." I slumped back on the sandy chair to wait for the letter that Mr Barnes was emailing to his secretary.

"Fine." He strode past me without another look.

The chair next to me was occupied by Derek from the year below and I looked across, seeking an empathetic eye-roll. Even I had to admit that the boy was good looking: blemish-free skin, short dreadlocks and a jaw line so firm he could rock a mask and cape if he wanted to.

Today though, he was so pale he looked green and his hands clenched and unclenched in his lap endlessly, like creatures independent of the rest of him. He was hunched over his bag, his whole body tense: a jack-in-the-box ready to spring.

Unable to make any sort of eye contact I turned away. What had happened to him? Until a couple of weeks ago he was the Justin of his year group then suddenly he was even less popular than I was. Hannah told me that if he tried to speak to someone they turned their back on him. If he sat at a lunch table, everyone else got up and left. He had become a ghost in his own classroom.

"Hey." I couldn't not speak. "Are you OK?"

There was no reply and I was leaning back in my seat when suddenly he spoke. "How do you stand it?"

"Stand what?" I frowned.

"Being what you are. So 'out' with everyone."

I inhaled sharply. "I have Hannah."

"So you do." His fingers twined in and out of themselves, the knuckles red raw. "I…"

"Yes?" I couldn't help noticing how sunken his eyes were. It looked as if he hadn't slept for weeks.

"I want to apologise. I was a dick to you. Just like everyone else. I know how it feels now." He cleared his throat. "You're stronger than I am, Oh."

"Derek Anderson, Mr Barnes will see you now."

"Listen," I caught his arm. "You should eat lunch with me and Hannah."

Derek snorted. "That's nice of you, Oh. Especially considering, you know, everything. But it's too late. I'm leaving."

"In the middle of term?"

"I've got a transfer, I'm collecting my papers now. I'm out of here. This place is effed up!" He gave a smile as fake as plastic fruit. "Don't let the bastards get you down, Oh."

I dropped my hand and watched him go.

Hannah stood in the courtyard waiting for me and she wasn't alone.

"Look who's keeping me company," she half sang.

"Pete." My eyes widened, but still I nodded at him as I went to her side. He grunted wordlessly and moved away, disassociating himself.

I sighed and turned to Hannah. "You didn't have to wait." I shook more sand out of my waistband. Would I ever get rid of it all?

"Last period's over. I'll get the bus with you."

Gratefully I stuck my arm through hers. Then I stopped and turned to our one-time friend. "You know, you could get the bus with us."

Pete just looked at me.

"Like old times."

"Right," he sneered. "Those times you pretended to like me, or the ones you refused to talk to me?"

"That's not fair." Hannah leaped to my defence. "We were friends."

Pete turned to Hannah. "Does she ever tell you what's going on with her?"

Hannah blushed and avoided looking at me.

"I don't know how you stand it, Han." He rubbed his palm over the darker mahogany of his head. "How can you think she's your friend if she won't talk to you?"

"We talk," Hannah snapped.

"Yeah sure. Look she's zoned out on us already. Obviously not that interested."

Pete's words had become a distant buzz, my focus shifted to the suited man striding across the flagstones. Was he living or dead?

The sun had moved and now the whole courtyard was in the shade so the first item on my mental checklist, to look for a shadow, was out. Pete and Hannah had their backs to him, so I couldn't tell if they were able to see him or not. I had to assume he was a ghost.

I prepared to run, slipping my arm free of Hannah's.

Pete caught my other elbow. "You think you're better than us."

"That's not true." I was forced to take my eyes off the approaching suit. "Let go, will you?"

Hannah still clung to one arm and Pete had the other. I was trapped.

The suit saw my predicament. His pace increased and he raised his head to look directly at me.

It was possible he needed to ask directions or something.

And it was about to rain kittens.

I had to get out of there. I tugged ineffectually at Pete, but he didn't move. "Did you ever like me the way I liked you?" he suddenly asked.

"I... I..." I blinked up at him. "It was complicated. And this isn't a good time."

The businessman reached us and smiled. I grit my teeth and tensed, but he didn't hesitate. He reached past Pete's arm and grabbed my hand, pressing his palm on to my knuckles. My skin froze as if I'd held my hand to a block of ice and an almost electric shock shivered up my arm. Then a familiar black Mark spread across my tendons like spilled ink.

"Crap." Immediately I yanked my hand free, terrified that I might accidentally touch my friend's skin.

"You're a cold bitch." Pete swung around and strode away.

The words to stop him caught in my throat. Pete had been wavering, maybe even considering leaving Justin's clique. Hannah and I could have had our friend back. Now he was gone again, utterly out of reach.

Venomously I glared at the ghost who had cost us our chance. Then I pulled away from Hannah who was staring after Pete with surprise.

"Did he just say he liked you?"

"It was a long time ago, when Mum was still around. I couldn't go out with him."

"I remember you had a lot going on."

"Yeah." The ghost drifted closer, wanting to speak to me. I pulled the white glove from my bag and tugged it over my hand.

"Hey, your eczema got bad fast!" Hannah caught at my wrist trying to see and I leaped back. I didn't dare let her touch me in case she was accidentally branded. The thought of the Darkness coming for my best friend made me sick to my stomach.

"It's OK, Han. Listen, I've got to be somewhere. I'll call you later."

Hannah nodded, but her face had fallen. She had waited for me, now she would have to go home alone.

Pete was right, Hannah put up with a lot from me and I wondered once more, with a shiver, how much longer she'd stick around.

6

A *twinge* of *sympathy*

I followed the suit away from Ken High Street leaving behind the shoppers, street hawkers and laughing groups of workmates heading for bars.

In this more sedate area shops were open by appointment only and metal grilles obscured half-glimpsed chandeliers and antiques. None of the retailers here were open past five but a few were still shutting up as I walked past. The rattle of descending shutters kept breaking the deathly quiet and making me jump.

The only other person on the road was a woman with a shopping bag from Whole Foods Market. She was obviously heading for home but she turned off before I reached the Crescent where tall white houses loomed like ribs in an elephants' graveyard, turned purple by twilight.

A glowing taxi passed the end of the road and disappeared.

I rubbed my hands on my skirt. "You're sure this is the place?"

The suit nodded. "This is it. It's been five years since she left the house. You'll have to go in."

My throat closed up as silence blanketed the street. But there was no way the Darkness was coming for me, not this soon; I'd only been Marked a couple of hours ago. The usual London noise was simply unable to penetrate the labyrinth of high white houses.

"Let's get this over with."

The gentle creaking of a tree seemed frighteningly loud and I jumped as a pigeon flapped almost apologetically to roost in its branches.

The murderer's home was dark and still. "Maybe she's out."

The suit shook his head. "No chance. After she had me killed and he left her anyway she lost it. My so-called wife is in there, trust me."

"And you're sure she won't answer the door?" I flexed my hands, hoping he'd say no and that I could simply ring the bell and shake her hand when she answered.

"Not if there's no delivery expected."

I sighed and checked out the house opposite. It had high walls, but lights glowed in the upstairs windows. I couldn't see anyone, but I still opened the gate to number three and walked down the path as if I had a right to be there. The first lesson of breaking and entering that Mum had taught me was that skulking draws attention.

The suit preceded me down the side of the house. I risked one furtive look over my shoulder and when I saw that the street remained quiet I followed and breathed a sigh of relief as the road disappeared from view behind the hedge.

At the back of the house large windows overlooked a decked garden. A few plants in urns provided glimmers of green, but mostly the space was decorated with stone sculptures and mirrored water features.

I turned my back on the centrepiece of a jagged, rippling mirror and regarded the house.

The windows were all shut fast. The double doors that opened on to the decking were locked and a security alarm blinked above them.

"There's an alarm."

The suit shrugged. "Can you do this, or not?"

I glared at him and removed the glove from my stained hand. "Thanks to you I don't have a choice."

I looked closely at the lock. It was a pretty standard deadbolt. Nothing I couldn't handle with a tension wrench.

Which was at home. I'd come straight from school. I opened my bag with a sigh and pulled out my History homework amidst yet another small sandstorm. The papers were connected with a metal paperclip and it was the work of a moment to create a makeshift pick.

I tapped my teeth with it and fixed my eyes on the alarm. It was a home security system from Everest. I sucked air in through my teeth, knowing perfectly well that Everest used pre-entry detection.

"I can't get in while that alarm's on."

I was glaring at the blue logo when the light on the box blinked.

"She's switched it off." I frowned. "Why?"

The dead guy shrugged. "Maybe she's letting the cat out."

"Jeez." I threw myself behind the water feature as a dumpy figure appeared in the darkness and cracked the door. A soft yowl told me a cat had just joined me in the garden. Briefly I considered rushing the killer. Then I shook my head. She might get back inside before I could reach her, then I'd lose my chance to transfer the Mark. I had to stay hidden.

After a slow count of one hundred I peered around the side of the mirror. The rear of the house remained dark and the figure had vanished.

I ran across the decking on my toes and stood outside the French doors. In the growing darkness my reflection appeared in the window. It was as if my own ghost had come to warn me to stay out. I put my nose closer to the glass and peered past my pale face to the room beyond. Before my breath fogged the window I saw a sitting room; uninhabited, cold and dark.

I flexed my fingers, shook my head and inserted the paperclip into the lock. Quick as I could I turned it, then I found my little metal nail file, slid the tool into the key hole and began.

Sweat made my grip uncertain and the roaring blood in my ears almost stopped me from hearing the pins fall into the housing. The hair on my arms rose and my back prickled. I was certain I was being watched.

Despite my mother's rule to appear as if I belonged, I had to look over my shoulder. Movement caught my eye and my breath caught. Frantically I pulled my tools free, and tried to look like as much like an ordinary visitor as possible.

I heard no challenge. When my heart stopped hammering I realised that I'd reacted to my own movement reflected in the mirrored sculpture. The only audience I had was the cat who was peeing loudly in the gravel. Nice.

I rolled my shoulders, inhaled and pressed the heel of my hand to my forehead; then I started again.

The final pin clicked into position. I took a deep breath and turned the file. The plug rotated, the lock snicked open and I pulled my tools free.

My hand shook on the handle. I added enough weight to push it downwards. The patio door swung open on thankfully silent hinges and I stepped into the house.

My shoes squeaked on the tiled floor and I froze. I pulled the door closed behind me, tucked my tools away and rubbed my arms. The house was cold. Very little light followed me in from the garden and the room was grey with shadow and shade. A piano stood in one corner and two large, overstuffed sofas faced a well-stocked drinks cabinet. A crystal decanter distilled the dim light and turned it into a tiny constellation.

Carefully I tiptoed to the doorway and peered around. There was an alcove opposite me displaying an empty vase almost as tall as I was and to my left was a carpeted dining room. It too was quiet. I sped past the large rectangular table and ornate chairs and cracked the door open.

Voices made me hold my breath. Then I recognised a familiar theme tune. She was watching *EastEnders*.

I poked my head around the door and faced a long hallway. Doors flanked black and white tiles that led all the way to the front entrance. Light came from beneath only one, the farthest away from me.

I retreated back into the alcove and glowered at dead guy. "I'm going to wait here. Tell me when she falls asleep and I'll Mark her."

"You're not going to confront her? I need her to know who's doing this to her. That bitch ruined my life."

I ground my teeth. "She *ended* your life. I'm here to get justice, not to let you go on a rant. If you want a medium, go find one."

The suit opened his mouth.

"Just forget it. I'm not risking myself so you can go on a power trip. You'll get your revenge. So go. Get the alarm code so I can get out of here later, and don't come back till she's asleep."

The stairs were carpeted and the carpet was thick; my shoes only whispered on the pile and the stairs supported my weight uncomplainingly. At the top I swung around the nearest wall and leaned against it. All the doors up here were closed, as if the house had been shut up for a holiday.

The suit was standing outside the only one that was slightly ajar.

"She's in there?" I mouthed.

He nodded resentfully.

"You're sure she's asleep?"

He nodded again.

I slipped into the room and found the middle-aged woman passed out on the bed. She was snoring and her eye-mask had slipped so that only one eye was covered. A bottle of pills lay on the nightstand next to her. I edged closer. By the look of what she'd taken I could start playing the trumpet and she'd sleep on.

One arm lay on top of the covers, fingers twitching in sleep. She snuffled as if she could sense me, but did not move.

A twinge of sympathy wormed in my chest as I held my hand above hers. She hadn't gained much from her dark deed. But I'd been Marked and it was her or me. I pressed my hand to her palm as if we were holding hands. She mumbled again, pulled away and rolled over. Her eye-mask slipped all the way off and her blackened hand flopped over her face in its place.

"Sorry." I couldn't prevent the apology from slipping out.

The suit opened his mouth but I ignored him and slipped out of the room. He'd have his revenge and if she was as reclusive as he said, no one would even know.

7

So disappointed

Dad had fallen asleep at his desk again. *The Tale of Oh-Fa* lay open beside his microscope. If I took it I could get it back in place by the morning. I ached at the thought of actually reading the words that my mother had once spoken. Automatically I picked it up and opened it to the front page. The familiar sentences danced in front of me, drawing me in.

THE JOURNAL OF OH-FA,
*translated from the Chinese
by his daughter, Oh Yehao*

*Entry the first
I have consulted the I-Ching. That is how I know my son will be born on this date. The fact that I will not see him until he is near walking is a source of great pain. But my heart's ache is unimportant; our family needs this salary.*

Today we begin working on a new grid so maybe we will find the sign the Professor seeks and this interminable misery will end.

I sit on my tiny camp bed to write. The overseer I call Sunbird, because of his bright red hair, permitted me to use these old requisitions once he witnessed my industriousness. Not all of the company work so hard. Even now, despite the brutality of the sun burning through the tent, I see the lankiest of them still fast asleep, one arm slung over his face, knees off the end of his too-small bed. The others have gone for breakfast. The last of them stumbled and cursed into the glare only moments ago. Only he and I remain, one too lazy and the other too excited to eat.

I am tempted to waken him, but the last time I did so, he attacked me and today I am happy to let him lie.

Today I become a father.

First bell is ringing, calling us to work. I must go too. Still it occurs to me before I put down this charcoal that hours in different lands flow inversely. Although it is early here, in Egypt, it may be late at home. I wonder if I will feel different once the time comes.

Is it possible that I am already a father?

A wave of exhaustion rocked me and I stroked the soft paper, almost pitying the man whose story had begun with such hope but ended in despair. One more entry and I would waken Dad.

Entry the second
A miracle has occurred. The discovery has been made and, incredibly, I myself was the one to make it. As I brushed sand aside, just as I have done a million times, the visage of a dog's head on a man's body resolved itself from the sand. It was just as the Professor had described.

The Sunbird overseer was the first to notice my shock. Sand puffed around him as he slid to a stop by my feet, barely able to believe after all these months of failure. Then he wheezed his way to the Professor's tent, calling for our employer who swiftly emerged with his wiry daschund, Titus, dogging his heels.

Due to an excess of coffee and lack of hygiene, the Professor's teeth have become dark yellow. The colour ensures that his tombstone incisors are the locus of his narrow face. When he reached me, he bared these decayed markers and leaned so close to the stone that his breath shifted fine dust around the dog's carved muzzle.

"The jackal," he breathed. "At last."

Then he had the company clear a four-metre space around the cell where I had been digging. Once we had laboured to board back the sand and provide a canvas shade, he banished us.

Several card games have now sprung up and I have returned to our tent.

I cannot help but wonder if the ancestors are smiling on me. Today all my dreams will come true, I feel it.

What an idiot; if only he could see what was coming. With difficulty I pulled my eyes from the text. There was no point taking the book with me, I'd be asleep before the end of the next page and if Dad noticed it missing he'd never trust me enough to let me have Mum's notes.

I placed it carefully back down with a sigh and nudged him awake. "Dad?"

Groggily he sat up and pulled a document off his face. Smudges of ink blackened his chin and his wedding ring had dented his cheek.

"You should be in bed."

"I was waiting for you." His shoulders cracked as he stretched. "You're still in your uniform. You haven't been home before now?" He focused on his watch with a frown. "This is ridiculous. You have school in the morning."

"I know. I'm sorry, I wasn't expecting it to take this long."

"It – another 'murderer'?"

I nodded with an inward groan, waiting for Dad's lecture on hallucinations. But he just turned to his microscope with a sigh.

"I don't know what to do any more, Taylor." His hand rasped over his stubble. "I can't control you."

I swallowed. "About that…"

"What?" He narrowed his eyes.

"I have to give you this from the school." I handed him the rumpled letter. "You need to sign it and write a comment so I can get it back to Mr Barnes tomorrow."

"What is it?" Dad put his glasses on to read and I let the letter speak for itself. "You attacked a boy in the playground?" His shoulders dropped and his hair fell into his eyes; I couldn't see his reaction.

"It was Justin Hargreaves, Dad. You know what he's like."

"I know you don't like him." He shook his great head, took his glasses off and rubbed his eyes. "This has to stop, Taylor. The path you're on doesn't end well."

"He started it."

"The letter says it was unprovoked. I've had enough, Taylor. I'm going to have to ground you for the weekend and as of Monday you have a curfew. I expect you in the house, doing your homework, by 8pm every single day."

"But–"

"It's reasonable, Taylor."

I rubbed my bare hand. It wouldn't be too bad to stay in all weekend; thanks to Mum the ghosts couldn't haunt me inside the house.

I nodded and as Dad scribbled a note on the letter I wished, not for the first time, that my parents had allowed me to be home-schooled once the curse had struck. If I stayed at home I wouldn't have to risk encountering ghosts at school and I wouldn't have to put up with Justin Hargreaves. But Mum had wanted me to have a normal life. I closed my eyes and thought of her once more.

"I have you and your Dad to keep me sane. You need friends; people your own age. You need to have time to think about pop music and clothes and – yes – boys. Otherwise..." Her eyes darkened and I know she was thinking about her own mother, who had killed herself

when I was a baby. She shook herself then. "Anyway, you have to be on the lookout."

"I'm always on the lookout for the ghosts, you've told me."

Mum shook her head. "When your ancestor agreed to our curse, those of his line that bore it were each promised a great love. It's our reward and a way for Anubis to ensure the legacy gets passed on. Somewhere out there someone is waiting for you. That's who you need to look out for – and you can't do that if you never leave the house." She sighed. "Also, Taylor, your dad doesn't believe in the ghosts, so there's no way he'll agree to home-schooling to protect you from them." She ruffled my hair. "You have to stop thinking of the departed as the bad guys. They're souls seeking justice and we have the honour of being able to give it to them. Try and have a normal life." The ruffling hand turned soft. "Look forward to finding the love of it. And in the between times, be proud of what you do for the dead."

Dad folded the letter and rolled back from the table with a groan. "I'm just so disappointed in you, Taylor."

8

Lucky day

There was an odd atmosphere in the school corridor and it was unusually quiet for a Monday morning. Hannah was just ahead of me. I couldn't suppress a grin as I watched her kiss her fingers and press them to the Dean Winchester poster that decorated the inner door of her locker. She was so in love with him.

With a sigh she slammed the sticky door until the latch caught, then started to walk on. I stopped her with a shout that felt strangely out of place among the whispers that dogged my heels.

"Hey, Tay." Hannah gave me a tight smile and chewed the purple tips of her hair. "Did you hear?"

"Hear what?"

"There're policemen in Mr Barnes' office." She cut her eyes in the direction of the closed door.

"So?" I stowed a few books from my bag and glowered at Justin's dogs, who were blocking most of the lockers. "They're probably here for a safety talk or something."

Hannah shook her head. "I saw them arrive; Mr Barnes was surprised to see them."

"Oh. Then it's probably drugs." The idea brought a smirk to my lips and I glanced at the obvious candidates: James and Harley.

Hannah kicked her locker door with thick soled shoes. "Something isn't right."

"Nothing's ever right in this place." I glowered at Pete. He didn't acknowledge me. "Look at them."

"Yeah, I know." Hannah shoved her bag higher on her shoulder and lowered her eyes. "Time to run the gauntlet."

Together we headed past the tables opposite the lockers, the tables where Tamsin Harper and her hags held court.

I pulled my sleeves over my hands and half hunched my shoulders as we drew level, but no barbed comments flew after us.

At the stairs I looked back. "That was easy." Hannah was right; something was off. I scanned the room.

The boys were lined up like they were at a club but James' blond hair hung messy and unkempt and instead of his usual alert posture he was slouching with his muscles bulging unflatteringly. Harley, whose jackal laugh could usually be heard wherever you were, was silent and he had dark circles under his eyes. Even Pete's shirt was already hanging out of his trousers.

Only Justin looked together, but he was watching Tamsin like he was on a diet and she was dessert. Normally they'd be all over each other but Tamsin was looking everywhere but at Justin.

So that was why we'd got past so easily, the "it" couple were having a fight.

I nudged Hannah as one of the girls said something to Tamsin under her breath and she ran to the toilet.

"What's gone on there, d'you think?" Hannah cocked her head at the fleeing queen bee.

I shrugged but didn't take my eyes off Justin. He watched his girlfriend go, but made no move towards her.

As usual he stood a little bit away from the other lads. Five years on and he still lightly wore that sense of exotic newness he'd arrived with on his first day. Adding to the sense of slight unreality that always surrounded him, his eyes now darted restlessly from student to student, never stopping in one place. As his gaze landed on me, they narrowed and I couldn't resist giving him the *Loser* sign.

"Hey." He straightened up as if I'd shoved him and I lifted my chin. I didn't *really* want to get in a fight with the jerk, not again.

"Come on, Hannah." I grabbed her elbow and steered her up the stairs.

Justin's voice rose above the general clamour of the common room. "Get back here, Oh."

"I don't think so," I muttered and stalked away.

"I know you heard me. Turn round."

I grit my teeth. Only a few more steps and we'd be outside Mr Barnes' office. *He won't dare start anything there.*

Year eight girls clustered at the top of the stairs. I used my shoulder to barge our way through. They moved slowly, glowering at us, but weren't far enough up the food chain to say much.

A gap opened ahead, but before I could dive into it, my bare right hand was caught from behind.

A shock both familiar and unutterably terrifying ran up my arm.

Suddenly the signs hit me: the strained hush, the policemen, Tamsin's upset. It hadn't been a fight that had prevented Tamsin from meeting her boyfriend's eyes.

I dropped Hannah's elbow and turned.

Justin's hand was locked around mine. The cold flesh of his palm was flat against my own. The darting of his eyes – he'd been looking for a sign that someone saw him. Too late I recognised his flickering gaze as the confusion of the newly dead.

I swayed as his wintry touch continued sending spikes of ice up my arm and pulled away before the chill bit me to the bone. It was too late. I stared at my hand in sullen comprehension. Swirling on the palm like a smear of black ink was a Mark.

How dare he do this to me?

As my brain struggled to get past the shock I stared into Justin's dark eyes, those eyes that said he hadn't yet come to terms with what had happened to him.

Great. Sometime over the weekend Justin Hargreaves was murdered... and now I have to avenge the idiot.

A younger boy was standing behind Justin.

He glared at me. "What's your problem?"

"I'm not looking at you," I snapped.

"Freak." He stepped around me and I turned to Hannah. "You go ahead. I've left my homework in the locker."

Hannah headed for the classroom, unaware that she was leaving me with the ghost of my worst enemy.

"*Outside.*" I spoke from the corner of my mouth, whirled and headed back down the stairs.

At the bottom I stopped. Mr Barnes was standing in the common area with two policemen at his back.

"We'll speak to each class individually," he was saying, "but just so you know, one of our students has disappeared. If anyone hears from Justin Hargreaves, please contact the police. If you know anything about what's happened to him, if you aren't comfortable talking to the police, come and speak to a teacher and we can do it for you." He glanced back and one of the policemen nodded. He was holding his hat like a shield.

"You couldn't have come out of your office five minutes ago?" I muttered.

Mr Barnes looked seriously at each group of students then shook his head sadly. "The bell's about to go, you can start making your way to your classrooms." He turned and left. I waited for a moment to make sure he was gone and then marched to the door.

Justin fell into step with me and I grit my teeth. Once in daylight, I hesitated.

"Where're we going?" Justin's voice in my ear left no impression on the air, no breath on my skin. Still I jerked back, not wanting to be in the same airspace.

I held my hand over my mouth. "Somewhere private so we can talk."

"You don't want to be seen talking to me? It can only improve your reputation."

I whirled on him and one of the younger kids who took my bus stumbled over the step in his hurry to get away.

"Shut up if you aren't going to help."

He shrugged and gestured. "Bike sheds?"

I glanced contemptuously in the direction of his pointing hand. "Full of losers getting a smoke before class."

My rucksack started to slide down my shoulder and I nudged it into a more comfortable position. As I did so I remembered my mobile. We weren't supposed to use them, but if I stood at the bus stop people would probably leave me alone and I could talk to Justin without looking like a nutcase.

I set off towards the gates and pulled the phone free.

With the scratched bus shelter propping me up, I squinted into the reflection of the sun as it glared from a multi-storey office block. Rather than look at Justin, I lowered my gaze to watch the cars and taxis belch past.

A few late students were sprinting from the tube. As they passed, each looked at me curiously, wondering why I wasn't running with them, trying to get into class before registration.

The number ten rounded the corner and I felt in my pocket for my pass. I hadn't intended to bunk off school, but I couldn't stay now.

As the bus pulled up I looked around. There was no one to stop me getting on.

The doors opened with a mechanical hiss. I gestured at Justin to follow and climbed on board.

As I swiped my Oyster card the driver glared disapproval. Almost too late I remembered the school speaking to the bus company about truancy. Quickly I groaned and clutched my stomach. With a shake of her head she waved me past.

The bus was practically empty, the work rush ended. Holding the phone to my ear I dropped onto the back seat. Justin sat in the seat behind.

"You're skiving," he muttered delightedly.

Hannah was going to kill me. She hated it when I left her alone at school. I glared out the window as the distinctive mix of architecture zipped by in jerks and starts. Finally I gave up and looked at Justin. He was slouched along his own seat, one arm draped over the back.

"So, what happened to you?"

He tensed. The humour left his eyes and he sat up. He knitted his lean fingers. "Would you believe I was starting to think no one could see me?" He stopped. "It's stupid."

"Why do you care what *I* think?"

He stayed quiet.

"So, what do you think now?"

He swallowed. "I... I don't know. It's some sort of trick, right? Everyone's *pretending* not to see me and those policemen have to be in on it." He thumped the seat and raised his voice. "This isn't funny, guys." He turned around. "I'm on YouTube, right?"

"You're *dead*."

He blinked. "You're crazy."

"Then why am I the only one who can see you?"

"You're the only one not in on the joke. No offence, but it's not like you're part of the in-crowd, Oh."

"Right… and Mr Barnes is?"

"Shut up." He clenched his fists on his knees.

"You came with me. You'd never do that if you didn't know I was your only hope."

"Only hope for what?" He sneered, but his voice was hoarse.

"It's your lucky day, Justin. I'm your only hope for vengeance and you can't move on without it."

9

You don't believe you're a ghost?

"Right." Justin regarded me from under raised eyebrows. "You'll 'avenge' my 'death' so I can 'move on'." He used his fingers to create quotation marks. "You are in on it, aren't you? This is your dare. See how far you can make Justin go? They don't usually go all in like this, but I guess they have been spicing things up lately. Go on then, what do you have to get me to do?"

I exhaled noisily. "I don't know what you're talking about, dipwad. I don't want you to do anything. Just tell me what happened."

"What happened when?"

"When you died. Tell me who killed you."

He crossed his arms. "You do what you have to, but I'm not going along with this." He glowered around the bus. "C'mon you guys. Haven't you had enough?" His voice had a quaver in it, so slight I could barely hear it.

Anger made me hiss. "How can you not believe this?" I pressed the heel of my hand against my forehead. The longer I carried the Mark, the more likely it was that the Darkness would come for me. I'd never had to deal with the newly dead before. I should be gentle with him...

My memory flashed up a scene. It was well-worn, but bright, like a silver locket often taken out of its box, rubbed and replaced.

"Dad! Are you alright?"

He looks like hell; his face so bruised and swollen that the only way I know it's him is the wedding ring chained over his collar bone. It catches the light as he twists towards me. His arms are in bandages and he's in plaster up to the waist.

He looks around anxiously. "Where's your aunt?"

"She brought me in, I wanted to see you."

He shakes his head and wheezes with the pain of movement. "I told her to keep you at home."

My eyes fill with tears. He doesn't want me here.

"She wanted to see Mum too, you know."

He gives a little jerk, as if he wants to hold my hand, but he can't get to me. Suddenly the curtain around his bed twitches open. A nurse picks up his chart, checks it and gives me a smile.

"Here to see your dad, love? He looks scary at the moment, doesn't he? Like a mummy. But he's going to be alright." As she says it, her eyes darken. "Do you have any sensation in your feet yet, Mr Oh?"

Dad shakes his head and beneath the swelling his jaw tightens. There is silence for a moment as she updates his chart.

"I'm just going to check your temperature and give you a dose of morphine." She smiles down at me. "Your dad's going to be a bit out of it for a while, love. Who are you here with?"

"My aunt." I find that, nice as the nurse is, I can't speak above a whisper. My whole body is prickling, as if something's coming: a monster I can't quite see. "She went to see how my mum's doing. She's still in s-surgery." The word feels foreign on my tongue.

The nurse nods. "Let me go and find her for you." She finishes taking Dad's temperature just as the curtain moves behind her. I hold my breath and a doctor steps in. He looks exhausted.

"Have you given him morphine yet, Andi?"

The nurse's smile freezes. "I was about to." She hesitates with her hand in the air. "Will I need…?"

"Something stronger, a sedative, yes please." The doctor comes to sit on the end of the bed. "And who's this?"

"The daughter." The nurse is pressing her lips together. They are white as her shoes.

"And she's with…?"

"An aunt. I'll send her in."

Andi, the nurse, almost runs from the cubicle. I stare at the doctor. There's a tiny speck of blood on the wrist of his gown. His eyes are bloodshot and he avoids looking at me. Dad is saying nothing. As soon as the nurse mentioned the sedative he went cold and still. It's as if he thinks speaking will bring the monster into the room.

"Dad?" I touch his nose with my finger tip. It's the only part of him that doesn't look bruised.

His mouth stretches into a false smile; a rictus that fails to reassure and instead makes me shiver. "I hear your aunt."

I turn. Dad's ward is quiet but I can still hear a ringing telephone, running feet, a baby crying. Then my aunt's voice. "I can't believe it. I just can't."

I whip round and catch Dad's expression; his features have collapsed like scaffolding. Then Auntie bursts into the room and throws her arms around me.

"We did everything we could…" the doctor begins.

He was kind. But hearing that Mum had died was the worst moment of my life. Wouldn't finding out that it was you who had passed on be just as bad? Or worse?

I should be kind.

But it was *Justin Hargreaves*.

"You think this is all a big joke, right?" I wrapped my bare fingers around the rim of my chair. "Go on then, touch my seat."

He blinked. "I'm sitting right here just fine."

"Yes, but I want you to touch *this* seat."

"Why?" His eyes narrowed. "What've you done to it?"

"Nothing. All you have to do is knock on the back of my seat with your fist. What's wrong, scared you can't?" I tilted my head in a mocking challenge.

He exhaled. Then all of a sudden he leaned forward and knocked on the back of my seat. At least, he tried to.

As his hand went through the cushion he lost his balance and fell forward. His forearm appeared above my lap and I caught his clenched fist in mine.

Justin yelped and tried to pull away but I kept hold of him, forcing him to look at his arm as it vanished through the chair-back.

"I-it's a trick of some sort. The seat isn't there, it's a… a projection."

Wordlessly I knocked on the metal rim.

"It's a *trick*." He yanked and I had to let him go. The whites were showing in his eyes and he scooted back against the window. He cradled his hand as if I'd burned it and he was shaking. I was getting through.

"Justin, you're a ghost."

He licked his lips. "You touched me, you held my fist."

"I'm the only one who can touch you. For the same reason I'm the only one who can see you."

"I'm ending this." Justin leaped to his feet and addressed the air. "This isn't funny any more." He strode down the juddering bus until he reached an art student who was sitting near the sliding doors.

"Hey, pal." He waved his hand in front of the guy's face. "I don't know who you are, but the joke's over."

The student rubbed his cheek and settled lower in the seat.

"Idiot." Justin kicked out viciously and his foot connected with the art case that stuck out from the seat opposite. It rocked and fell to the floor with a thud.

Justin stared at his foot and the student swore and reached for his case. His arm went right through Justin's leg.

Justin yelled and jerked back as the student checked his artwork with a relieved sigh.

I watched Justin desperately patting his leg. It looked like he was on fire. Finally he ran back to me. "Did you see that?"

"You're a *ghost*. I've seen it before."

He stared at his legs then slumped into the seat next to me. "It doesn't make sense," he whispered.

"You're dead," I growled without looking at him.

"Not that. How did that guy's arm go through my leg after I was able to kick his case? How come I can sit on the bus?"

Surprise pulled my eyebrows upwards; I hadn't expected him to be able to think clearly about his situation. "I'm not sure how it works exactly. I know you can't touch anything living, attached to a living thing, or that a living thing is touching directly. The art case was on another seat, that guy wasn't touching it." I gestured towards the student, who'd gone back into stasis. "You can sit on your seat, but you can't touch mine while I'm sitting here. You can't affect the living in any way. Mum thought it was something to do with resonances. I don't know."

"So I could pick up a knife, but not stab someone with it."

"You don't have any substance, Hargreaves. You can feel yourself touch things, even knock things over. But you can't pick anything up; people would notice stuff floating around."

He frowned. "OK. You're touching this bus. Shouldn't I fall through the floor?"

"Everyone on the bus is wearing shoes, Hargreaves. No one is touching the floor directly. You won't fall through it."

Tentatively he reached for the back of my seat again. His hand continued through wood and plastic until he groped my shoulder.

"Get off," I hissed and shrugged him away.

Justin stared at his hands. "You're the only one I can touch. Ever?"

"Sorry." I loaded my voice with sarcasm. "Look, once I've found your killer and transferred this Mark you left on my hand, you can move on and we'll never have to see each other again."

"But…" Justin looked up and his eyes swam with tears. "But I never…" his voice trailed off. His hands dropped to his lap. "I'm going travelling after A-levels. I thought I'd go back to Dubai for a bit. I'm applying to do engineering at Cambridge next year." His voice broke. "Tammy and I…"

I saw his throat move like he was trying to swallow a huge lump. "I never did anything."

I bit my lip. "I'm sorry," I said and I actually was. "If you can tell me how it happened, we can… OK, we can't make it right but I can avenge you. It's what I do."

Justin looked up with red-rimmed eyes. "This is bull." He hurled himself from his seat and lunged for the back of the bus.

"Come back." I grabbed for his jacket, but missed.

Ignoring me, he leaped off the bus and onto the Hammersmith overpass, dodged through the traffic and disappeared from view.

Stunned, I stood and wobbled with the movement of the vehicle. "Dammit." I examined my hands, one clean, the other stained with a blemish that screamed murder. The Darkness was coming. And without Justin, I had no way of getting rid of the Mark before it came for the one carrying it.

10

I should have taken you away

Dad holds my hand as I squirm. His new wheelchair digs into my side, but he doesn't loosen his grip. I'm supposed to be looking at the coffin, or maybe the priest, but there's a man striding towards us across the graveyard.

He's wearing a white coat: a doctor's uniform. A stethoscope bangs against his chest as he nears. Why would a doctor be coming to the funeral? Even if I recognised him, or if he was one of Dad's new friends, wouldn't he have dressed in black like everyone else? The signs are there: he's a ghost.

I try to pull free of Dad's fingers and he leans across to put his mouth to my ear. "Stop it," he hisses. His anger heats my face.

"But–"

"This is your mother's funeral, have the grace to stand still."

"There's a g–"

He shakes my arm. "Your Mum's being buried, Taylor. Stand still."

Frozen by Dad's anger I watch him approach. Tears blind me and when I can refocus his face looms above mine. I can't stop myself flinching when he grabs my hand. Ice spikes into my arm and I jerk.

He shows teeth like tombstones. "That was easy."

I stare at my hand where a black stain has splashed me to the wrist. Dad gives me another shake and wordlessly I raise my arm to show him the Mark.

His shoulders shudder then he fixes his gaze back on Mum's grave.

"Mum says the Darkness will come for me."

"Your Mum isn't here, I am and I'm not having my daughter going out and approaching strange people."

"But what if the Darkness comes?"

"It won't."

"Look at my hand." Over the last couple of days the Mark has darkened. Now it looks like a hole through my palm.

"It's just a skin condition." Dad won't meet my eyes. "You'll be fine. If I have to lock you in your room I will."

"You have to let me out. It's school tomorrow."

"We'll see." Dad rolls awkwardly in his chair towards the living room.

I lie in bed and stare at my hand. I can't take my eyes off it. The Mark seems to grow every time I look away.

I know the ghost is waiting outside. I've seen him. At least when Dad lets me out he'll be right there. But I'm afraid it might be too late by then.

A compilation CD is playing on a loop. My ears are tuned into the sound rather than the song. I'm terrified that the noise will suddenly cut out. I know that means the Darkness is coming.

I hear the mechanical rumble of Dad's stair lift. Then it falls silent. My heart stops.

It's here!

No, my music is still thumping loud as ever.

My heart stutters back to life and I clutch my chest as the stair lift coughs and continues to climb.

Finally Dad rolls into my room. I lie with my back to him and refuse to turn.

"Taylor, it's time to get up."

"A-are you going to let me out?" Hope trembles in my voice.

"No." The carpet shushes as Dad comes nearer. His hand falls on my back. "This is for your own good, when you see there's no Darkness coming, you'll be able to get better." In the periphery of my vision I see him pick up *The Tale of Oh-Fa* and remove it from my bedside.

Still I cradle my fist under my chin and refuse to speak. My skin is numb where the Mark stains it. When the Darkness comes will my whole body feel the same way?

"Taylor, come to the kitchen. You have to eat something."

I shake my head.

"I'm angry with your mum, you know." His voice is low and I almost look at him.

"Why?" My eyes fall on a shadow on the wall and I jerk. Is it moving?

"She's done this to you with her horror stories. I should have been stronger that day, when it all started for you. I should have taken you away."

Staring through the dawn-brushed window I realised I was looking at the spot the ghost had occupied for those three weeks after Mum's funeral. During the final week I didn't eat or sleep. Dad considered hospitalising me, I know he did. But finally he relented and let me out. Luckily the killer had been easy to find and Mark, even for a young teenager, so the Darkness hadn't taken me. It had been close though. Everywhere I looked the shadows had been trembling.

So I had around three weeks to find Justin and get him to take me to his killer.

The school corridors were quiet once more. Hush reigned where usually there would have been pre-class chaos. One of the boys from the lower school jostled me as he ran through the common room. I caught him with a frown, but he had already stopped dead with one foot raised in ridiculous apprehension. He licked his lips as he slowly put down his foot and edged between the static groups. I watched him break into a self-conscious jog as soon as the double doors closed on his back, then turned as Hannah closed her hand around my elbow.

"You're here early." She dragged me towards an unoccupied table. "You missed the police yesterday. They talked to us in assembly, then Tamsin went home." She lowered her voice. "Justin's missing. Isn't it awful?"

I nodded as we skirted the news-thrilled whisperers. Then I stopped, pulling Hannah short.

Tamsin had leaped to her feet and now stood over her hags. Her blonde hair was in its usual perfect waves, but her make-up was just that little bit off, giving her face the expression of a plastic doll left too long by a roaring fire. The reddening of her cheeks added to the effect of heat-blast Barbie.

"What would you know about it?"

She slammed her hand down on the table, making books jump. Her girlfriends avoided her eye and one in particular leaned from her wrath, so unbalanced it looked like she'd fall off her chair any second.

Tamsin spun to face the rest of us. "You're all thinking it, aren't you? That he's run away and it's my fault because he was my boyfriend. Well, you're wrong." She tottered away from the table, fists clenched. "Anyone else want to say it? Come on." Her eyes narrowed as she zeroed in on Hannah and me: somehow the only others standing in her eyeline. "How about you, Oh?" She angled towards me, propelled by fury. Her face thrust against mine, her hot breath slightly sour. This close I could see how the whites of her eyes had become yellowed and bloodshot. They were eyes I'd seen in the mirror often enough. She had been crying. A lot.

"You want to say something?"

For once I stepped back, my instinct to provoke dead in my throat. Tamsin placed both hands flat on my chest and tensed to shove. I raised my hands and Hannah spoke over my shoulder.

"We don't think it's your fault, Tamsin." Her soft voice soothed. "No one does. They're just trying to make sense of what's happened."

"You'd have been the first to say it if it was someone else," I snapped. So maybe the bitch was still kicking in there. Behind me Hannah groaned.

Tamsin snarled and raised a hand. I knew the slap was going to land and had barely a second to brace myself for head-spinning contact. But it never came. I blinked to see Pete standing with one hand around Tamsin's wrist.

"Get off me." Tamsin wheeled on him. "I'm going to kill her."

Pete tilted his head meaningfully. Behind him James stood with his arms folded, Harley at his side.

"This isn't the time." James' eyes raked me from head to foot and I shuddered, feeling as if I needed a shower. "Pull it together, Tamsin."

Slowly she nodded and Pete released her. She stepped into James' orbit. "You'll get yours." Her lips twitched and James curled a big hand around her shoulder, holding her still.

"Mr Barnes wants to talk to us." He spoke to Tamsin, but remained looking at me. "Let's go."

The whole common room watched as the four headed towards Mr Barnes' office. Breathless silence persisted for a moment, only the rustling of paper and nervous clearing of throats filled the air. Then heads closed together and the gossip started up more persistent than before. Where was Justin Hargreaves? Why would he have run away? Had something sinister happened?

Only I knew that he wouldn't be coming back. And I very much needed to speak to the dead bastard.

"Your eczema's bad again." Hannah poked at my glove. "Is that why you ditched school yesterday?" Her tone held a gentle accusation.

"I'm sorry, Han. It came on really fast."

"It always does." She rubbed her fingers through her dandelion hair. "I just wish you'd let me know. I looked for you all morning. After that assembly, I was worried."

"I didn't realise." I shouldered my bag. "I really am sorry."

"You could have answered your phone, or replied to my texts. I couldn't even concentrate on *Supernatural* I was so worried."

I nodded, thinking of my phone turned to silent in my pocket the whole time I was breaking into the mariticide's house. It was late when I'd picked up Hannah's worried messages, too late to get back to her. "I can't say it won't happen again, but I'll try harder." My heart played a panicked staccato; Hannah couldn't be mad at me.

Hannah sighed. "It's just been happening a lot lately. I wish you'd–"

"What?"

"I wish you'd tell me what's going on. I could do something to help."

I exhaled slowly. "Is this about Pete?"

"No." We stopped outside the classroom. "Maybe. I shouldn't let him get to me."

"No, you shouldn't." I squeezed her arm inside mine and pulled her to one side as our classmates pushed to get through the door. Finally the black rings round her eyes registered with me. "A *Supernatural* marathon, or did your mum keep you up late again?"

Hannah sagged. "She made me clean the house before Carl finished his shift. The Winchesters kept me company."

"What about your homework?"

Hannah shrugged. "I did it after."

"Damn it, Han, what did your mum do while you were cleaning her mess?"

Hannah's mouth curled bitterly. "She went down the pub then passed out in front of *CSI*."

I squeezed her tighter; there was nothing else I could do. "Bet Carl was pleased."

"They had a fight when he got in. Then they made up. Loudly." She winced and I pressed my lips together. Sometimes I wished I could kick Hannah's mum, but there was always this tiny traitorous voice inside saying, "at least she still has a mum". I squashed it into silence.

"You should come over after school."

Hannah nodded. "Your dad won't mind me staying?"

"Does he ever? So... what colour this time?"

Hannah grinned. "I'm working my way through the neons. What do you think?"

"Love it."

Her hair had long turned into a frizz, but it was the one thing her mum couldn't take away. I understood that. Hannah had control over her hair and she made it glow.

I glanced back down the corridor towards Mr Barnes' office. Tamsin and the others were still inside. "I forgot something in my locker, see you in class?"

Hannah looked alarmed. "You aren't skipping out on me again?"

I shook my head. "I'll be back before bell. Save me a seat."

Hannah inhaled and didn't move.

"Honest, Han, I'm coming back."

She glanced at my gloved hand.

"What?" Self-consciously I folded my arms, hiding the glove from sight.

"You bail on me a lot when your eczema is bad," Hannah shrugged. "It's a pattern."

"Oh." I worried at the glove with my nails. "I hadn't noticed."

"Whatever, it's no big. I'll save you a seat."

"I *will* see you in a minute."

"Sure."

Hannah followed the last of the hags into the classroom and she didn't look back.

I wanted to go and check the waiting area outside Mr Barnes' office. I hoped Justin might be hanging around waiting for his girlfriend. But the hallway was empty and the chairs sat unused. There was no sign of any dead.

I flexed my Marked hand and looked at the clock. There was still time for him to show up in class. If he still believed he was alive, he would come to school.

As I prepared to head back to the classroom, the door to Mr Barnes' office opened. Pete stood with his back to me, still holding the handle down, but he made no further move to leave. Mr Barnes was just finishing up.

My breath shortened as I realised that I was alone and about to come face-to-face with the whole group. I wasn't sure who I was more worried about, James or Tamsin. Normally I'd deal, but today they were unpredictable and with Justin missing, the teachers would let them get away with more than usual.

Swiftly I slipped into the shadow behind the drinks machine. It wasn't the best hiding place, but it might keep them from noticing me.

I stared at the ceiling, pressing myself into the cool metal, as the door clicked shut.

"Tamsin, you gotta chill." That was Harley.

"Mr Barnes says everything will be alright." Pete. "He has a contact in the force, a bloke from his club. There's nothing to worry about."

"You – you think they'll find Justin?" Tamsin's voice wobbled and I almost felt sorry for her.

"Yeah, they'll find him." That was James. "Let's get to class."

"We're still meeting this week?" They were moving further down the corridor and I risked a look around the drinks machine. Tamsin was clinging onto James' arm as if it were a lifebelt.

James nodded at her. "We have to show. People depend on us."

At the back of the group Pete hesitated, then turned. I pulled back too slowly and his eye caught mine. He shook his head: disappointment, exasperation? I wasn't sure. Either way, he said nothing, simply turned and trailed his gang into class.

I knocked my head against the drinks machine making it rattle and Mr Barnes emerged from his office.

"Are you waiting for me, Miss Oh?"

I clutched my bag. Moron. "No. I was just on my way to class."

He frowned at me over his glasses and his pudgy fingers worked around his tie. "I don't want any trouble today, Miss Oh. I'm thinking particularly of Justin's friends. They are having a difficult time and I do not want to hear reports of you antagonising them."

"That's not fair–" Heat flushed my chest.

"I don't want to hear it, Miss Oh. Get to class."

He closed his door in my face and I stood for a moment, shaking. My gloved hand wound around the straps of my pack and I tried not to picture winding it around his neck. Then I closed my eyes and exhaled. If only he was the sort to commit murder, I could stamp him with a one way ticket into the Darkness.

Stifling the fantasy I smirked, Mr Barnes wouldn't be earning a trip to Anubis any time soon. But I could dream.

Above my head the class bell rang. Still no sign of Justin. I ground my teeth and ran down the corridor. If he didn't show up in school today I'd have to start looking elsewhere. In a few short weeks the Darkness would be coming for the bearer of the Mark and I wasn't going to be the one wearing it.

I slid into the chair next to Hannah, earning a tut from Mrs Pickard.

"I'm writing you up for lateness, Taylor." She made a note in her book.

I nudged Hannah as I opened my bag. "Told you I'd be here." I pulled out my pencil case and tried not to be stabbed by the fact that Hannah was relieved that I had shown. My heart tied in knots as she forced a grin.

"I know." She cut her eyes towards Tamsin. "Check out the new seating arrangement."

I hadn't noticed. I raised my head and my eyebrows followed. James was now in Justin's seat and Tamsin had left her table of hags and moved onto his right. Pete and Harley sat facing them, still opening their books.

We weren't the only ones who had taken note. Murmurous comments blew through the rest of the class, earning defiant glares from a flush-faced Tamsin.

Mrs Pickard sat for a moment at her desk then seemed to come to some sort of decision. She stood.

"Right, class, I know that one of your number isn't here today and that things aren't quite as normal. I know you all have questions and we hope and trust that Justin will be back with us very soon and that he will be able to answer some of those questions for himself. In the meantime…" she glanced out of the window. "You won't be taking much in today. I wasn't going to do this till later in the term, but we've been looking at *Romeo and Juliet*, so I've got two films for you – one by Franco Zeffirelli and the other by Baz Luhrmann. Over the next few lessons I'm going to let you watch both." She glowered at us as she patted towards the light switch. "I give you fair warning, next week I'll want essays comparing their treatment of the material, so this isn't time off. Pay attention and take notes. It'll be Zefirelli's version first. Boys, I don't want any silliness during the balcony scene." She turned off the light. "Harley, get the blinds will you?"

I tensed up. I was probably the only person in class who hated it when the teacher put on a film, purely because I couldn't see out of the window. From my seat I normally had a good view of the entrance and of any ghosts drawn to the school.

"Taylor, are you with us?"

"Yes, Miss." I dragged my eyes away from the tiny slice of car park revealed by the pulled blind. Justin remained absent. I shifted my chair so I would have a good view of the classroom door. If he came in, I'd spot him.

Halfway through the lesson I gave up. Justin wasn't coming. I shifted my attention to the screen. Juliet had just discovered Romeo's true name. I sighed and reached for my pencil, knocking my notebook onto the floor as I did so.

Mrs Pickard glared pointedly and I bent over to pick it up. In the darkness beneath the table across from us, James and Tamsin were holding hands.

••••

"I'm back." I dropped my bag in the hall. Not one
teacher had given us homework and we'd spent the day
watching films or reading quietly. During break nervous
energy overspilled into fights and races around the quad.
Tamsin had gone home at lunchtime. I'd considered
following her, hoping Justin might be lingering at her
house, but I'd shelved that idea. Hannah needed me to
be in school for at least one full day and I still had time
to find him, at least for now.

Dad rolled out of his office, his face grave. "Hannah's
mum called. She said there's a kid from your class gone
missing." His face told me what he thought of Hannah's
mum calling him. He liked her as much as I did.

"Is she worried?" I sat on the stairs so I could be at
his level.

"I think she just wanted to gossip." Dad pushed his
chair closer. "It's that boy you were in trouble with last
week, isn't it? Are you OK?"

"I didn't even like him." I shrugged.

"Sometimes that makes it worse." Dad pressed
forward. "Do you feel... guilty?"

"Why would I?"

Dad cleared his throat. "No reason." His eyes froze on
my white glove. "You didn't tell me your condition had
returned."

I shoved my hand behind my back. "It was yesterday."

"Still." His chair pinned me to the stairs as he reached
for my arm.

I snatched it out of reach. "Do you really need a
sample?"

Dad dropped his hand. "No, that's not it. I just wanted to make sure you were alright."

"I'm fine, Dad." I tried on a smile. "Hannah's coming over later."

He glanced at my gloved hand again. "You aren't… going out?" *Out after a killer*. He hated saying it and didn't believe it anyway.

"Not yet." There was a loose thread on my glove from all my picking. I tugged at it, avoiding his eyes.

"Good." He glided back, gave me some room. "I have to do a bit of work – a teleconference with the bank. They want to talk about diversifying the mutual fund we got with your mum's life insurance. And I need to check on our stocks and shares, make sure her family money is still working as hard as it can." He rubbed his hands through his hair and glanced at his office. "We're fine financially, but my research has thrown up a couple of ideas I want to run with, so I'm going to set some wheels in motion with the patent office. Anyway, when I'm off the phone, I thought I might take you out… and Hannah of course. We could go down the river. I know you usually prefer to stay in, but it's such a nice day."

Was it? I'd spent the whole journey home watching for Justin and keeping an eye out for other restless dead. I looked out the window and saw the sun streaming through Mum's ivy in a lacework of green and gold.

I closed my hand around the Mark on my fist. Normally I'd argue to stay in and order a pizza and it was true that I didn't want to risk getting a second Mark, but I'd seen Justin hanging out at the river before.

He hadn't been at school, so I'd have to start looking further afield.

"OK, Dad." I smiled at him. "We'll go out."

"We will?" For a moment surprise made his face comical. Then he grinned. "You can push me from Hammersmith Bridge and I'll feed you guys at the Blue Anchor. What do you think?"

"Sounds great, Dad." I remembered that there was a good view from the tables there. I could sit and keep watch while I ate. "I'll call Hannah." I jumped to my feet and Dad's arms pumped purposefully as he rolled towards his office.

"I'll be as quick as I can," he called over his shoulder. "It'll be great to have a date with my favourite girls."

I sniggered. "Right." I ran upstairs already pulling off my uniform and his wistful tones trailed me up the stairs.

"It's been such a long time."

11
No sign of Justin

My burger was growing cold and I was half listening to Hannah and Dad talking about school, half watching out of the pub window. There had been no sign of Justin. Dad grunted irritably and placed his pint meaningfully on the table.

"Are we keeping you from something, Taylor?" he snapped.

Hannah laughed uncomfortably. "She's always like this, Mr Oh, I think it's her eczema. It's distracting when it's bad."

"How many times have I asked you to call me Gabriel?" Dad reached for her hand, squeezed it and withdrew. "Oh was Emma's name, she wanted me to take it when we got married, a family tradition. Now when people say it, well... it reminds me what I've lost."

"Sorry." Hannah looked mortified. "I can call you Gabriel. It's a nice name."

"I didn't mean to upset you." Dad took a drink of his beer. "If we can just stick with Gabriel, or even Gabe, from here on out…"

"Of course." Hannah looked at me, panic stricken.

"You're right, Dad, it is a nice day." I tried to focus on his face as I changed the subject, but my eyes kept slipping to the walkway outside. Was that man in jeans and a jumper really dressed for the weather? Was that woman casting a shadow?

Dad sighed and rolled his eyes at Hannah. "It's just like being with her mum, she never gave me her full attention either. I started to feel like the most boring man alive. And now she's older, with the glove and that hair, it's easy to think I'm out with Emma."

"The glove? Did Taylor's mum have eczema too?" Hannah frowned at my hand.

"I'm sure she's told you." Dad smiled at my friend. "Emma shared Taylor's condition."

"No." Hannah twisted her drink so that it made wet circles on the wooden table top. "She never said."

"Oh." Dad cleared his throat awkwardly. "Well, that's her glove Taylor wears." It was his turn to change the subject. "Is that a rowing team at the bar?"

Hannah gave me a final glower, before leaning to look. "Oh yes. Tay, check out the muscles."

"Muscles?" I grabbed gladly at the change in direction. "Where?"

But my gaze never reached the bar. There was an old man in one corner. He had been slumped over an empty pint glass since we came in. As I watched, a waitress emerged from the kitchen area and started clearing away empties. She had a smile and a word for every customer, but not this guy. He nodded at her when she picked up his drink, but she didn't even acknowledge him.

My heart started to sink. The corner in which he sat was shadowy and I hadn't seen him looking at us, but still…

"Hannah, do you see that old guy over there?"

Hannah squinted. "Which one?"

"Under the picture."

"I can't see who you mean. Anyway, I'd much rather be checking out biceps than some old bloke. What are you thinking?"

She leaned back towards the bar with an exaggerated sigh that made Dad laugh. Then he touched my hand. "Taylor?"

Hannah couldn't see the old man. We had to leave. "I've finished, have you?" I said brightly, pushing my burger away.

"Well, yes. But I thought you might want pudding."

"No thanks." I twisted to grab my coat from the back of my chair. "Let's walk back while it's still nice. Hannah wants to dye her hair anyway."

"Hannah?" Dad looked at her. "Do you want anything else?"

I widened my eyes in silent warning and she sighed. "No thanks, Mr… Gabriel… I'm OK. We can head back."

Dad snorted. "I've got to get the bill, Taylor. We can't just run from the restaurant, sit back down."

"We'll meet you outside." I grabbed Hannah and backed towards the door. The old man had raised his head, but made no move to follow.

As I reached the exit I stopped. Why hadn't he come after me?

"You still can't see the old guy with the red scarf?" I asked.

Hannah peered around the pub. "I must be blinded by the lovely rowers, who I would've been happy to watch for longer," she grumped.

"Huh." I tilted my head at the dead guy. With a wry smile he raised one hand, but made no other move. Maybe he was newly deceased. I waggled my fingers in tentative response and he returned to regarding the beer mat that had sat under the empty glass. I exhaled, relief lightening my shoulders.

I'd never had a ghost just let me go before.

"Taylor, that was rude."

Dad was so annoyed with me that he hadn't even let me push his chair on the way home. Hannah had done a stint then he'd rolled himself the rest of the way. Now she was in the bathroom getting the dye out of her bag and his arms were shaking.

"Dad–"

"Even on the way home you were hardly paying attention to your friend. Let alone to me." The bags under his eyes had grown, tiredness made him look older. "I just wanted a nice meal out, to spend some time together and you couldn't even do that. I know why you made us leave early."

"There was a–"

"This is getting out of hand." He rubbed his trembling fingers through his hair. "Do you treat Hannah like this all the time? She didn't even know about your mum having the same skin condition."

"It's not something I talk about," I snapped.

"Not even with your best friend?" Dad glided forward. "I know what women are like and I know how important friends are. Your mum had her sister. She didn't share her illness, but she knew about it. You don't have a sister. As far as I can tell, you only have Hannah."

I hung my head. "What am I meant to say? By the way, I see ghosts."

"Of course not." Dad sighed. "There's no such thing and don't be clever. Maybe I can speak to her. I can tell what we know: that it's genetic, that you have hallucinations. You don't want to lose her."

"Right, and telling her I have hallucinations, that won't freak her out."

"It's *Hannah*." Dad's chair hissed across the carpet. "She truly believes 'the truth is out there'."

"Dad!"

"You aren't giving her enough credit."

"Leave it." I glanced towards the upstairs bathroom. "I'm handling this."

He shook his head. "I'm worried about you. You're going to end up alone."

"I mean it. If I want Hannah to know, I'll tell her. But right now I'm not taking the risk."

"I'm ready." Hannah's voice called out from the bathroom. "Check it – neon pink and we're going to try frosted tips this time."

"Coming." I glanced at Dad and sighed. "I really didn't mean to ignore you."

Dad looked at his dead feet. "Like I said, Taylor, I'm used to it."

That night I fell asleep to the memory of words from Oh-Fa's journal. I clenched my fists as I curled up in bed. If only I had enough of me left to keep my dad from feeling so alone.

As the day teetered on late afternoon our employer called us back. Our excited mutters were silenced when he stood with his arms spread; a showman with an elixir to peddle.

"I have it." His round glasses glinted in the blazing sun. "Nefertiti's tomb is…" He paused, enjoying his moment. "Right here."

"Where?" Sunbird's head bobbed and the Professor grinned at the man's confusion and then tucked his notebook into the satchel he habitually carried over one shoulder.

"Anubis is pointing with his flail. The tomb is right beneath our feet."

Sunbird roared at us to gather our tools and sledgehammers, but his instructions were unnecessary, activity had transformed the camp.

Yet as the Professor directed the first hammer

blow into Anubis' jackal snout I became apprehensive. Desecration of the image of a god, even that of a foreign deity, did not seem providential.

As the ancient stone boomed and shards of rock shattered on stone far below, a hole opened up beneath the carving and I, temporarily surplus to requirements, made my retreat.

"This is your early warning." I looked sideways at Hannah. The candyfloss of her hair finished with platinum ends that caught the sun like puffs of cloud. "You look great, by the way."

"I know." She fluffed it with her fingers. "Mum hated it."

"Excellent," I grinned.

"So – early warning?" She swung her bag higher on her shoulder.

I cleared my throat. "I'm skipping out at lunch."

"What?" Hannah stopped in front of me. "Why?"

"It's an eczema thing." I flashed my gloved hand briefly in front of her. "Doctor's appointment."

"You have a letter?"

I blinked. "I don't have to show you a letter, do I?"

She sighed. "I guess not. Mrs Pickard will want one though."

"I've got a letter." I'd been forging Dad's signature for three years. Mum always took me out of school when the Marks made it necessary, but Dad, not so much.

"You didn't mention it last night."

"It's boring. I'll be back in tomorrow, probably."

"Probably? They're not going to keep you in, are they?"

"No, nothing like that. I'll let you know as soon as I do, promise."

"Fine." Hannah stepped to one side so we could walk to class. Her feet dragged all the way.

Getting hold of Justin's address had been a matter of getting hold of Tamsin's phone. I'd simply waited until she was showering after second period gym and snagged it from her bag. As I suspected, her contacts were up to date with email addresses, phone numbers, Twitter and all sorts, including physical addresses. Quickly I memorised Justin's postcode and house number, and stuck the phone back in her bag when her hags weren't looking.

Then at lunch I headed over there.

He lived in Brook Green, or he had, and his house was not actually that far from mine, which explained why I'd seen him down at the river a few times.

It was a smart Georgian townhouse. Justin had only been in the country five years, so his parents must have bought at the height of the market. They were well off. Not a huge surprise.

Unfortunately, it wasn't the kind of area that was good for loitering; no benches or bus shelters anywhere nearby and a police car was parked at the end of the road. I walked up and down the street half a dozen times, keeping my eyes on the blue front door. There was no sign of Justin.

Movement in the living room caught my attention and I increased my speed. A tall woman was standing at the window, one hand on the curtain, slow and elegant in grief. With the other she clutched a phone to her chest. Even from a distance I could see that she hadn't slept in days. It had to be Justin's mother, waiting for a call that would never come.

Was he in there, watching her?

I considered going up to the front door and knocking. I could offer my sympathies and try to get inside.

But I couldn't face her. Not knowing what I knew.

I tugged at my glove, pulling it free. The black Mark staining my hand seemed to mock me. I had to ask Justin who killed him and put that look on his mother's face. Still, I had time left; time to stake out the house and local area. And there was another obvious place for me to look.

Bothering his mother would be a last resort.

I texted Hannah swiftly. "*Do you know where Tamsin lives?*"

It turned out that Tamsin lived in a portered apartment on the other side of the borough, an easy walk from High Street Ken tube. I curled my lip. She'd have parquet flooring and downstairs a gym, maybe even a swimming pool. I leaned in the shadows of the building opposite and my eyes darted. The day was getting busy and any one of the people milling past me could be dead. Every minute I spent out here I was opening myself to the possibility of gaining another Mark and hastening the arrival of the Darkness.

The porter buzzed in a woman with an armful of shopping bags, calling her by name. It wouldn't be easy breaking in and Tamsin certainly wasn't going to be inviting me over any time soon. Again, my best bet would be to hang around outside until Justin turned up.

I closed my fist. The black Mark seemed to throb and the shadows around me grew darker. Breath held I stepped carefully out into the light, where I exhaled. Suddenly I was no longer comfortable with my hiding place.

A wave of anger lifted me onto my toes. "Justin, where the hell are you?"

It was almost 4 o'clock when Tamsin came home and my feet were itching with the need to run. I'd never stayed in one place for so long, so exposed. I felt as though ghosts were converging from all around the city, surrounding me with hands outstretched, ready to cover me with Marks, enough to blacken my whole body.

I was shaking like a junkie by the time she turned up.

Finally I saw her turn the corner with a couple of hags. At the end of the road she waved them off and as soon as they had given her cloyingly sympathetic hugs and turned away, her shoulders sagged and her whole body seemed to gain weight. She almost heaved herself along the street, bag dangling from her fingertips, barely skimming the filthy pavement.

I felt an unfamiliar twist of sympathy. Now would be the time for Justin to show up. I scanned every face, jerked when I saw a dark haired young man approach her. But he wasn't in school uniform and he walked on without saying a word.

"Cheer up, love, it might never 'appen." A grinning builder gave her a nudge as she passed and Tamsin glared poison.

"Piss off."

With a low whistle he backed away and I shook my head with a half smile. Tamsin could look after herself. But where was her boyfriend? The shadows teemed at my feet. Suddenly it seemed like there wasn't so much time after all.

By the time I got home it was dark. After I'd seen Tamsin enter her building I'd taken the risk and walked back via Justin's house. He remained conspicuously absent. The frustrating thing was, I could be just missing him. He may well have been at school today while I was at his house, or at home while I was at Tamsin's. There was only one of me and a whole city to search.

I had less than three weeks. He had to turn up some time. Didn't he?

I decided that the best thing to do was choose one place. Given that he hadn't gone to school, I thought Justin's most likely hangout would be his own house. I wasn't keen on staking out his street so obviously, exposing myself to local police as well as ghosts and nutters, but I took a sketch pad and pretended I was drawing. It was at least an excuse to be loitering.

It was a total waste of time.

••••

By Thursday night I'd stopped wearing my glove inside. Looking at my hand had become an addiction. It didn't hurt, but the numbness throbbed and I checked it obsessively every few minutes. Had it grown darker?

If I didn't find Justin I was going to be the one stuck wearing the Mark when the Darkness came. There was no way I'd be able to identify his killer without him, I was no Sherlock Holmes. And without knowing who his killer was, I couldn't pass the Mark on.

I'd been fortunate as far as other ghosts had been concerned. Somehow I'd successfully avoided the dead since Justin had Marked me, but I couldn't be lucky forever. When another ghost touched me, I would be carrying double the stain. That would summon the Darkness faster and shorten the time I had to find him.

I shivered, tore my eyes from the invisibly throbbing black Mark and tucked my hand under my arm. I needed more information. I had to speak to someone who knew Justin better than I did.

My hand hovered over the phone, tendons standing proud. I had to call Pete.

Viciously I punched in his number from memory, hurting my fingertip as I jammed the digits.

"Hello."

"It's Taylor."

There was silence for a moment and I wondered if Pete had put the phone down. Finally he spoke. "Right. Why are you calling me?"

I exhaled. "I know they haven't found Justin yet–"

"What do you care?" His anger shivered down the line.

"I was just going to ask if you could tell me some of his hang outs. I-I thought I could help, maybe spend some time at one or two this weekend in case he turns up."

"*You* want to help." His scorn burned, but then I had no cause to complain. He was right; there was no way I'd be making this call if Justin hadn't Marked me.

I swallowed. "I guess there're a lot of people out there looking for him, but a fresh set of eyes can't hurt, can it?"

The phone sat silent in my hand. I closed my eyes, wondering if my one-time friend would believe me.

"You haven't been at school much this week." Pete's tone was accusatory. "Hannah's been on her own."

"I know." Guilt hoarsened my voice. "I've been ill."

"Yeah, like always. Her mum's been a bitch. Have you even called her?"

"I... Not yet." I looked at the Mark on my hand again. It was all I could think about. Hannah hadn't even crossed my mind.

"But suddenly you're worried about *Justin*," Pete sneered. "Hannah deserves better."

"I know." I closed my eyes.

"And I've been telling her so."

"You've no right." My eyes snapped open.

"I've every right. I have no idea what's going on with you, but then I never did. Neither does she."

"I'll be back at school soon and back to normal."

"This *is* normal for you."

"Pete..." My eyes were caught by my own hand. As if it were under a spotlight that suddenly dimmed, the stain darkened right in front of me. I almost gagged. "I was calling to find out about Justin, I'll sort things out with Hannah, but–" I remembered what Dad had said when he asked if I felt guilty. "I fought with him just before he went missing, I feel really bad. I just want to know that he's alright. That it isn't my fault." The lie felt like ashes in my mouth, but it was enough to give Pete pause.

"If you're trying to pull something–" he said finally.

"I honestly want to find Justin." Every atom of my body trembled with sincerity. He'd hear it. He knew me.

Eventually he sighed. "Fine, whatever. We went to the Empire quite a bit and we hung out at the Walkabout a few times, but I can't see him in there without Harley. He and Tamsin loved Camden and..." He paused. "I guess it doesn't matter if I tell you. He spent a lot of time at the Science Museum."

"The Science Museum." Something about that made me sit up.

"Yeah. Don't laugh."

"I'm not. I might check out the Museum then."

"Fine." Pete didn't hang up. The sound of his breathing reminded me of all the time I'd spent on the phone with him over the years. I was tempted to ask what he thought of last night's telly or what I'd missed at school. The words quivered on my lips, but never surfaced.

Then the dial tone hummed in my ear.

And in my mind the fourth entry of Oh-Fa's journal:

Less than an hour later the hole is wide enough to admit two men and of the original icon, only the feet remain.

Now stairs descend from the sand but, despite the blazing sunlight, I can see no further than five treads; the sixth is covered in darkness as impenetrable as treacle.

I have returned to the tent to collect my tools and admit that I am reluctant to go back to the crypt. Pimples speckle my arms in defiance of the heat. It seems strange that we have been camped above the dark-tombed dead this whole week.

I cannot shift the words of the I-Ching from my head, they circle like hawks: The way that can be described is not the true way.

Something about this feels wrong and I would give a lot not to have to descend that staircase.

I think of my son, perhaps newborn. Not that. Never that.

It is time to go.

12

Trapped inside the circle

Instead of going to school I stood on Exhibition Road, leaned against the railings that hemmed the street and looked up at the flag above the building. It snapped in the wind but I couldn't hear it over the road noise. My eyes followed the lines of columns that bordered the windows, down the smog-stained stonework, to the worn gold name above the huge doors.

I hadn't been to the Science Museum since I was a kid. The website had said there were five floors and I had no idea which of them Justin might have headed for.

I shaded my eyes and peered at the windows, secretly hoping for some sort of sign. But there was nothing to see but sun glinting from darkened glass.

A stream of people poured from South Ken station and knocked my elbow as I glared at the printed map scrunched in my gloved hand.

Irritation forced speed into my pulse. There were too many people here, too many ways for the dead to disguise themselves. I had to get off the street. I shoved the map into my backpack and dodged through a gap in the crowd to run up the museum steps.

Then I paused. The shadows around the great doors seemed too dark, too cold. I licked my lips and strained my ears. The street sounds continued, noisy and normal. Shaking my head I ran in, towards the well-lit security checkpoint.

Time was getting tighter. Justin had to be here.

I queued behind a school group then handed my backpack to a guard whose smile was already looking strained.

"Got any sharp objects?" He raised his eyebrows at me.

"No."

"Any of this?" He gestured to a laminated sheet showing a range of lethal weaponry.

"No."

"Alright then." He briefly lifted my cardigan from the top of my pack so he could see my purse, Oyster card, keys and can of drink. Then he handed my pack back to me. "Enjoy your visit."

I stood by the information desk in the gaping entranceway. There were too many options. I was planted like a rock in a sandstorm, my feet unsure which way to turn. Should I take the lift? Start at the Garden and work my way up to the fifth floor? Maybe I ought to head straight on, past the ticket booth for the iMax? According to the map, that route would take me through an area dedicated to space travel and into a display about energy.

Above the ticket booth there hung a huge metal hoop. It was so big it reached the third floor. An electronic display inside its rim drew my eye. The little lights danced endlessly, trapped inside the circle, seeking a way out that they would never find. It spoke to me. I headed towards the glowing ring.

Beyond the light-filled ring I caught my breath. Ahead of me a space shuttle hung in a dark-shrouded room. People walked towards me in pairs but I ignored their irritated huffs, refusing to move and forcing them to part in order to pass me. It was dark in there, full of shadow. I took a step backwards; I didn't have to go this way. There was no guarantee that Justin was on the other side.

But then his voice came back to me: "I was going to study engineering."

If he was here, he would be in the Engineering section and that was on the other side of the cloying darkness. I straightened my shoulders and walked into the false night-time.

To get out in record time I planned to march through the exhibit, looking neither left, nor right, but then glimmering displays caught my eye. There were whirling representations of planets and stars, and engines from real shuttles. They looked like Dalek mutations but had propelled man into the vacuum of space and brought him safely home.

Awe filled me and instead of striding straight on, I faltered and my eyes flickered from plastic astronauts to their replica equipment. Then I saw a quote on the wall.

"An unseen force pressed me to the couch as if lead had been poured over me. Breathing became more difficult. The weight bearing down on us robbed us of the ability to speak. It ate all sound, leaving only wheezes and grunts."

I stood reading and rereading it. *"It ate all sound"*. In my mind there was no doubt; astronaut Vasili Lazarev had experienced the Darkness.

Panting like a long distance runner I darted from the space exhibit and burst gratefully into the light of the Energy section.

I bent over until my breathing felt more normal then I straightened. A giant silver plane was suspended just ahead of me as if flying through the giant hall. My shoulders twitched before I managed to suppress the instinct to duck. Embarrassed, I pushed my hair back over my shoulders. The hall was bright, light, silver and white. The only dark patches were on the aged metal of machines from earlier centuries.

I adjusted my bag and walked forward. Shadows were not permitted in this realm of science.

This was more like it.

The hall was crowded, but my eyes moved, constantly seeking the missing ghost. I clenched my gloved fist as he failed to materialise.

In case I'd missed him I circled the energy section twice more, growing familiar with the locomotives, cars and planes surrounding me. He wasn't there.

On the way towards the exit, shoulders sagging, I passed Stephenson's *Rocket* and hesitated. The first of its kind, it looked utterly out of place in front of the shiny engines that had superceded it.

I took a tiny step forward. My hand lifted as if to touch the huge wooden wheels, but I couldn't reach past the stand. *Rocket* was to look at, not to touch.

Without *Rocket* there would have been no *Apollo*. I shook my head and willed my feet to move, but they didn't. The metal barrel of its body led my eye to the black chimney... and Justin dropped out of the bottom.

I gasped and relief almost knocked me to the floor. I had found him. Nervously I exhaled, if he ran off again I was in deep trouble. Somehow I had to keep him calm.

I watched in anxious silence as Justin stepped backwards out of *Rocket*, wiping his hands as though he'd been doing maintenance on the locomotive's innards. He didn't turn his head to acknowledge me, but he knew I was there. He froze and put one hand on a wheel that was almost as big as he was.

"Did you know Stephenson was basically uneducated?" His voice was loud in the hall. All the suspended technology invited a church-like silence but Justin's voice boomed.

I blinked at his words and he carried on, still refusing to look at me.

"When he was seventeen he went to night school so he could read and write. He learned all about engines in the collieries and invented a safety lamp that would burn without exploding. Then this 'educated' scientist accused him of nicking his idea."

I swallowed, unable to bridge the gap between us. "I didn't know that."

"Then did you know that *Rocket* killed a man?"

I shook my head, but he talked on, as if I hadn't moved. "William Huskisson, Member of Parliament for Liverpool. He was attending the opening of the Liverpool and Manchester Railway. He was the first ever guy under a train." He hesitated and his fingers stroked the killer engine. "Bet you've seen a few of those."

I shuffled my feet. "Not really." He didn't show that he'd heard me. "Are you coming out of there?"

"*Rocket* changed the world." Justin still didn't look at me. "Did you know they're testing a network of personal driverless pods at Heathrow? They could be all over the world by the time we're... *you're* fifty."

"Justin..."

"I was going to change the world."

"Yeah, sure."

Now he looked at me and I took a step back, almost tripping over the wheels of a pram. I weathered a glare from the mother and turned back to Justin.

He finally moved his hands from *Rocket* and spread them wide. "I know people say that, but I had ideas. We could have made them happen, Dad and me, just like Robert and his son."

I gestured to the train he'd dropped from. "You get it then? You're dead."

He put his hand through the engine then pulled it free and nodded. "It's been nearly a week and I don't need to eat or sleep. I haven't even been able to touch anyone since you." His eyes met mine.

"Well, you aren't touching me again." I wrapped my hands around my elbows. "Tell me who killed you and you can move on."

Justin shook his head slowly. "I don't get this. I don't get why you can see me when no one else can."

A Japanese family moved towards me and I pressed my lips together. Then I gestured curtly for Justin to follow me and headed towards the lift.

We stood in silence as we rose towards the fifth floor. Justin said nothing more about engineering, Stephenson, or his Dad and every time he moved, I moved too – away from him, as though we were opposing magnets.

Finally the lift doors opened onto a white corridor with two exits. In one I could see a plastic replica of a skinned cow. I shuddered and turned the other way.

"The Science and Art of Medicine?" Justin frowned.

"I'm betting it'll be quiet." I paused with my hand on the door. A security guard glared at me through the glass but I was thinking about the dim lighting. I considered changing my mind and heading for the skinned cow, but apart from the guard, the room was empty; we'd be able to talk.

I opened the door and went in.

The air was cooler and drier here and the low lighting gave the impression, not of age or mustiness, but of importance. The displays were sedately lit and invited long, slow examination.

The security guard lounged on his stool by the door and barely glanced at me as I walked past.

On our left there was an Egyptian display. Perfect. Immediately I led Justin towards the mummified corpse that formed the centrepiece. We were shielded from the guard by a wall and there were no other visitors.

"I thought there'd be a picture of Anubis in here," I frowned. "There isn't one. That's strange."

"Who's Anubis?" Justin stood next to me, so close the hairs on my arms stood up.

"Egyptian God of embalming and mummification."

Justin eyed the mummy in the sarcophagus. "I can see why you thought there'd be something about him round here. Why, does it matter? You aren't Egyptian are you?"

"I'm half *Chinese*, Hargreaves."

"On your Mum's side, right?"

"Right."

He hesitated briefly. "Then… why're you called Taylor Oh?"

"Huh?"

"Shouldn't you be Taylor Smith, or something, whatever your Dad's name is?"

"Not everyone takes their husband's name," I snapped. Then I looked at the ceiling and took a breath. "If we all keep the same name it helps us keep track."

"Keep track?"

"Of who carries the curse." I cracked my knuckles, hardly able to believe that I was about to speak the words. But Justin was dead; he had no one to tell. If he thought I was crazy or didn't believe me, what would it matter? Suddenly I was desperate to talk and the words tumbled from me like sand through an hourglass.

"Anubis is meant to be the reason for all this. My ancestor was a member of an expedition of... I suppose you'd call them tomb robbers. They found Nefertiti's tomb but it wasn't empty." I looked at the mummified Egyptian, my memory taking me back to my mother's book. *Scattered lanterns illuminated the bodies*.

For a moment the mummy had looked as if it were bathed in blood. I caught a skeptical twitch of Justin's eyebrows.

"Oh-Fa was the last survivor of the slaughter. Anubis offered him life in exchange for his service. Oh-Fa agreed and now, at a certain age, unlucky members of my family start to see ghosts – murder victims. I was ten."

"Ten." Disbelief vibrated in Justin's voice.

I sighed and focused on the bandaged corpse. "It was your first day at school."

"Oh, please..."

"Really. It was my birthday, remember?" I closed my eyes, allowing the memories to wash over me. "I'd been seeing this clown all day. At first I thought Dad might have hired him – you know, like a really cruddy birthday treat. But it was creepy the way he was hanging around the school. I kept seeing his balloons, but no one else noticed anything."

Justin shook his head. "You're making this up."

I pushed my hair from my face. "Why would I?"

He leaned close to the glass case, close enough for his breath to have fogged the glass, but no fog appeared. Then he leaned back. "So then what?"

"I started hearing the flap-slap of his giant shoes. Clown shoes, you know?"

Justin smirked.

"That sound." I shuddered. "Pete said I could be having a migraine or something, so I called Dad and he took me home."

"And that was the end of it?"

I snorted. "I wish. Somehow the clown followed us back. Dad couldn't drive me to the door, there was a Volvo or something double-parked at the end of the road. He dropped me off and went to find a space." I swallowed, the recollection still filling me with a ten year-old's terror.

"I only had to pass nine houses by myself. I could hear the rumble of the underground line and a dog barking in someone's garden. Then I heard those damn shoes..."

13

Worst birthday ever

Flap-slap.

I froze.

Flap-slap.

The hairs on the back of my neck stood to attention and I spun around. For a moment I saw nothing out of the ordinary then I caught my breath as a single red balloon floated at head height from behind the house at the end of the road. It bobbed as if it couldn't make up its mind which way to go, then the breeze carried it in my direction.

The balloon weaved towards me unhurriedly and I took a step backwards, gaze fixed on its plastic skin. My eyes were reflected in its shiny surface, wide and staring. It jerked towards me, as if to tap me on the head and I jumped, snagged my heel on the kerb, lost my balance and fell. I sat hard on the pavement and quickly looked for the balloon. It was floating on past our house.

It's only a balloon. Get a grip.

I caught my breath and put my hands on the warmed concrete, ready to push myself up.

Flap-slap.

I cried out and turned, one hand covering my mouth. Maybe he had finished toying with me because this time, when I expected to see nothing, the clown was there.

When he saw that I'd noticed him, he started walking towards me again.

Flap-slap, flap-slap… flap-slap.

I scrambled to my feet, stumbled, and with one frightened look backwards, started to run for the house.

Flap-slap, flap-slap.

The clown didn't hurry, the footsteps didn't get any louder, but when I reached my steps and looked over my shoulder he was only a few steps behind me.

He was wearing a multi-coloured wig. Underneath the bobbing curls he had bloodshot eyes sharp with purpose.

He reached for me with one gloved hand and I screamed, threw myself up the steps and fumbled for Dad's keys. My fingers touched the ring and I dragged it out of my pocket. "Go away!" I shrieked. "Leave me alone."

Flap, slap.

The clown had mounted the steps.

Flap-slap.

He was coming.

I jammed the key in the lock and looked over my shoulder. The clown's balloons bounced jauntily as he reached for me. His fingers brushed my rucksack, but before they could close and tug me backwards I leaped into the house and slammed the door.

Justin was watching me now, his eyes narrowed. "It wasn't over?"

I shook my head. "I had to open the door for Dad. The clown was standing right behind him. He reached round and touched me – like you did – transferred the Mark. I didn't know what was going on. I freaked out, couldn't believe Dad had let this creepy guy put his hands on me. But as far as Dad was concerned there was no one there.

"Mum came home just in time, before I touched Dad and accidentally transferred the Mark to him. Instead of a birthday dinner Mum took me to the fair on Clapham Common."

"Sounds nice," Justin shrugged.

I shook my head. "Not really. The killer worked there…"

The sun was going down and the evening had turned close. My T-shirt had bunched under my armpits and my tongue felt fluffy and strange as if I'd eaten too many sweets. I'd never been more nervous.

Mum pinned me with a look. "I'll point out the man we're looking for. All you need to do to transfer the Mark is touch his bare skin with that hand. It'll be alright. It's easy."

I nodded as around us rides whirled and the shrieks and screams of teenagers blended into a din with the blare of tinny rock music.

Mum walked confidently by my side, one hand resting lightly on my wrist. Quickly she guided me past the big wheel and the hook-a-duck towards the Hall of Mirrors.

"Is he there?" I gestured.

Mum nodded, keeping her face down. "He sometimes works the candyfloss, sometimes the Hall of Mirrors. He has a bulldog tattooed on his arm."

"Why did he do it?"

Mum snorted. "His girlfriend had left him."

"For the c-clown?"

"No, actually. He helped her escape to a women's shelter."

As we walked my trainers skated through a mixture of brown grass, mud created by spilled fizzy drinks and ketchup covered cones of half-eaten chips. "So he was hitting his girlfriend and the clown helped her?"

Mum sighed. "That's right. He couldn't get to his girlfriend so he killed Tony."

"Tony's the clown?"

Mum nodded. Until that moment my feelings about the clown had been straightforward: he was the boogieman. Mum's words released a wave of pity that dampened my fear. Then we were almost at the steps of the funhouse and I had to raise my head.

"Two tickets please." Mum pulled her purse from her handbag and nudged me forward. The man was paying no attention to me. His piggy eyes were fixed on Mum's maroon top, so I stared at him unashamedly.

He was wearing a stained white vest over baggy jeans. A money filled pouch was tied round his waist and as he took the money, he flexed his biceps and made sure his fingers touched Mum's hand. Then he licked lips like slugs. I gagged a little and Mum nudged me again. His left forearm had a bulldog on it.

I didn't want to touch him. I knew I had to, but my arm wouldn't move.

"Why don't you take the tickets, Taylor?" Mum's voice was tense and I knew what she wanted me to do. I just couldn't.

Now the man was pressing the ticket stubs into Mum's hand, taking the opportunity to paw her again and it was too late to touch him without being suspicious.

"Taylor." Mum's voice was urgent.

I swallowed. "Um… wow, I like your tattoo." As if in a dream I reached up to press my palm against the snarling bulldog.

"My brother has a matching one." Proudly he rotated his forearm. "It's from our army days."

Mum knocked my hand down before I could transfer the Mark. "Does he work in the fairground too?"

"Oh yeah." He winked. "We both work the Hall of Mirrors. He's gone on a break, but I'm the handsome one."

Mum tried a smile. "So, do you have a girlfriend?"

The man shook his head. "No way. Been single for three years now. My brother's the one for committed relationships." He waggled his eyebrows suggestively. "I get off in ten."

Mum grabbed my elbow. "We'd better go in. Thanks." She steered me up the steps.

The trailer bounced as we opened the creaking door and entered the Hall of Mirrors. Ahead of me a corridor appeared to stretch for miles yet I knew we only stood inside a lorry. I looked to my left and my body seemed to stretch like an elastic band. My head span. "He didn't do it. Now what?"

I heard the crunch of Mum's teeth. Things weren't going as smoothly as she'd planned. "You'll have to stay in here. I'll go and wait for the right man to come off his break. When he turns up I'll say you hurt your ankle and ask him to help carry you out."

"Then I have to touch him?"

"That's right." She hesitated. "It'll be fine, Taylor." Then she left me alone.

I wrapped my arms around my chest and stared at my reflection. The lump in my chest resolved into a ball of tears but I held it down and wondered what would happen when I touched the man. For some reason I imagined him melting away like the Wicked Witch of the West.

"Taylor? Are you alright?" The door opened; Mum was back and she wasn't alone. "You haven't tried to move, have you?"

"No." I leaned one hand against the oddly warm surface of a mirror. My heart thudded in my ears and I couldn't look away from my reflection.

A man appeared behind me. His image lay beneath my hand, so it looked as if I was pressing him into the glass. This mirror made us into stick people and I couldn't tell what he really looked like, so I turned around.

The man in front of me looked like an action hero!

He wore the same vest as his brother, but on him it looked really good. Like Danny Zuko from *Grease*. His hair was shiny and black.

"Taylor?" Mum pressed her hand to my shoulder. "This is Bill. He's going to carry you down the steps."

"But…?"

"Don't be shy, honey. Remember what we talked about?"

My mouth went dry and I tried to lick my lips.

Suddenly the man's arms were around my shoulder. Before I could help myself, I inhaled. He smelled of lemon shower gel. Underneath there was the sour smell of sweat, cigarettes and something unidentifiable and sweet that would forever remind me of the fairground.

He half lifted me off my feet. "Alright, love?" He gave me a lopsided grin. "Got to be careful in here, it's dark."

I stuck my Marked hand resolutely inside my jacket.

"Taylor?"

I ignored Mum and limped alongside the man who held me in his arms, smiling gratefully up at him as if I really was hurt.

The door opened and the light hit his face. Away from the flattering darkness I could see flaws. His skin was more sallow than olive and his black hair had obviously been dyed.

"Mister, I was wondering, are there any clowns at the fair? I love clowns." The lie almost made me choke, but not as much as the fleeting look that crossed the man's face: a glimmer of rage that chilled me to my toes. Suddenly his fingers on my shoulders felt like claws.

"We just *lost* our clown," he said and his teeth were gritted, "but there're some good acrobats over in the main tent."

"Y-you don't like clowns?"

"Some clowns are alright, but ours was interfering." He pressed his lips together and I swallowed, making a decision. At the bottom of the steps I pulled my hand free of my jacket and offered it him to shake.

As the killer pressed his palm to mine I felt a tingle. He held my hand slightly too long and smiled when he released it. I stepped backwards and looked for the Mark. It had gone.

"Come on, Taylor, time to go." Mum grabbed my shoulder and I just barely remembered to limp. As we left I turned around. The killer stood with his hands on his hips and a grin on his face. But my eyes were drawn to the shadows around the Hall of Mirrors. They were darker than anywhere else and were moving towards his feet.

"Mum...?"

"Don't look, Taylor." She grabbed my shoulder. "Let's go home."

Justin looked impressed. "So you did it?"

"Yeah. On the way home Mum told me about the curse, how it's carried through the female line, how there's a fifty-fifty chance I'll pass it to my own children."

I looked at the white glove I wore whenever a Mark was on me. "I was ten and my life was over. Suddenly I was being told that I'd never stop seeing ghosts and I'd have to spend my life tracking down killers." I trailed my fingers along the glass case surrounding the sarcophagus. "And that I won't be able to have kids, not without giving them the same thing."

"Sucks for you."

I nodded. "Worst birthday ever."

"And your Dad can't see the ghosts?"

"He thinks I'm ill, that I have a skin condition and the rest is all in my head."

"That must be hard." Sympathy changed Justin's face. "So you've been seeing the dead for what, five years?"

"Since we met."

"Look, Taylor," he rubbed his face and stepped away from me. "Maybe your Dad's right."

"What?" I spluttered. "How can you not believe me? You're one of them."

"Obviously I believe you see ghosts." His hand lifted as if to touch my shoulder then changed direction as if repelled, and slipped into the glass case. "That part could be the illness at work, changing something in your brain, letting you see stuff that other people can't. But this thing about avenging murder victims. Maybe that's the part that's made up."

"You—"

"No, listen. What if you don't really need to avenge the dead? Maybe someone in your family came up with it as a way of justifying what happens to you."

My chest felt tight, like I was wearing a corset. I ripped off my glove. "Is this all in my head?"

Justin examined my hand as though I was holding out an interesting beetle. "I thought you wore that because of eczema."

"It happened when you touched me, just like the clown. Once we find your killer I'll touch *them* and this Mark will move from my skin to theirs. Then the Darkness will take them away."

Justin cleared his throat. "What *is* the Darkness?" His foot moved through the shadows that surrounded the sarcophagus.

I shook my head. "It's... the Darkness. It's meant to take murderers to Anubis for judgment."

Our faces were both reflected in front of the dead Egyptian and in the glass we both looked like ghosts.

Justin stood almost a head taller than me. His hair and eyes toned with mine; a brown so dark it was almost black. But my eyes were slanted almonds and his were round-edged and deep set, preventing a true match. He had lost his tan over the years and was naturally pale. The skin of his throat curved above his tie soft as the petals of a flower. Not for the first time, it struck me that he looked like someone I should really like. It was a shame I didn't.

Strands of my hair shifted around my shoulders as the air-conditioning blew over us so gently I barely felt it. Through our reflections I could see the face of the mummy and the phantom of the display behind us; tiny statuettes of Thoth.

Our eyes met. Then Justin looked down at himself and ran his hand over his jumper, flattening it over his chest. "I *feel* solid."

I said nothing as he pinched his sleeve between his fingers as if he'd only just realised what he was wearing. He offered a strained half smile. "I'm dead and I'm stuck in this crappy uniform."

I snorted. "As far as I know your consciousness resurrects you in the last way it remembers. You must've been wearing your uniform when you died. Look, after we find your killer you won't have to hang around here. I don't know exactly what'll happen to you but I'd have thought you had better things to worry about than the dress code."

"What happens if you don't transfer that Mark?" He pointed to my hand and I closed my fist around it.

"In a couple of weeks the Darkness will come for the bearer of the Mark. If I don't pass it on, it'll come for me."

"And me?"

"No, but you won't be able to move on. You'll be stuck here, unable to touch. No eating, sleeping, nothing."

"It might not be so bad." He shuffled his feet. "I could go to films, that sort of thing. You don't know what this whole moving on thing is. You don't know that it's a good thing."

"Ghosts all want to move on. Watching movies forever would get old, Hargreaves."

His eyes flickered.

"So you'd better tell me who killed you."

His long fingers twitched and he pressed his hands together. "There's one problem with your crazy theory, Oh."

My eyes narrowed and I wheeled to face him. "And what's that?"

His Adam's apple bobbed. "I wasn't murdered."

14

I wasn't murdered

I rubbed suddenly sweaty palms on my jeans. "You mean you don't know who killed you?"

"No. I *mean*, I wasn't murdered." He bent close to me. "That's why I think your Dad might be right."

"You must have been murdered." I stuck my blackened hand in his face. "If you weren't, your touch wouldn't have done *this*." My shoulders vibrated inside my T-shirt, rage fuelled. "This is so typical of you. Nothing can be easy, can it?" I dug my nails into my palms and tried to see reason. "I suppose it's possible you don't know who did it. Just tell me how you died and we'll see if we can work it out."

Justin looked at the mummy. "I-I don't want to talk about it."

I swung him to face me. "Didn't you listen to a word I said?" I growled. "I'm not going into the Darkness for you. Tell me what happened and we can be done with each other."

He yanked his shoulders out of my hands. "Why should I do anything for you?" he snapped.

I blinked. "Are you kidding me?" I realised that my voice was raised and lowered my tone to a hiss. "You aren't doing *me* a favour, Hargreaves, I'm doing you one. The dead chase me all over London trying to get me to do what I'm trying to do for you. My life is a bloody nightmare because of you."

"Me?"

"All of you, the damn dead." I gestured angrily at the body before us. "And let's not forget you made my life hell at school. If I could walk away from you and leave you alone, believe me I would. But I can't, so tell me what happened, you selfish, arrogant *jerk*."

He jumped as if I'd bitten him and landed in the middle of the case, wearing the mummy like crazy fancy dress. "I've just found out I'm dead."

"Get over it."

"Pete's right about you. You're cold."

His words made me gasp as if he'd thrown cold water at me, but I felt as if I was standing on the edge of a furnace. My face flamed. "You don't know anything about me," I yelled. And what was worse was that just wasn't true any more. Justin now knew more about me than anyone since my mother had died.

There was a noise and I spun around. I had finally drawn the guard.

"I'm going to have to ask you to leave." He fingered his belt, not quite touching his walkie-talkie, but the threat was there.

"Yeah," I mumbled. "Right. Sorry."

I stumbled through the small Egyptian display, past the guard's vacant stool and back into the white corridor.

I was so angry I could hardly see. I slammed my hand against the lift button and waited for the doors to open. Justin stood at my heels, also silent, tailing me like a mosquito.

Once inside the lift I whirled on him. "Are you going to tell me what happened?" I scrubbed at my face, trying to rub the fire away, but it only seemed to make it worse.

"I–"

I didn't give him a chance to finish. "Fine." I showed him the Mark again. "Your lot called me Godzilla for years because they thought I was scaly under the glove. I don't have eczema, I've got this Mark. Do you know what happens if I don't cover my hand up?" I advanced on him and it was his turn to step away. "I could accidentally transfer the Mark to someone."

"That's–"

"I could pay your girlfriend a visit. Tamsin treats me like dirt. Or what about your precious Dad? We could see how long it takes for the Darkness to take him."

"You wouldn't."

"You think I'm going to hell for you? If it's a case of me or Tamsin, I know who to pick." I curled my lip. "You don't believe in the Mark anyway." He lurched towards me and I stepped out of his reach. "Don't touch me."

"You… you bitch." The flesh of Justin's face was paler than ever. His hair flopped over his forehead and his eyes were wild.

"You think you can get away with anything because you're cool and good-looking and everyone likes you. Well, things have changed, Hargreaves. No one knows you're even here. No one but me that is. And I don't like you. So tell me how you died."

Justin's fists clenched compulsively. "I was going to tell you. You didn't need to threaten me. I just needed a bit of time."

I cradled my Marked hand as if it was burnt. "It's not simple any more. We've got to work out who killed you before I can Mark them. Who knows how long that'll take? You've *had* time. Now you have to talk."

Justin hung his head. "Can we at least talk outside?"

I nodded. "Fine. But you're telling me what happened."

The clouds outside were low and the late afternoon looked more like early evening. We stood on the pavement at the crossing outside South Ken tube station and silently watched the river of traffic pour past.

Justin shuddered each time a body passed through a part of him, but to the press of people heading to one of the three museums he was nothing but air.

I turned from his discomfort and watched two teenaged boys swagger from the station. Earphones still dangled from their ears and they talked loudly over their music. So loudly I could hear them over the other noise.

"Dude, did you hear? They found a dead kid in the building site round the corner from me."

"No way, man."

"It was just on the news, aren't you listening?"

"Radio bores me." He patted his iPod. "I'm playing tracks."

"Whatever. They reckon he slipped from the scaffolding." The boy's watch jangled as he gestured. "It's creepy. The police have been looking for him and the whole time he was just lying there round the corner from our bus stop. If the developer hadn't run out of money they'd have found him a week ago, but no one's been working on the site."

His friend hissed. "Nasty. Maybe he was high then his crew ran out on him."

"Or he's a total Darwin Award." They nodded together.

I turned my head to track the conversation.

"I must've walked past him, like, three times."

"How old was he?"

"Our age. I'll get such a lecture when I get home." He put on a falsetto voice, his Mum's. "*You keep away from that building site. No climbing on scaffolding.*"

I couldn't help myself. I shouldered a tourist aside and took a step away from the road. "Excuse me." The boys turned. "The boy you were talking about, the one that's been found. What was his name?" Their eyes widened at the interruption and I quickly explained myself. "There's a boy at my school gone missing."

The boys relaxed and the taller one gestured at his iPod. "It was just on the news. It was Justin something. Hargreaves I think. Yeah, Justin Hargreaves." He scratched his chin. "So, is it him? Did you know him?"

"Yes. That's him." In front of me Justin had frozen.

The smaller of the boys shuffled his feet. "Harsh."

I glanced behind me as Justin's shoulders started shuddering. I pressed my lips together. "Well, thanks."

"See ya." The boys took off and I moved back to the edge of the pedestrian crossing. The light remained red and the traffic still sped past.

I took a breath. "You heard?"

Justin said nothing. I didn't dare step forward to look at him in case I was knocked into the road, but his back was stiff as marble. "I guess you did."

Slowly he started to shake his head. His hair flipped around his collar as he moved faster and faster.

He was about to run. Without thinking I touched his sleeve with my fingers. A businessman standing next to me moved sideways with a frown. I ignored him. "It had to happen some time. Someone had to find your body."

"No."

Terrified I was going to lose him again I closed my hand around his forearm. "You knew you were dead," I murmured.

"Not like this. Not…" He fell silent. Then he shook his arm free of mine. The traffic screeched to a halt and the green man started to flash. "Let's go."

We crossed the road and Justin carried on walking.

"Where're we going?" I scurried to keep up with him and adjusted my bag.

"Princes Gardens, it isn't far."

"Right."

We turned the corner and I disturbed two pigeons pecking at a discarded McDonald's wrapper. My looming shadow made them jerk back, but they kept pulling at the manky bun with frantic beaks, as if their heads were on elastic.

I shook my head and tucked my hands under my armpits. Then the boy's words came back to me: *his crew*. Maybe Justin hadn't been on drugs, but he hadn't been alone either. I thought about the last time I'd seen him alive.

"Were you with Tamsin?"

"Huh?" Justin's eyes when he turned to me were red-rimmed.

"You're in your uniform. You must've died Friday night."

Justin turned his head to watch the pecking birds.

I was about to push him further when my palm tingled. I clenched my fist and the shadows beneath a Kensington-monogrammed bin caught my eye. I shivered; right at that moment there was nothing passing to make those shadows move, yet they were twisting as if caught in a trap.

15

Remembered as an idiot

A breeze lifted my hair from my ears as I did a quick scan of Princes Gardens. It was filled with gasping grey-tinged trees choking in the polluted London air. They weren't dead enough to bother me.

Apart from Justin and myself, there was only an old guy slumped in the shade on a bench next to a building marked "The Goethe Institute". His hat was pulled down low over his ears; who knew how long he'd been there.

Satisfied that the place was safe for me, I sat with my back against a tree and wriggled between its roots until I was comfortable.

Justin looked as if he wanted to lean on the tree himself but it had too much life-force to support him.

He stretched out on the grass. "I can't even feel this." He went to pluck a blade and his fingers came up empty. "It's like lying on cardboard."

He fidgeted and rolled until my glare pulled him up short. "Did it go down like those boys said?" I asked.

"That I was climbing scaffolding?" Justin rolled until he was staring at the cloud-pocked sky.

"Were you?"

His head lolled towards me, his expression such a blend of defiance and misery I knew what he was going to say.

"Yes." He cast his elbow over his face. "I'll always be the stupid waster who killed himself climbing wet scaffolding. That's going to be all anyone remembers about my life. What a legacy."

I shrugged, scraping my shoulder against bark. "At least you'll be remembered."

Justin jerked.

"I mean it." I inhaled and the scent of shorn grass relaxed me. "Sometimes I have to look people up, find addresses, that sort of thing, and when I start asking questions *no one* remembers the dead guy. It's like he never lived. That must be hard to find out. For the ghost, I mean."

Justin thumped the ground. No dirt puffed under his fist. "I'll be remembered as an idiot."

I shrugged. "If it helps, I would have remembered you as an idiot anyway."

He inhaled sharply and I raised my hand. "Sorry, let's not do this again. Can you talk about what happened now?"

Justin exhaled. "OK." He continued to stare up through his crooked elbow. "It's all blurry, like a bad dream."

"That could be because of the trauma," I shrugged. "Or maybe you haven't really accepted what happened.

Most of the dead that track me down have been that way for years. They've had time to get used to it, to dwell." I scraped my scalp on tree bark as I shook my head. "Just tell me what you can."

"I still don't think I was murdered."

There was nothing left to say. I glared and Justin's lower lip disappeared under his teeth. "Fine, OK. I don't really know where to start."

I twitched and anger started to fill me again as if I was a waiting jug.

"No, listen, there's stuff you don't know. Background. It's important."

Across the path the trees shadows lengthened as if the sun had jumped across the sky. I held my elbows and watched the movement closely. It stopped.

"Go on then," I sighed. "Tell me everything."

Justin rolled onto his stomach and rested his chin on his palm. For one tiny half-second with the scent of grass in my nose and the feel of the tree at my back, I forgot to hate the boy lying in front of me.

It didn't seem so bad that he'd called me Godzilla, or that he was now one of the hounding dead. It felt like a normal moment with a boy from school, something I hadn't had for years. Five years.

Then his dark eyes looked inward and he gave a sort of shrug. "It started on my first day. James made me play Truth or Dare. You told me to take the dare." His eyes narrowed. "You had to have known how bad it would be."

My jaw slackened. "How could I have known?"

His glare intensified. "You knew James. I didn't." He shook his head. "I had to make Mrs Pickard cry. On my first day I told her she smelled and made the whole class laugh. Dad went nuts." His own jaw tightened. "James thought it was *great*."

I nodded. "The Truth or Dare thing was a bit of a craze for a while." I tried a smile that felt uncomfortably like a too-tight mask.

As Justin's face hardened my breath stopped. His eyes suddenly seemed darker than the tentacular shadows cast by the tree branches. "You thought the game went away?" His voice was bitter as dark chocolate.

"Well, yes. It was banned," I frowned. "Oz smoked that whole pack of cigarettes one break and had to go to hospital."

Memories swirled like fudge in the recesses of my mind. That time was kind of a blur for me. Back then it was as if school had stopped being real, as if my life only happened when the dead forced me to dance for them.

"The game didn't die." Justin shook his head. "It went underground. It evolved."

"You make it sound–"

"It isn't really a game, Oh." Justin was no longer looking at me. His eyelids seemed half closed, threaded by a network of tiny blue veins as he stared downwards at an ant scurrying through the grass. "It's more like a way of life. If you want to play, if you want to be 'cool', you have to join the V club. V for Veritas. Truth."

"James came up with that? It doesn't sound like his style."

Justin shook his head. "The club isn't James' baby. It's been around for a while. I think his stepbrother put him onto it. There's even a motto: *Qui audet vincit*. Who dares wins."

"Wait a minute, didn't Mr Barnes say that?"

Justin nodded. "I think the club has been around for longer than even James realises."

"But Mr Barnes..."

Justin's eyes flashed upwards. "Once you've done the initiation and joined the club, you're in for life."

"You think *he's* an old member? Don't you think we would have heard something about it?"

Justin shook his head. "There's no talking about it with outsiders, no telling what's said in the confessional, that's where we hear truths. There's no discussing the dares. If anything goes wrong, there's no admitting that you were doing something for V."

"Pete's in your stupid club, isn't he?" I thought about my friend, how, just after our fight, he'd suddenly become popular.

Justin nodded.

"But how can you say you're in the club for *life*? What happens when you all go to uni or whatever?"

Justin swung into a sitting position and crossed his legs. "Something was going to happen at the end of this year. James had a dare, something huge involving everyone. Something so big it would tie us together for life."

I leaned forward. "Why don't you just say no?"

Justin's long fingers weaved in and out of his fists. "You don't understand. When you're there, with everyone watching, you follow the rules. You just do."

"So take truth. After all this time there can't be much they don't know about you."

Justin fidgeted. "The rules are a bit more complicated than that, mostly it's easier to take the dare." He twisted his tie between his fingers. "Anyway, what's important is what happened Friday night, right?"

He dropped his tie and his hands lay on his lap like poisoned spiders.

I nodded. "Tell me."

His fingers twitched, but didn't rise. "You can probably guess, I was doing something for the club."

"A dare."

"I was hoping it was my last one."

"It was."

His hands curled into fists. "I had a plan. It should have got me out. But I had to do this one last big thing. I had to climb to the top of the scaffolding and walk along one of the pipes. It was only maybe fifty centimetres or so without a handhold."

"If this is what the dares are like, I'm surprised no one's died earlier."

"The stuff we've been doing, it's only been getting really dangerous recently." He groaned. "I know how it sounds. It's one reason I didn't want to talk about it." Justin looked away from me. "So now you know."

"I need to know more. Did you go to the building site alone?"

"Dares have to be witnessed by at least three other people, and videoed. I went with–"

"James, Harley, Pete and Tamsin."

"Right." He hunched his back. "You saw us on the bus after we checked it out the first time."

"Well, what happened when you went back?"

"We got to the building site, there was a bit of banter and then I went up."

"You didn't see anyone else?"

"It was deserted, I wouldn't have done it otherwise."

"So... you went up," I prompted him.

His shoulders tensed as if he was still climbing. "I must've reached the top. I-I remember stepping out onto the scaffolding. It hadn't looked so high from down on the ground. The others waved to me. Tamsin blew me a kiss. I waved back."

"And you fell?"

"No. I was holding on tight." His hands closed around a bar that wasn't there. "I gripped the best I could with my trainers and edged towards the bit without the handhold. Maybe I should have taken my trainers off." He glanced at his feet.

"Maybe." I rubbed my eyes. "Then what?"

"I-I reached the bit with no handhold."

"And you let go."

"No! I could hear the wind below me. I could barely see Tammy. I stretched out as far as I could, so I wouldn't have to be too long without holding on. But I didn't let go of the bar behind me. I edged forward and my foot just slipped. It flew out from under me and I-I swung out. I was only holding on with one hand. I think I heard Tammy shout, but I'm not sure. Then I f-fell."

I was silent for a moment. Justin's cheeks were colourless and his hair was a black wing against his face.

I inhaled. "No one pushed you. No one distracted you."

"No." His voice was as colourless as his face. "See, I wasn't murdered."

I looked at my hand and then across at the barely twitching shadows. Across the park the old man had shifted position. I turned back to Justin. "You *were* murdered. I wonder if…"

"Hey, do you know that guy?" Justin pointed. The old man had levered himself up and was ambling across the garden towards us.

"No," I dismissed him. "He's just leaving the park. You need to focus."

"It's just that he keeps looking at you and there's something about him."

I lifted my spine from the tree trunk. "He keeps looking at me?" I frowned. "It looks like I'm talking to myself, Hargreaves, I'm going to get odd looks." Still, I shifted onto my heels. "How long's he been looking at me?"

"I haven't been paying him much attention, Oh."

As the old man drew near I studied him. His trousers were frayed at the bottom and his great coat was warm for the weather. But he was old. Old people liked to keep warm, didn't they?

He kept his eyes cast down. When he reached the tree nearest me his head rose. Our eyes met. He touched the brim of his hat with twisted fingers, nodded and went as if to walk on. "Kids."

Hope lit Justin's eyes like a sunrise. "You can see me?"

"Crap." The old man's face twisted and he lunged at me.

I dove sideways and his arm hissed through the tree trunk where I'd been sitting.

"Geezer, what're you doing?" Justin scrambled to his feet. The ghost ignored him, focused completely on me.

"I can't take another Mark right now," I cried. The Darkness was already moving and if he touched me I'd be carrying two Marks, with no idea who had killed Justin.

The ghost lurched towards me, grinning hugely. "You can help me. It won't take long."

I tried to get to my feet but slipped on the grass. "Leave me alone."

The old man bent over me. His hooked nose had a bead of moisture on it. It trembled above my face as he reached for my cheek with cracked fingers. I scrabbled backwards but he was faster than he looked.

Suddenly he grunted and flew sideways.

I blinked. Justin had tackled him and now he had both arms round his waist. "Run," he shouted.

I leaped to my feet. "Justin–"

"Go."

The old man was wriggling and swearing viciously.

"Meet me at my house. Do you know where it is?"

"Pete pointed it out once." He renewed his grip on the great brown coat. "Go."

I looked back once. The old guy had removed his hat. He was hitting Justin with it and tears were streaming down his face.

Bloody dead people.

16

The house is cursed

When I got home the study was shut tight. *The Book of Oh-Fa* however, was sitting on the dining room table. I bit my lip, but the temptation was too strong to ignore. Swiftly I grabbed it, stuffed it under my top and, with the pressure of the ancient leather on my skin, I tiptoed upstairs.

Once in my room I leaned against the door. There I stuck my tingling hand behind my back. It was too tempting to just keep looking at it, like picking a scab.

Under the bed the shadows pulsed. I slammed the lights on, all of them. A long time ago Mum had installed a bulb under my bed. Now there was no part of my room that wasn't brightly lit.

I exhaled heavily. I had less than two weeks before the Darkness came for me and I had no idea what had really happened to Justin and who I should be Marking.

Swearing under my breath I crossed to the window. As I passed the dresser I automatically stroked my picture-board of Mum. My fingertips caressed a snippet of her favourite jumper, her old hair band, a silky piece of the skirt I had most liked her in. My fingers bumped over her turquoise beads and lingered on the three photos: one of her smiling over her shoulder, one where she looked sad and serious and hid her gloved hand behind her back, one of her holding a baby – me. In that one her eyes were half-closed and her expression unreadable, but her bare hands were curled around my back as if I was the most precious thing in the whole world and might break.

Her book pressed against my stomach. I tugged it free of my waistband and opened it with reverent fingers. I closed my eyes to bring her voice to mind then started to read.

Entry the fifth
My hand shakes as I write this, trembling so hard that I can barely make sense. The Professor paces outside and his demands have become increasingly urgent. Perhaps his gun is trained on me even now. Still, I cannot move without finishing this, my family needs to know what happened.

If only there was a way to beg my child's forgiveness. Even if I make it home now, I do not deserve to look upon the faces of my family.

The sack of blood money at my feet is not compensation. How could I think it would ever be enough?

Perhaps I should let the Professor shoot me.

It began when I returned to the hole in the ground, a moment that already seems a lifetime ago.

Despite the queue of lantern bearers who had entered the tomb ahead of me, a preternatural darkness still covered every step below the sixth. Miserably I sought the Professor. The glare of the sun on his small round spectacles erased his eyes as he gestured me downwards.

On the fifth step I caught up with the man in front. Like lovers entering an icy sea we felt together with our toes. Step-by-step we descended and the tide of dark rose first to our thighs, then our chests. My bare legs prickled with cold then the darkness enveloped my head.

My lantern revealed walls decorated floor to ceiling with hieroglyphs. As I wondered what ancient curses surrounded us, we rounded a corner to find a large antechamber, riddled with tunnels like black mouths. In the centre the overseers were waiting to take the light.

"We're setting up base there." Sunbird indicated the lanterns already clustered by the far wall. "Stay out of the way until you're needed."

I followed the muted speech of my fellows, stumbling blindly towards the noise until I thumped into another of the men. I ignored his curse and wriggled into a space to try and meditate.

I should have fled.

There was a shout outside and I almost dropped the book. "Taylor Oh!"

I opened my window and leaned into the air. Justin was standing on the street, hands cupped round his mouth. "I can't get in."

A secret smile touched my lips.

Of course he couldn't.

"I'll come and get you." As I passed the dresser I put the book down carefully and looked, not at Mum this time, but in the mirror. Something made me pick up my hairbrush. Swiftly I dragged it through my hair, shaking it out over my shoulders. Then I opened my bedroom door, sucked in a breath at the sight of the dimly-lit hallway and sped as stealthily as possible to the vestibule.

I opened the door and peered out. Justin stood at the top of the steps. "I tried to walk through the door, but it's solid. Don't tell me your front door's cursed too." He sounded grumpy and tired and I couldn't help smiling as he tried to walk past. "Ow." He rebounded onto the pavement and rubbed his shoulder. "I don't understand; there's nothing there."

I rubbed my palm on my jeans. "I'm not sure if this'll work but we can try. Here, you'll have to take my hand." My lip curled as I held my arm out to him.

Justin looked at it. "You don't mind?"

"It's the only way you're getting in."

I braced myself for the familiar hateful jolt, but when Justin's fingers wrapped around mine they just felt dry and cool; no electric ice.

I walked backwards, Justin walked gingerly forwards and he was in.

As he passed the front door he shuddered and dropped my hand. "What was that? It was horrible, like walking through jelly."

I checked behind me. Dad's door was still shut. "Actually, you were right," I whispered. "The house is cursed – Mum did it. She found these hieroglyphs a few years ago. They used to put them on Egyptian tombs to stop the ghosts of the pharaohs' servants from escaping. She figured if it stopped ghosts from getting out of a stone pyramid, it might stop them from getting into a stone house. They're engraved right there, under the ivy."

"So I'm the first ghost that's been in here." He sounded impressed.

I nodded. "For a while." I gestured towards the stairs. "Come to my room, dead boy."

"Taylor, is that you?"

Automatically I panicked and looked at Justin; but of course Dad wouldn't see him.

The study opened and he rolled into view. He looked exhausted.

"Are you alright, Dad?"

"I'd be better if I hadn't had a call from the school today, asking why you've hardly been in class this week."

I flushed and stammered, caught without an excuse.

"I told them you were ill." He rubbed a big hand over his eyes. "At least I didn't have to lie."

"I'm sorry."

"The only thing I can think to do for you is find a cure, but..."

"What?" My arms prickled with terrified apprehension. Was he going to send me away after all?

"I'm failing you, Taylor, and I don't know how much longer we can go on like this."

All I could do was repeat myself, but the apology sounded hollow even to me.

Dad sighed. "I need another sample. Give me your arm, please."

"D-Dad." My eyes flicked sideways. Justin had stepped towards the kitchen as if to give us privacy, but he was watching. "Can we do this later? I'm in the middle of something."

"I need it now. Are you sick at the moment?"

I showed him my gloved hand.

"That's... good." He rolled the syringe between his fingers. "Come on then." He waved me ahead of him into the study. "Our evening out was good for me, it cleared my head. I think I'm onto something."

A sigh quivered on my lips as I passed the threshold and took in the mess of equipment on the desk. "You've said that before," I reminded him.

"This time is different, there's a definite change in your blood when you're sick." He frowned. "I've booked a session with the electron microscope at Kings, but I can't get in for a couple of months. I think the change might even be at a mitochondrial level. That's where your cells make energy. But I can't see it clearly with this thing." He gestured angrily at his microscope, the best money could buy outside a real lab.

"Then why do you need more blood?" I huddled over my arm. "Can't I have a break? I'm sore."

He turned his frown on me. "You're right; your arm does need a rest. I'll take a few mils from your leg. Take off your trousers."

"Dad!" I looked at the door. Justin was staring into the room.

"Come on, Taylor, we haven't got all night."

"I don't want to do this any more."

He tapped his fingers on the wheel arch of his chair. "I know this is hard, Taylor, for both of us. But I'm close, I can feel it."

Looking for something to distract him I thought of *The Tale of Oh-Fa* that he'd left in the dining room. "Why were you reading Mum's book?"

Dad followed my gaze towards the door. "Obviously it's only a story, but there's a bit in it that's interesting, perhaps a kernel of truth. Oh-Fa's granddaughter writes that he drank something after he made the so-called deal. Maybe your ancestor ingested some infected blood when he was in the tomb."

"Blood?" I frowned.

"If you swallow blood containing a viral vector that carries an oncogene, it can insert itself onto host DNA and disrupt normal genes." Dad raised his eyebrows. "Whatever you choose to call it – curse or illness – what you have has to be genetic; a dominant gene on the x-chromosome with a marker that kicks in at puberty. If only I could work out how to find that viral vector..." he shook his head. "Well, it's only a story."

He pulled the wrapper from a sterile syringe and I stepped backwards.

"Taylor," he sighed. "Will it help if I overlook the conversation I had with Mr Barnes this morning?"

I pressed my lips together. "I want to keep Mum's book and see her notes."

The creases in Dad's face deepened. "I don't think that's a good idea. I put your Mum's things away because I don't want your hallucinations being fed with yet more stories."

"But–"

"I'm not ready to give up on you yet. Let me have this sample and I won't ask for any more for a while, you can have that break."

"Fine." I sighed.

"And you'll go back to school?"

I nodded, then paused with my hand over my belt.

"Taylor, I'm your father, just take them off."

Justin backed into the hall. When I was sure he couldn't see me I slid out of my jeans. Dad pointed at a stool and I brushed away a thin layer of dust before I lowered myself onto the seat. Then I looked away as Dad approached with the needle.

I held my breath as the point broke my skin and tried hard not to wince at the insistent tug of blood being taken from the vein.

"All done." Dad pressed a pad of cotton wool over the needle and pulled it free. An ampoule sat on top of his desk, ruby in the light that shone through it.

I took over the pressure on the pad. "You really think you're close?"

Dad considered the brimming vial. "If I can duplicate the effect I'll be nearer to the cure. Now I've seen a difference between your blood samples I'm going and try infect a sample of ordinary blood – my blood. If I can do that, then we know it's an illness and reversible."

"It isn't an infection, Dad. If it was you'd have caught it already."

"Not if it's passed directly from blood to blood."

"Like AIDS you mean?" A shudder went through me and I grabbed my jeans from the floor. Quickly I pulled them on, feeling exposed and grubby.

"Taylor." Dad reached for my ungloved hand and I dodged him.

"I'm tired, I'm going to bed."

On the landing Justin moved into my peripheral vision. He followed me silently and I closed the door behind him.

"Don't say anything," I warned. I hurled myself onto my bed and pressed my face into the pillow until the heat in my cheeks was cooled by the smell of laundered cotton.

17

A *weapon in his arsenal*

"Your Dad must really love you."

I rolled over. Justin was standing by my picture board of Mum and staring into her serious eyes.

"What makes you say that?" I growled.

His fingers hovered over Mum's face. "He's working so hard to make you better."

"He's not trying to make me better," I snapped. "Well, he is, but that's not the real point."

"That's not what it looked like." Justin cocked his head at the baby Mum cradled in her arms.

I swallowed. "That's because you don't know everything." I rose and stood next to him, soothed by the image of Mum's knowing expression.

Justin shrugged. "Tell me."

"There isn't that much to tell. Mum died in a car crash." I looked at her picture, then at Justin.

"I remember it happening." His face twisted into sympathetic lines and my stomach soured.

"Yeah, well, they'd gone to a party and Dad had drunk a bit much, so Mum was driving. Apparently she suddenly jerked the wheel left, like she swerved to avoid something."

"A dog?"

"He says there was nothing there."

Justin was quiet for a moment, then understanding dawned. His eyes widened. "She saw a ghost, and she didn't realise."

I nodded. "I've thought about it a lot. Maybe it was a kid in pyjamas or something. She'd have had a split second to ask herself: is it a ghost, or has the kid just managed to wander out of her flat and into the road?"

"She had to assume it was a real person."

"I know. I'd have made the same call."

"But your Dad…"

"The curse is his enemy. It's taken Mum *and* his legs. He's trying to defeat it. I'm a means to an end, a weapon in his arsenal. As long as I'm around he has a way of getting to it."

"He's your Dad, I'm sure there's more to it than that."

"Yeah." My fingers trailed over Mum's face and I gave my shoulders a shake. "We would have lost her at some point anyway." My smile was a fragile papier-mache construction. "My family doesn't have a long life expectancy. As if tracking down killers isn't dangerous enough, we pretty much always go mad." I tried to sound matter of fact, but I knew my voice was drum tight. "When I was a baby my grandmother hanged herself. My uncle was shot by a man he was Marking. Those of us who don't die go to live in the middle of nowhere, or in institutions where we can be basically drugged off the planet."

Justin pressed his lips together. "You think that'll happen to you."

"One day."

"But you know what you see is real. You're not mad."

I turned to the mirror. "I have to be on the alert all the time. I have to pay attention to every single person anywhere near me, just in case they're a ghost. Can you imagine what that's like?" I didn't wait for his answer. "You get sort of frozen at the moment just before death, so some of you are easy to spot. If you'd died in the bath, you'd be naked and wet, so if I see a fat man streaking towards me down Oxford Street I can avoid him pretty easily."

Justin snorted and I gave a half smile. "But what about the guy in the business suit? Is he a ghost?" I went to straighten my duvet. "I don't know why I'm telling you this."

Justin grinned, a bit too smoothly for my liking. "I'm easy to talk to."

"No, you aren't." I retied my ponytail to busy my fingers. "I don't like you and you don't like me." Blood was seeping through my jeans; my vein wasn't closing fast enough. I moved to my wardrobe and selected a skirt. I pulled it on over the denim then pulled my jeans down underneath. Justin watched, fascinated.

I was shoving my jeans into the laundry basket in the corner when I stopped. "I'd checked that old guy out before I sat down, I'm used to spotting the out-of-place, but I didn't notice that he wasn't right, you did." I spun to face Justin. "You said there was something off about him." I pointed at him accusingly. "How did you know?"

Justin took a step back as if I held a knife on him. "I'm not sure," he muttered. "It was like... you know when you meet someone you sometimes have a feeling about them. You know if you'll be friends."

For some reason my memories flashed to the day I'd first met Justin.

"It was like that," he scuffed his feet in my carpet. "I just felt as if he was similar to me."

"Not right." I gave a small genuine smile.

"Yeah." It was Justin's turn to paste on a fake. "That's right."

My limbs felt like lead; tiredness had crept up on me. I glanced at the clock. It was later than I'd thought. I'd forgotten Justin didn't need to sleep; I couldn't keep up with the dead.

"I've got to get some sleep." I covered my mouth as I yawned and Justin nodded.

"Should I leave?"

For the first time I wondered where one of the bothersome dead would go while I slept. "What will you do?"

Justin inhaled and his full lips twitched downwards before he got them back under control. "I'll find a cinema or something."

I nodded and he stepped backwards.

"Wait." I pushed my hair off my forehead. "You could watch telly downstairs. Dad won't hear – he'll work late into the night then take some painkillers; they knock him out. You should be able to work the remote as long as you don't turn it up too loud. The sofa's comfy."

"It's not like I'm going to sleep on it." The sullen words didn't match the sudden brightening of his face.

"So you'll be downstairs?"

"Sure. You can find me when you get up."

"OK." I stood up, legs brushing my duvet. "Night then."

"Night."

There was an awkward moment when I thought he was going to try and shake my hand or something. Then he backed out of the door. Without opening it.

I hesitated then reached for Mum's book. Until Justin settled downstairs I would read and bring her voice back to life; that way I would not feel so alone. My hands caressed the leather cover and I inhaled the scent of the fragile paper, like dust in my nose. It took me a few moments to find where I had left off, kicking off my shoes and ghosting towards the bed on bare feet as I searched. I knew the book so well, it was hard to locate the place I had last finished. Finally I sank down and began to read.

A dreadful sound disturbed my contemplation: a low snarl on the edge of hearing.

For a moment I thought I had imagined it, then the boy next to me exclaimed with a trembling voice. "Do you hear that?"

As the rest of the workers drew together I held myself still and tried to pinpoint the source.

However, the growl echoed strangely and seemed to come from more than one direction.

"There's more than one of 'em. Can you hear?"

Voices raised. "We need a lantern, t-there's something in here with us."

The darkness carried the Sunbird's reply. "You lazy Lubberlanders, don't you want to find the treasure? All you have to do is stand still while we wait for the Professor to come and work out where it is." His footsteps pounded angrily, but the workers exhaled relief; he brought with him an island of light.

Then the overseer stopped. "What was that?"

The snarling grew louder and shuffling cloth told me that panicking men had raised their tools. Forcing the numbness from my limbs, I managed to edge away.

In the centre of the chamber the Sunbird span and his beacon left a trail in the darkness; a dimly glowing spiral which surrounded him like a cage, but illuminated nothing. He began to retreat and immediately a howl went up from the workers beside me. As one, they rushed the escaping glow.

Horrorstruck I watched my fellows fight over the lantern. As it was torn from hand-to-hand it revealed scraps of faces contorted with terror and rage. The brawl reverberated from the walls until the room filled with voiceless thunder and the beast stopped snarling and began to roar.

Fleeing men tripped on their comrades and in the confusion the myriad of tunnels leading from the antechamber became a labyrinth, trapping us inside. Although my feet itched to run, I thought my best chance of finding the exit was a slow creep along the wall.

With rising terror I soon realised the babble had quieted. Now the only sound in the tomb was made by my chattering teeth. Quickly I inhaled and held as still my shaking limbs would allow.

Every sense burned yet I heard nothing.

When the silence continued I took one tortoise-like step to the right, then another. Finally my hand found empty space and I looked to see that around the corner, high above me, there was a square of light. I had found the way out.

As noiselessly as possible I felt for the first step.

The distant barking of a small dog called to me and I climbed as fast as I could. When the line of daylight was a mere body length ahead I took a deep breath and something whistled by my face to thud on the tread in front of me.

A clawed foot slid towards me and wet warmth on my thighs and the smell of urine betrayed my terror.

Yet the beast did me no harm, only drove me back into the tomb.

I put down the book and rubbed my gritty eyes. It was time to leave Oh-Fa. I needed to shower and crash. I opened the door to the hallway and stopped. Like an invading force the shadows pressed against the border of light that projected from my room.

My legs trembled and I rubbed my ears frantically. The house was too quiet. If only I'd asked Justin to stay upstairs.

I heard the faint strains of the television starting up and stared into the darkest of the shadows, as if challenging them to move. My eyes started to blur. The light switch was two steps more into the darkness.

Only two steps.

But I jumped back into my room and slammed the door. I could have a shower in the morning.

18

I have to get into the V club

"Alright, Hargreaves." I scooped Weetabix from the bowl. Dad hadn't gone to bed until the early hours, so I wasn't worried about talking to Justin while I ate. "We have to work out who killed you so I can avenge your death."

"Who says?" I opened my mouth and Justin quickly clarified. "I mean who decides I need avenging?"

I paused with the spoon halfway to my mouth. "I've never thought about it. It's something that has to be done before you can move on, so maybe it's something to do with the other side. Perhaps you can't take that kind of baggage through."

Justin swallowed.

"Look, something, or someone, has ruled that your death wasn't just an accident. We might not agree, but somehow we have to think like they do. What wasn't accidental about what happened? How could it have been prevented? Maybe that's where we should be looking."

"I know what you're thinking." Justin leaned against the work-surface and crossed his arms. "You're thinking the person who set the dare must be to blame."

"Aren't you?"

"No. Like you said, I didn't *have* to do it."

"What about whoever started the V Club…"

"What about the person who came up with Truth or Dare in the first place? What about the builders who put up the scaffolding? What about the company who erected the crumbling building? Come on, Taylor."

"Fine." I bit my lip. "You said your foot slipped. Could it be something to do with that?"

"I don't know."

I chewed slowly, enjoying the feel of the sunlight on my back as it swept through the long kitchen window. After a moment, I pushed the bowl away. "If someone in the V club knows something they aren't saying, wouldn't they have to tell in the 'confessional'?" I emphasised the word with my fingers.

Justin spoke slowly. "Truth or Dare."

I nodded. "It all comes back to the game. I have to get into that club."

Justin was awkward when he turned on me. "Taylor, I don't think it'll work."

"Why not?" But I already knew the answer. It wasn't that he didn't think I'd be able to find the answer in his dumb club, he just didn't believe I'd get in. "I'm not cool enough for you." I clenched my fists.

"Basically."

Flushing, I jumped to my feet. The Mark on my hand was black as pitch now. If I squinted it looked like a hole through my palm. "There has to be a way."

"You need a sponsor. No offence, but I can't think of a single club member who'd stand up for you."

I licked my lips. "There might be one."

Justin frowned.

"Pete's a member… isn't he?"

"Well, yeah, but Pete… he doesn't like you much… you know that, right?"

My heart gave a little jump and I inhaled sharply. "Of course I know."

If only he hadn't tried to change things.

"Pete, I can't come over tonight."

"You're always cancelling stuff on us. This is the third time this week and you didn't make it to the cinema last weekend."

"I know, but it's–"

"Family stuff, yeah."

"You can speak to Mum if you don't believe me."

"You never used to have all this 'family stuff' going on. I think you just don't want to hang out any more."

"That's not true. If I could come over I would." I glower at the Mark that is forcing me to cancel on my friends again. The ghost who had grabbed me had huge hands. The stain spills onto my wrist like a pointing finger.

"Whatever."

I bite my lip and look at Mum. She makes a "hurry up" gesture. We have a long drive ahead of us and she wants to get going.

"Can't we do something tomorrow?"

There's a long pause. "I'm sick of waiting for you. You've been acting strange for ages. You never tell me what's wrong and now you don't even want to hang. I've got other friends. I don't have to wait around to go out with you."

"What do you mean?"

I hear the hiss of his breath. "You know what I mean."

I inhale shakily. "You want to go out, go out?"

There's silence on the end of the phone. Why did I say that?

"Yeah. I did. I do. So, what about it?" The phone leeches none of the hope from his voice. I picture his round, brown eyes. What do I say?

Mum's hand falls onto my shoulder and I look up. She isn't trying to hurry me any more; she's heard my last question. She gives me a squeeze and I close my eyes.

I imagine what it would be like to date Pete. We've been friends forever, I love him, but do I fancy him? I picture kissing him and something low in my tummy gives a little flip.

Then I imagine a ghost appearing behind him, reaching round his back, grabbing my hand as I hold him close. The whole thing is bad enough now and we're only friends. How hard will it be to cancel dates? What if I have to run away when we're out?

Mum told Dad about the curse – could I tell Pete?

He'd laugh his head off.
"I want to Pete... but..."
He slams down the phone.

"I-I know he's down on me. He's our best hope though... Isn't he?"

Justin hesitated.

"Or I could ask Tamsin."

A snort of laughter bent Justin almost double. "Yeah. Pete's your only chance."

My legs were curled beneath me on the love seat in the hall and my hand was sweating over the receiver. I could have gone to my room and used my mobile, but I'd spent so many years chatting to Pete on the house phone that it just seemed wrong to use anything else to make the call.

Justin stood at my shoulder. "When did you last speak to him?"

"Just before I found you. He told me where to look."

"I mean–"

"I know what you mean. It's been years since we were friends. Since before my mum died."

"He might not be up for this."

"I know."

Swiftly I dialled the number. My fingers moved automatically over the pad, I didn't have to try to recall a single digit, the pattern was so familiar.

"Pete?"

"Twice in one week, I am lucky."

"I know we haven't been close in a while."

"Yeah." His voice betrayed nothing.

"Talking to you the other day I-I just realised how much I missed you." Justin raised his eyebrows and I turned my back on him. "I know we aren't really friends any more."

"We aren't friends at all."

"Does it have to be that way?" He didn't respond. The phone hummed and I rushed to fill the silence. "I know you've got other mates. I know we can't hang out." I swallowed. "It used to be we could talk about anything."

"Sure." His voice sounded rough. Was I getting somewhere? Then he carried on. "I remember that I used to talk to you and you'd tell me *nothing*. All that weird behaviour, you'd never tell me what was going on."

I licked my lips and thought fast. I only had one card left to play. One thing he wanted from me. "Listen, Pete. I know you're part of a club."

There was a sharp intake of air and the silence on the other end of the phone grew weighty. "I don't know what you mean," he said finally.

"The V club. Truth or Dare."

"Who told?" Whip fast, sharp as a blade; the words promised retribution for whoever had spoken out of turn. I shivered. I'd never heard that tone from Pete before.

"Does it matter? It sounds fun and it would give me a chance, you know, socially. I'm sick of being picked on every time I walk into the common room."

"You can't–"

"There's something in it for you."

He hesitated. "What?"

"Well, it's called *Truth* or Dare. Isn't there some stuff about me you want to know?" I swallowed a knot of nerves. Would he still care why I'd grown away from him? Why I was so different now? Maybe he didn't want to know anymore… but his earlier words suggested that my secrecy still rankled.

He gave a laugh so cold it almost froze the phone to my ear. "I suppose you won't just tell me now."

"What would be in it for me?"

He lowered his tone. "You don't want to join the V club, Taylor."

That was probably true, but I also didn't want to get taken by the Darkness and right now I saw only the two options. "You're in it."

"Well, yeah, but I'm different."

"What's that supposed to mean?"

"School's over in a year. Can't you put up with things the way they are for that long?"

My eyes narrowed and anger made me snap. "It's easy for you to say. How do you think Hannah feels having to run through the common room with Tamsin Harper calling her names? Don't you think she's got enough to deal with at home? I join your V club and I can help her as well as me."

I imagined Pete at his end, fist tightening on the receiver, guilt darkening his face.

"You think I haven't tried to get them to leave her alone?"

"If they aren't dogging me any more, surely that'll extend to her."

He hesitated. "Maybe. But you don't know everything about the V club. It isn't your kind of thing."

"What's my kind of thing then?"

He snorted. "Not being told what to do, for starters." I heard his exhalation. "Taylor, there are loads of rules and I don't think you'll be happy with them."

"That's my choice."

"I don't know who talked to you about the club and what they told you about it, but you can't talk about the club to anyone outside of it. If you get in you won't be able to tell Hannah. She'll want to know why you've suddenly got popular."

"I can make something up."

"You're good at that."

"So?"

"I can ask for a meeting."

"Great."

"But it doesn't mean you're in. You'll need a second to agree–"

My shoulders tensed. "He didn't say anything about a second."

Pete pounced. "Who didn't?"

"No one. What else?"

"You have to complete a dare."

"And then I'm in."

He hesitated. "I propose, someone else seconds and sets a dare. If you manage to complete it, then you're in. But the dares aren't what you're thinking."

"Whatever it is I can do it."

"I don't think you–"

"*You* got in."

"That was a while ago."

"If you're doing these dares, I can too."

"Whatever. Don't say I didn't warn you. I'll call James and we'll set a meet for tomorrow. But if you try and fail, things at school will get even worse for you."

I glanced at the shadow beneath the table. Was it my imagination or was it closer to my feet than it had been?

"I won't fail."

Pete inhaled. "I'll let you know about tomorrow." He hung up without saying goodbye.

19

Don't worry about it

As soon as I arrived at the bus stop Hannah's face froze over. "I'm sorry, Han." When she didn't even look at me, I stood awkwardly in front of her. "You know what I'm like. I had–"

"Stuff, yeah, I know what you're like."

"So we're cool?"

Hannah shook her head. "We're not cool. You dumped me at school. You didn't call or text or anything *for days*. You left me on my own without a word. Pete's right. I'm right at the bottom of your list. I get that crap from my Mum, I shouldn't have to put up with it from my best friend."

"I'll make it up to you."

Hannah glowered for another minute; then she relented. "Tonight?"

"Tonight – we'll do a movie or something. You can come over."

Hannah's face thawed. "Popcorn?"

"Of course."

"Salted?"

"I hate salted."

Hannah raised her eyebrows.

"Fine, salted. You're absolutely right."

"Yes, I am." She threaded her arm through mine. "Now let me tell you what my mum did to Carl."

Just before the bell went Pete walked past. He appeared to be ignoring me completely, but as he strode by his hand flicked out and a piece of paper dropped into my lap. Hannah had her head buried in her bag, so I quickly opened it.

It had today's date, a postcode and a time: 7pm.

I inhaled sharply. I'd thought the meeting was going to be at school. Quickly I scribbled on the back. *Can we make it earlier?*

Then I grabbed a folder, took a deep breath and walked to Pete's table. Thankfully James hadn't arrived yet, but Harley grimaced like a gargoyle as I approached. "Hey, Chickety China," he leered, but I could see his heart wasn't in it. Justin's ghost was present, even when he wasn't.

I grunted a reply and turned my back on him to put the folder in front of Pete. "Here's that work you wanted."

Pete glared up at me. "What are you doing?"

"You don't need it anymore? Fine." I lifted the folder, leaving the paper behind. Harley gave a desultory finger wave as I left.

When I reached my seat I looked back at Pete to check he'd got the message. He was just screwing the paper into a ball. He met my eyes, curled his lip and shook his head. Message received. My only chance to get into the V Club was at 7pm tonight, which meant I'd have to cancel on Hannah again.

My chest tightened. "Han?"

"Got it." She rose from her bag clutching her lucky pencil. "Thought I'd lost it."

"Look, about tonight..."

"I'm thinking old school *X-Files* marathon. We can start right at the beginning. It'll be great."

"Can we do it another time? I've just remembered I've got something on."

Hannah leaned away from me. "Family stuff, right?" Her voice was cold and each word had sharp edges.

"That's right." I spoke carefully, as if the wrong word would bring a blade down.

"Don't worry about it." Hannah turned her back on me and laid her lucky pencil next to her work book.

"So we'll do Thursday?"

"I said, don't worry about it. Don't worry about rearranging, or fitting me into your busy schedule. Just don't worry about it. Not that you ever do."

I tugged her arm with my gloved hand, trying to get her to look at me. "We'll do Thursday, definitely."

"No, we won't. I'm done." Finally she raised her head and her eyes were red-rimmed. "Either you see me tonight, or we don't hang out ever again."

I swallowed. My hand seemed to throb under the glove. I couldn't think of any other way of getting to the truth about Justin's death. I had to join the V Club.

"I-I can't do tonight, Han."

"Whatever." She scooped up her things.

"What are you doing?"

"Moving."

She stalked away from the table and the sunlight caught in her hair, turning it into a neon halo. Her lucky pencil rolled from her book and landed on the floor in front of her.

"Hannah, wait." The whole class heard. Like vultures they rotated to watch as Hannah's foot came down with a crunch. She wobbled and tilted, then went crashing down, her books flying around her.

As I leaped up to help, she glowered at me with poisonous eyes. Her face was completely colourless. "Leave. Me. Alone."

My breath caught as she dumped her bag by a spare seat on the table furthest from me, and started rearranging her things.

Laughter reverberated from the doorway; Tamsin and James had arrived.

Trembling, I sat back down. My legs felt like jelly and my chest ached. I ducked my head and caught sight of my gloved hand.

"I hate you, Justin Hargreaves," I muttered.

20

How bad could it be?

"Don't speak to me," I snapped, glaring at the piece of paper in my hand. I'd copied the postcode from memory, and had got it wrong.

"Bad day at school, dear?"

"Seriously, Hargreaves, if you don't shut up..." I turned my glare up and down the street. It was a quiet residential road with a large modern church right in the middle.

"What, you'll kill me?" Still, he took a step to one side.

"I don't have to let you stay in my house." I shoved him so hard he staggered. "And I'm more than happy to transfer the Mark to Tamsin bloody Harper."

I swung back round, clutching the paper to my heaving chest. I wished I really did have the guts to Mark Tamsin; that would teach her.

After a couple of bitchy remarks she'd pretty much left Hannah alone for the rest of the day, turning all her vitriol on me. I hadn't realised how much Hannah's quiet presence gave me the strength to put up with her. Now I was on my own and my ears still burned.

Hannah would forgive me in a few days, she had to. Until then... I growled under my breath... until my friend came back, I'd focus on getting rid of Justin Hargreaves. Which meant Marking his killer so he could move on.

And that meant finding the V Club.

"Fine." I exhaled noisily. "I'm lost. Where am I supposed to meet them?"

"Seriously – here?"

Justin shrugged. "See, you weren't lost. Where did you think you were heading?"

"Not a church hall."

He steered me forward by my elbow. "We're a youth group."

As we walked I peered around me, challenging the eyes of passing tourists and checking every group for outliers.

Justin shook my arm. "You aren't going to get a second to stand for you if you keep shoving the weird down everyone's throats."

"I have to check for ghosts," I hissed angrily.

"I'll do it for you."

I hesitated in my scan. "Really?" I whispered.

"Sure. I had a feeling about the old guy. I'd probably be able to ID any others, right?"

"I-I guess."

"Do you trust me to do this for you?"

Did I? Justin had never liked me. He didn't believe he was murdered and he didn't particularly want to move on. This ghost had no incentive to help me find his killer. His only real motivation was that I'd threatened to Mark his girlfriend.

I swallowed. When I came to think about it, if the Darkness came for me, it probably wouldn't bother Justin at all.

So if he saw another ghost, would he tell me?

I thought about how he'd fought the old guy to stop him from Marking me.

"Well?"

Reluctantly I made the decision. "Alright, but be alert and let me know if you see one of the dead. This kind of place attracts them."

His grin widened. "You trust me."

"Just look for the ghosts," I hissed and strode up the steps into the church, eyes straight ahead for the first time in five years.

It was a Catholic church, I knew that much. It was called Saint Benedict's and the sign on the door said the Priest was Father Harding and the Deacon, Don Lomas. I paused to savour the sound of those titles: Father, Deacon.

I looked up. It was a modern building, but even from the outside I could see that the windows were stained glass.

The door was ajar. I pushed it all the way open and stepped inside.

There was a bowl of water by the door and a notice-board that was full of newsletters, notes about the parish and information about charities. A letter from the Bishop was the centrepiece. A group of children were being confirmed in two weeks time and the choir practised on Tuesdays. Mrs Christophers was winner of the one hundred club this month.

To my left a wooden bookcase contained hymnbooks. I imagined a line of people trailing past, each taking a book before going through the glass doors in front of them. I blinked and looked away. I was spending too much time taking in sights that I normally skipped over in my search for the dead.

There was another door, a wooden door, to my right. I assumed I would have to go that way, but first... I wanted to see.

I moved towards the glass doors. The early evening sun was catching the windows just right and rainbows painted the pale wooden pews and spilled on the floor like oil on water.

A statue of the Virgin Mary opened her hands to me above a vase of lilies. My shoulders started to loosen and I allowed my eyes to skim lazily towards the altar. It was covered with a gold edged cloth that would have been white, but the light made it so many colours I couldn't even tell what picture the window was supposed to be casting. I let my gaze follow the fractured image to the crucified man hanging above the altar.

Like the mummy in the museum this was one of the dead that couldn't bother me. He should have been in agony, I'd heard crucifixion was a horrible death, but whoever had carved the image had given him a loving smile. My hand was suddenly hot inside the glove and I rubbed it on my trousers.

For the first time I wondered what would happen to Justin when he passed over.

"What're *you* doing here?" The drawl could only belong to one person. My eye twitched and I turned. All thoughts of kindness fled.

But I needed someone to second me. "I'm here for the V club, Tamsin. Pete's proposing me. He didn't tell you?"

"Harley said he was proposing *someone*." She snorted. "What a waste of my time. I had to come all the way over town to get here and now I'll just have to turn around and head home again." She tapped her nails thoughtfully on the glass. They made a snick-snick sound, like claws. "Maybe we'll go out for a Chinky or something, when you've been sent on your way." She tossed her blonde waves. "Oh sorry, was that offensive?" she sneered. "What was Pete thinking?"

The dry scent of lilies tickled the back of my throat as I inhaled. "He has his reasons." I forced my fists to remain open. "I know a little bit about your club. I'd like to have the chance to be in it. Tell you what, if you second me you can set my initiation dare, that's a thing, right?"

Tamsin hesitated and her eyes filled with calculation. "James sets the initiation dares."

What had Justin seen in this girl? I glanced to the entrance where I knew he lingered. Instead of watching for ghosts, Justin's eyes were trained on Tamsin's red cross-over top.

My heart thudded and I resisted rolling my eyes. The dead would easily get past him and I'd have an early trip into the Darkness because his girlfriend was wearing a tight shirt.

I pasted a smile on my face and forced down the instinct to guard the entrance myself. "So what do you think, Tamsin? If you second me I'll do whatever dare you set."

"No double dares at an initiation." She dragged her nails along the door handle, apparently relishing the feel of her manicure on metal.

"Pete told me."

"He told you all the rules?"

"Just what I needed to know for tonight." I didn't tell her that Justin had filled me in on the rest. And he was right, it was a creepy and dangerous club they had going here.

Her smile was predatory now. "He told you what happens when you don't complete your dare?"

I nodded, nonchalant. "Social death."

She licked her lips. "People have hurt themselves, changed schools. Derek was the last."

I blinked. Justin hadn't mentioned that Derek had been in the club.

A frown creased my forehead. "I thought Derek was mates with you lot."

She shrugged. "Rules are rules."

I caught sight of Justin. At Tamsin's tectonic shrug his eyes had glazed over. I shook my head. "To be honest, I'm not sure how failure would change things for me." I grimaced. "I'm already at the bottom of the social scale."

Outside the church a dog yipped, but Tamsin never took her eyes off me. They were pale blue and slightly slanted. I'd never noticed the slant before. She reached up with her claws but stopped before she touched my skin.

"Oh, you have no idea. Right now, you're pond scum. We don't like you. Sure, we're mean. But we haven't been *trying*. You can't even imagine how much worse things could get for you."

She was wearing *Poison*. The perfume filled my lungs and my stomach gave a flip like it wanted to hurl my dinner. I made myself ignore the desire to see her covered in half-digested hamburger.

"Sounds like you'd enjoy that," I murmured.

She tilted her head and regarded me balefully. "Maybe I will second you. It'll be a lot of fun when you fail and I've been saving an excellent dare for a special occasion."

I had what I wanted. But the skin on my neck prickled. She turned to go through the open door.

"By the way," I said through clenched teeth. "I heard they found Justin. I'm sorry."

She stopped with her back to me. Her bare legs trembled slightly; then she carried on walking as if I'd said nothing at all. As she disappeared through the other wooden door Justin met my eyes sheepishly. I gave him a single glower, but had to remain silent; it was time to go in.

The room was pretty basic. A couple of religious paintings decorated the walls. I didn't know what they showed exactly. One was an angel, I knew that much; he held a spear through some sort of writhing monster. Another was a saint-like figure, haloed and dressed in white, floating up to heaven on a cloud.

James was busy tacking a photo-shopped poster over the image. It showed an image of Icarus flying too close to the sun and underneath it read:

THE V CLUB
Qui Audet Vincit

I was frowning at the poster when James turned around. "What's the problem, Oh?" His muscles bulged under his shirt; I'd heard he'd been drinking protein shakes to bulk up. Most of the girls thought he was hot, but to me he looked deformed, like someone had stuck a film star's head onto a wrestler's body. He pushed his sleeves up to his elbows and I finally got to see his full tattoo: "Veritas".

I fought a lip curl. "I just don't get the connection between Icarus and the club."

James laughed. "Icarus took a risk and dared to fly. We're all winners here, risk-takers." He pumped his fist and I jumped as all the other kids in the room made a matching gesture.

I tore my eyes from the poster, wondering if James even remembered what happened to Icarus at the end of the story.

"We're all here?" James cast his green-eyed gaze around the circle of plastic chairs. For the first time I noticed Pete leaning against the back wall. He was the only one who wasn't lowering his hand from the winner's salute.

I nodded towards him. He didn't nod back.

James walked towards me. I hadn't actually realised how strong he was until he grabbed my arm. I wanted to turn to Justin, but James was dragging me towards an empty chair in the middle of the circle. "Sit here."

I sat and tried to ignore the sensation of all those eyes on me, but the pressure of the hostile gazes made my skin itch. The light from the single hatched window fell on my face and I shifted. As I moved a hand squeezed my shoulder. I jerked and looked up. It was Justin. I exhaled.

James sniggered. "Everything alright, Oh? You seem jumpy."

"A fly in my hair." I wriggled to get more comfortable. "Now what?"

There were two chairs still empty; one next to Tamsin, the other next to Harley. Harley lounged back with eyes half-closed; he wasn't expecting anything of interest to happen. His curls lay flat against his head, and his arms were folded. He made no move at all when Pete dropped into the chair next to him and sat with his fists in his lap.

James took the seat next to Tamsin and her hand immediately crept onto his thigh, her nails tickling his leg in a very familiar gesture. Next to me Justin stiffened. They'd found his body only a short while ago. She hadn't grieved for long.

"Pete, you're proposing Taylor for membership of the V club."

Pete nodded tightly and the light caught his shaved head. I tried to catch his eye, but he didn't look at me.

"Anyone second the motion?" James stretched lazily and threw one hand behind Tamsin's chair. She said nothing.

Around me cloth rustled as the others prepared to get up and leave. It was over. I'd never find Justin's killer.

Then Tamsin stood up. Her fingers trailed up James' torso, lifting his shirt slightly as she rose. Then she posed; one hand on her jutting hip, the other on James' shoulder.

"I'll second." She pouted as an incredulous chorus shattered the quiet. "But Jamie, will you let me set the dare? Just for tonight."

The others fell quiet. They'd seen through her, just as I had. This was nothing more than a way to torment me more. She was convinced I'd fail her dare. Their appreciation bit the air.

James frowned. "You know the rules."

Tamsin walked her fingers up his neck. "I've got a really good one and don't I have a few points saved up?"

James hung his head, thinking. Then finally he nodded. "Majority decides – if the club agrees, we'll suspend the rule for tonight." He looked around the group. Most nodded quickly, their faces feral with anticipation. Only Pete shook his head. I closed my gloved fist over the Mark on my palm.

How bad could it be, really?

21
The stupidest thing I'd ever done

I stood with my toes just over the yellow line and allowed another train to speed by without me. The passengers stared at me with sullen incomprehension: why wouldn't I want to cram myself into the carriage with them?

Sweat was pouring off me and I did a little jog on the spot. Crowded as the station was, I wasn't even looking for ghosts. I was about to do the stupidest thing I'd ever done. *Ever*.

I hunched my shoulders and glanced along the platform. A little way down, so it didn't look like we were together, James, Harley, Tamsin and Pete were standing in a group. Harley had his video phone out but he'd just turned it off, again. They were getting impatient.

How long did I have before they decided I'd failed the dare?

"I don't think you should do this." Justin hopped up and down behind me.

I ignored him. A bunch of late night commuters sprinted down the steps, glanced at me standing so close to the edge of the tunnel, then barrelled past, slowing only when they saw the display. Three minutes till the next Northern line train. They had time.

Of course, sometimes the displays were wrong.

I looked down at the yellow line again. It stood out, seemingly the only real colour in the filthy tunnel. There were posters on the walls opposite, flanking the station sign: large curved boards advertising Jack Daniels whiskey and "five star hotels at three star prices" in Sharm el-Sheik.

The picture on the Jack Daniels board was black and white anyway. The pyramids on the holiday board must have been bright once. Now the colours were muted and smeared with soot. My eye followed the curve of the tunnel down to the track. Black metal shone in oily lines. My feet trembled.

I leaned so that I could see a little way into the tunnel. It was a black hole, shuddering with the sound of distant trains, the stonework so stained I could barely see the pattern of interlocking bricks. A flash of movement beneath a rail drew my eyes to a small group of mice. There were probably rats in there as well.

In order to come down here I'd travelled on what Tamsin was quick to remind me was the longest escalator on the underground system. I'd felt sick and dizzy all the way, clutching the black rubber hand rail as the moving stair took me down and further down into the earth. I felt as though I'd been swallowed.

Crisp packets moved on the tracks, whipped up inside a sudden cyclone. The mice scurried away and another train appeared in front of me. I rocked back on my heels and Justin steadied me as doors opened a few steps down from where I stood.

A flood of people emerged, jostling, ignoring one another. The commuters who had run past me leaped on. The doors slammed with a high-pitched beep and the train heaved off again.

This time the display said three and a half minutes. I only had to stay in the tunnel for twenty seconds. I'd have three minutes to get there and back before the next train. If I was going, I had to go now.

I rocked forward and Harley raised his phone, but my feet wouldn't move.

"You're doing it, aren't you?" Justin hopped again. "I wish you wouldn't."

"I have to," I hissed.

"If you're going, you have to go *now*."

"I can't move." I glanced at Tamsin. She was openly laughing at me. "I can't let them see me like this." Tears came into my eyes. "I can't fail in front of them."

Justin swore viciously then exhaled. "I'm only doing this because... well, you'll thank me later."

Then he shoved me off the platform.

I shrieked as I stumbled forward and my feet met air. Then the back of my head smacked into the rim, my feet thudded on the ground and my shocked ankles collapsed.

I shunted forward onto my hands and knees and gasped as my hands closed on the metal tracks.

Above me I heard panicked cries and a woman's scream.

"Quick, take my hand."

I looked up. A man leaned over the edge of the platform and his tie fluttered in the breeze that told me a train was moving somewhere. The whites of his eyes showed as he jerked his arm. "Reach for me."

Justin landed next to me. "You're here now. Do this fast."

Tears wet my cheeks as I staggered to my feet. I looked into the tunnel. It was black as the Darkness. The Darkness could be just a few steps away waiting for *me* to come to *It*. My pulse raced until it felt like my chest was about to burst open. The only chance I had to save myself was to go into the dark. So I groaned and ran into the tunnel.

Ten steps in, that was the challenge. As I ran Justin ran with me, counting. "One, two, three, four, five, six, seven, eight, nine, ten. Stop, Taylor."

I screeched to a halt, heart pounding. Pitch black surrounded me like oil in a barrel. I couldn't breath, I could only whimper in bursts of terror that brought in no air, only soot, and filled my lungs, coating them with darkness, until there was only the dark outside and pitch inside and I couldn't see a thing.

"Taylor." Justin was shaking me. "Twenty seconds, that's all, come on, count with me."

"I-I…" I stuttered. I couldn't think, I certainly couldn't count.

"One, two, three, four. It's going to be alright. Seven, eight, nine, ten. Halfway there. Twelve, thirteen, fourteen. We're getting you out of here in a few seconds. Sixteen, seventeen, eighteen, nineteen, twenty. Go, Taylor, GO." He spun me and shoved me towards the end of the tunnel. I stumbled a few steps and my feet caught on something. I fell and smacked my head on a rail.

My ears rang as I touched the huge egg-shaped lump growing above my eye. My legs were moving though, as if I was still running. They knew what I should be doing.

"Get up!" Justin pulled at my elbow and I let him help me to my feet. Then a whoosh of air yanked my hair into a stream behind me. A McDonalds wrapper tangled on my ankles on its way into the tunnel and I tried to spin.

Suddenly the rush of air reversed. The train was on its way into the station.

Dimly, I heard more screaming. It wasn't coming from me. My mouth was open, but no sound emerged. The sounds were from above; from the platform.

"Go. You can make it." I couldn't see Justin, or the panic in his face, but I could hear it in his voice. I broke into a run.

When I scrambled out of the tunnel entrance the man who had offered me his arm was still there, shouting and cursing at me. I reached for him, but he was too far away.

Behind me the pressure of the oncoming train struck my back, as if it was pushing the air ahead of it, compressing it into a smaller space. "Oh God."

The words barely formed on my lips and Justin was there. Like a rugby player he slammed into my thighs and hurled me upwards. My gloved hand closed around the stranger's wrist and he hauled me up, tearing my shirt, hurting my shoulder, but pulling me out of the way of the train. My feet cleared the platform edge just as the engine screeched into the station.

I rolled and the man and I pitched into a clutch of white-faced commuters.

"What the hell were you doing?"

"Stupid cow."

"Jesus, are you alright?"

Their voices faded to nothing as the train doors hissed open and I spun back to face the tunnel.

Where was Justin?

An arm grabbed mine. "Move it." I blinked. It was Pete, shoving me through the cluster of angry watchers. "Security will be on their way. Head for the way out."

"Hey! I don't think you should be going anywhere." It was the man who had saved my life. He closed his fingers around my wrist, just above my filthy, soot-stained glove.

"Get off her." James slammed his fist into the guy's forearm to break his hold. Then Tamsin and Pete gripped both of my elbows and hustled me along the platform.

"I... I..." I wanted to say thanks. I wanted to find Justin. I'd never seen one of the dead hit by a train. Could you get *more* dead?

"I can't believe you did that." Tamsin was wheezing with laughter. "You should see your face. You should have seen all those people. That might be the best video yet. You reckon, Harls?"

Harley nodded. My feet barely touched the floor as they bundled me past the glowing Way Out sign and up the first staircase.

"Here, take my cap." Pete jammed a baseball cap over my hair. "The transport police will be looking for you."

"It'll take more than a cap." Tamsin was already removing her jacket. "Put this on. Quick."

Moving on autopilot I shoved my arms into the body-warm sleeves looking around frantically. Where was Justin?

"Where's your Oyster card? We can't stop at the gates." Tamsin shook my arm. "Get with the programme, Oh. Do you want to spend the night locked up?"

I shook my arm free of her grip and pulled my card from my jeans. I showed it to her wordlessly.

"Come on then."

We were facing the giant escalator. Tamsin pushed me onto the stair ahead of her and the others crowded on. "Run, Oh." Tamsin gave me another shove and I forced myself to speed upwards, trying not to trip as my eyes blurred the lines on the stairs and turned the escalator into an illusory slope.

There was an angry shout behind us and I paused long enough to turn around. A guard stood at the bottom of the escalator, walkie-talkie in hand.

"We're not going to make it," Tamsin gasped.

"Harley, Pete – diversion," James snapped.

Pete and Harley shouldered past, sprinted to the top of the moving stair and vanished.

I grimaced and held onto my side as a stitch drove a spike through my kidneys.

Above me Pete began to shout.

"They'll close the station any minute," Tamsin called.

My legs felt like jelly and I was shaking all over, exhaustion, adrenaline… rage. I forced one last effort from my body and hurtled up the final steps. I staggered off the escalator like a drunk and doubled over.

"Only one more." Tamsin patted the middle of my back then gave me another push. "Not so long this time."

"I know," I gasped and stood up. James and Tamsin hemmed me on each side and forced me to move faster. We ran up the last escalator and emerged into daylight. Only one gate was open and guards were checking cards and faces.

"You'll be fine," Tamsin whispered. "We've got out of stations before."

I nodded, too shattered to disbelieve her, and got into the queue.

Just as I was about to place my Oyster card on the gate, shouting broke out. I turned along with everyone else. Pete and Harley were having a fist fight. My mouth fell open. I'd never in my life seen Pete hit anyone.

They rolled to the floor, howling and yelling at one another and all but one of the staff ran through the gates to separate them. The single guard remaining wasn't too interested in peering beneath my cap, especially as they were looking for a bare headed girl in filthy clothes. I ducked into the fresh air, where I inhaled as if I'd never breathed before.

Tamsin and James flanked me once more. "There's a Pizza Express down the road. You can clean up and we'll wait there for the boys." Tamsin fingered her jacket with distaste. "You'd better keep this till you get home. Dry clean it before you give it back."

I wrapped my arms around myself with a sigh. Now I was in the open air I could smell the *Poison* seeping from the designer threads. My stomach lurched, but she was right. I had to stay covered up for the journey home. I glanced down. My jeans were blackened and torn at the knee; who knew what my shirt looked like.

While Tamsin and James slid into their chairs I sidled past the tables and ran down the steps into the toilet. I cleaned my clothes up as best I could with paper towels and water, then pulled off the cap and stared into the mirror.

My right cheekbone was scraped and bleeding and I had a lump on my forehead that was already bluish purple and surrounded by angry red swelling. I touched it gingerly and winced. My left hand was also scraped and I ran it under the tap as I pulled the filthy glove from my right. I couldn't go home without it. I hesitated for a moment then put it back on. I held a wet towel against the lump on my forehead and tried to run my fingers through my hair. They came up against another bump on the back of my head and a snarl of knots so tight there was no moving it.

I rammed the cap back on. I'd deal with it later.

Then I stood and just looked at myself. I barely recognised the girl in the mirror. That was it then, I was in the V club. I was… popular. But I felt as if maybe I'd been hit by that train after all.

When I got back to the table, Pete and Harley were already sitting down. Harley actually had a bruise forming on his cheek and Pete had a cut lip. I winced; they hadn't held back on each other.

There was a spare chair between the two of them.

"So you're in. How does it feel?" Tamsin leaned against James and stroked the inside of his forearm. "I'll be honest, sweetie, I didn't think you'd do it."

"I didn't think I'd do it either." My legs gave out and I dropped next to Pete.

James regarded Tamsin from under lowered brows. "Not sure the others are going to like this, babe. The V club isn't for the likes of her." He brushed his tattoo as if to remove dust from the ink and glanced at me. "No offence."

I shrugged. He didn't have to like me, just let me ask for a truth. "So can I set a challenge now?"

Tamsin laughed and leaned back. "You are funny. Your initiation got you in the club. You don't get to be a challenger until you've been selected by the wheel and completed another dare."

"What?" I pressed my throbbing palm between my thighs and my head reeled. "How long will *that* take?"

"That desperate to get me back, huh?" Tamsin sneered. "The next meeting is in three days. I suppose there's a chance the wheel will land on your name. James is the challenger though, so you don't *want* it to land on you." A flicker of remembered terror blurred her blue eyes. "Trust me."

22

I haven't seen a light

There was a dark haired boy in school uniform standing outside my house. Of course, he hadn't known where we'd gone, after.

I hadn't realised how heavy my tread had become until I rushed towards him, my shoes apparently filled with air. "You're alright!" It was automatic to raise my arms but, just a breath away, I stopped myself from embracing him.

"You thought I was what? Dead?" Justin drawled, with a sardonic twist of his lips.

"I…" I flushed and lowered my arms. "I've never seen one of you hit by a train. I wasn't sure what it would do."

"It dragged me as far as Moorgate then I managed to get back onto the platform."

"Did it hurt?" I wrapped my arms around my chest.

"It was more scary." He started climbing the steps to the house. "Shall we?" He gestured ahead of himself like an old fashioned gentlemen.

I opened the door and Justin held out his elbow so that I could take it. With a single deep breath I wrapped my arm around his. "I'm in the club."

He nodded. "Sorry about knocking you off the platform."

I nodded. "I wouldn't have done it otherwise. It was the most freaking stupid thing..." I suddenly remembered how Justin had died and choked my words back down. We were in my hallway but hadn't pulled away from one another. The feel of his arm in mine reminded me of something else. "I'm sorry too, about Tamsin. Are you OK?"

Now he pulled his arm free. "I couldn't expect her to stay single forever." He shrugged, but his eyes were hooded.

"A couple of days would've been nice." I shut my mouth when I saw his face. "You don't want to talk about it. I get it." I checked the clock and headed towards my room; it was almost nine, curfew time.

"Taylor?" Dad appeared from the kitchen, a mug of tea balanced on the arm of his chair. I froze. He rolled into the hall and gasped. "What happened?"

I looked down at myself.

"I had an accident."

"An accident? Christ." His elbow knocked the cup from his chair. A tannin rainbow splashed as the mug spun and bounced on the carpet. Tea spattered the wallpaper and a wet stain spread under his wheels. He ignored the mess and pushed himself towards me. "Look at you. What sort of accident?" His fingers fluttered over me, light and desperate. "Are you alright?"

"I'm fine." I shifted, uncomfortable beneath his frantic regard. He reached up and caught my face, turning my cheek. "You're covered in bruises. Was it a car?" His voice cracked. Then he looked at his own fingers. "What is this? Soot?"

"I fell over, on the tube."

The wall clock ticked as Dad inhaled. "On the tube?" He gripped my arm. "You're black."

I swallowed. "I-I fell off the platform. It was so crowded."

"Oh my God." Dad's face blanched, his cheeks so white it looked as if he was going to faint.

"Dad, breathe. I'm alright."

With one hand he dragged me backwards into the kitchen. My feet squelched through tea-drenched carpet. Once at the table he forced me under the low-hanging light.

"This needs Dettol." He stroked my cheek then forced me to sit.

His hands trembled as he washed my face with kitchen towel and gently applied the antiseptic to my grazed skin. I winced, but remained quiet.

Finally he spoke. "You were almost hit by a train."

"No, honestly. I was pulled straight back up. A friend helped me."

"Hannah was there?" Dad froze.

"Not Hannah, someone else."

He pressed his lips together and wiped at my neck. I

felt the pressure of his eyes on my gloved hand. "Were you... doing your usual thing?"

I forced a grin that felt more like a grimace. "Actually, I've joined a sort of youth group. I was with some of them."

"A youth group?" Dad pulled back and his face lit up like my bedroom. My heart hurt a little at how much that cheered him.

"It's some of the guys from school."

"Hannah and Pete."

I rolled my eyes. "Dad, Pete and I haven't been friends for ages."

Dad dragged his fingers through my tangled hair. "I liked him."

"Well, he wasn't happy with our friendship the way it was. And Hannah... she's not talking to me at the moment."

"Oh." Dad's face fell as if I'd slammed the lights off. "I'm sorry." He patted my hair and dropped his hand. "So, who's in this group?"

"You know, people from my class, some from the years below."

"A youth group." Dad rolled the words around his tongue as if testing them out.

"We meet in a church."

"In a church?" This time Dad's eyebrows shot upwards and I knew he thought V was a religious thing. I didn't disabuse him.

He cleared his throat. "Taylor, is this something to do with the boy in your class who died? With Justin."

I caught my breath. "You heard that they found him?"

"I'm in a chair, not an isolation ward."

"Right. Sorry."

"If you're looking for answers, you and the rest of your class, I suppose a church isn't the worst place to look." He rubbed his stubbled chin and I said nothing. "You know you can come and talk to me if you want to." He tugged the arms of my chair until our knees touched. "You've had to deal with too much death already. If there's some way I can help..."

I shook my head. "I'm OK, Dad." I glanced at the door. Justin had drifted to the open jamb and was leaning against the frame. "I know Justin's still with us."

Dad closed his eyes. "I wish I had your faith." He pushed back. "Go and get properly cleaned up. I've got a heart attack to recover from and a complaint to write to the Transport Authority."

"Don't do that, Dad."

I stood up and he moved his chair so I could get past, at the last moment he caught my arm. "Taylor, I don't like you going out after school like this, but I won't take away your chance to make new friends. You just have to be more careful. You know how to travel in London. Be more aware of the world around you, will you?"

I nodded. "This won't happen again." I gestured at myself and he sighed.

"You look so much like your mum these days." He half turned away. "Don't let what happened to her, happen to you."

••••

Justin followed me to my room. "Your Dad was pretty spooked."

I winced at my reflection. "He had good reason to be." I peeled off my glove and held it for a long minute. It was wrecked and should go in the bin. But it had been Mum's. I dropped it in the laundry.

"So I'm in the club." I touched the Mark on my hand. "But I'm running out of time. The next meeting isn't for three days. I don't get to set the challenge till I complete another dare and I can't do that until I'm chosen by some wheel. What are the chances of that?" I clenched my fists.

Justin nodded. "I think I can help."

"You can?" I raised my eyebrows, then I realised who, or rather what, I was talking to. "Of course. So I do another dare." I ignored my sinking heart. "*Then* I get to ask for a truth."

Justin looked at my blackened hand. "There's one more problem, Tay. Once you complete the dare, you don't get to be challenger for another week."

I inhaled, desperately clinging to my calm. "Ten days, I'm not sure I've got that long." I slumped onto my stool in front of my picture board. "Maybe James will bend the rules again."

"We'll think of something." Justin's hand fell on my shoulder and I jumped. "You need a shower."

I fingered my bruised head with a wince. He was used to looking at his perfectly groomed girlfriend. Ex-girlfriend. "Right. I look like hell."

••••

I turned the nozzle onto *massage* and let the water hammer at my sore muscles until they ached. Then I lathered my hair up, rinsed and did the whole thing again, until the water ran clear instead of grey.

The room was lit with four halogen bulbs, there was a towel warming on the rail and there was plenty of hot water. I didn't want to get out. So I stayed, leaning my head against the glass door and watching the shower gel foam around the plug.

When the water started to run cool, I stepped out and wrapped myself in the towel. Then I dragged a comb through my hair, brushed my teeth and pulled on some flannel pyjamas.

The thought stuttered through my head: Not exactly sexy.

I bit down on it as I ran through the dimly lit hallway. Who cared about that anyway?

I was surrounded by a fog so dense I literally couldn't see my hand in front of my face.

"Justin?" I spun around, seeing nothing. No sound penetrated the whiteness; I seemed to be all alone.

Experimentally I stepped forward. I could feel the ground beneath my bare toes. It was cool, but not cold, hard, but not uncomfortably so. Was I on a road, a path?

Wait a minute… why were my feet bare?

I squinted down at myself and pinched my top between my fingers. Why was I wearing pyjamas? Had I come outside?

I tried to remember. Had I head a noise or something, maybe left the house?

"Justin?" I tried his name again, but there was no reply.

I took a breath and the air in my lungs felt oddly dense. "Dad?"

If I was on the street, surely I could find my house. I kept turning in a circle, hoping to see something to guide me home. There was nothing but endless whiteness. No glowing streetlamps, no outlines of cars. My toes didn't bump into a kerb.

My neck prickled. "Who's there?"

No answer.

"I know there's someone out there I can feel you watching me."

My heart thudded and without thinking about it, I broke into a run. I didn't consider what I might crash into in the weird whiteness, just that I had to escape the intense presence. Some primal instinct told me it was a predator and I was prey. So I ran, hands out in front of me, breath stirring the air until it swirled like smoke but revealed nothing.

"Taylor, can you hear me?"

At first the voice was so quiet I thought I was imagining it. The tones only tickled my ears, making me turn in search of it. Now at least I had a goal. I would run towards the voice.

"Can you hear me, Taylor?"

I stopped. The voice was still muffled, but I could hear it much more clearly. "Mum?"

"Taylor, it's coming. You don't have much time."

"The Darkness, you mean? Where are you?" Desperately I swung my arms, frantic for her touch.

"*You have to be careful. Some things were not meant to be.*"

"*What wasn't meant to be?*"

"*I love you, but I have to go, so you've got to listen. He's waiting for you in the Dark, Taylor, and he's hungry, hungry for the world.*"

"Taylor... Taylor... wake up."

I bolted upright with a gasp, clawing at my sheets. Finally my hands closed around Justin's biceps. For a moment I stared at him and I could feel how wide my eyes were, wild and straining. I knew I was digging my nails into his arms, but I couldn't let go. My breath came in hitching pants and I couldn't get enough air. "J-Justin?"

"It's me. You were having a bad dream."

"The Darkness is coming and we're not even close to finding your killer."

"Calm down." Justin carefully peeled my fingers from his arms. "Let me switch the overhead lights on."

I slept in the gentle glow of my standard lamp and my bed floated on the light beneath it, but he was right, the main light would help. He found the switch and I sobbed out loud as the brightness immediately dispelled the lingering shadows.

"You're shaking." He hesitated then crouched next to me. His torso protruded through the bed turning him into a strange sort of centaur but he was able to put his arms around my shoulders.

I flinched automatically – this was Justin after all. Then I forced myself still, the nightmare remained with me and even the touch of someone I did not like was better than hugging my knees alone.

His skin was cool against mine. At school I'd brushed against him once or twice and I'd always been struck by how warm he was, as if he had an internal furnace that burned harder and brighter than other people's. Now he was cool.

"You're dead," I whispered.

I felt the swift brush of long eyelashes against my forehead as he blinked. Then he pulled back. "I thought we'd established that," he murmured.

"Yes, but you shouldn't be."

He snorted. "Preaching to the choir here."

I thought of my dream. Was it possible that Mum had really visited me?

"What do *you* think happens when you move on?"

He tilted his head towards the wall in a silent question and I nodded. He leaned back, keeping one arm around me and I curled into him, exhausted and oddly grateful. "I don't know." His voice was low, as if he was afraid of being overheard. "I wish I did. Mum used to go to church, but Dad wasn't into all that stuff. I always figured if you were an OK person it would work out alright in the end…" His voice grew fainter and I felt his muscles tense beneath his blazer.

"And now?" It was my turn to pull back, to examine his face.

He shook his head and his Adam's apple bobbed. "You know how they say people see a light when they die?"

"I guess." I frowned as I remembered all the dead I'd seen move on. The way the light fractured them into small pieces, or dissolved them away like chemicals on a photo negative.

"Well, I haven't seen a light. I don't remember any light when I died and I haven't seen one since." He looked at his fingers. "I think it means if I move on I…" he stopped.

"You think you're going somewhere bad?" I sat up, legs crossed under me. My face felt tight, like I was wearing a clay mask. Surely not? Justin hadn't been nice to me at school, but I must have tracked down killers for worse people over the years. Everyone went into the light.

He pulled his arm from me and I shivered. "All I know is, there hasn't been a light. So maybe you're not the only one the Darkness is coming for."

I reached for his hand but he moved away. "Do you think you can get back to sleep now?"

I snorted. "Yeah. Nice bedtime story, Hargreaves."

His lips twisted into a smile. "You want a bedtime story?"

"Guess not." I scrambled back under my knotted sheet, straightened it out and lay back down. But my eyes stayed open, restlessly darting around the room, looking for shadows, movement, anything out of place.

Justin shook his head, detangled his arm from my hair and moved to my dresser. "What about this?" He was standing over Mum's book.

I caught my breath. "Actually, yes, please. You could read that." I padded over to the dresser and brought the book back with me, glad I hadn't returned it to the dining room.

I settled back down and Justin stood at my side. I opened the book and his eyes scanned the page. He looked at me, surprised. "Are you sure you want me to read this? It doesn't look very calming."

"It reminds me of Mum."

"Well, alright then. From here?"

I nodded and Justin started to read. At first his voice blended into my memory of Mum's but soon his own tones took over and were all I heard.

Enchantments opened a hole a hand's span from my outstretched arm. In it my eyes perceived the glimmer of gold. To my shame I could not drag my gaze away.

"Yours if you pledge yourself to me. In return I will ensure that your line cannot die. Each of your descendents that belongs to me will find... love." The beast offered a throaty snort. "I am offering you both treasure and immortality, of a kind." I bowed my head.

"So, do you agree?"

"I agree."

As the words left my lips the beast caught my face. Claws dug into my cheeks and I gagged as liquid dripped into my mouth.

"Swallow and it is done."

As soon as I had been allowed to collapse onto the floor, the Lord of Death vanished. Almost in a dream state I scooped the promised treasure into a sack, caught up a lantern and began to seek the exit.

Stumbling towards the sunlight, I stopped only when I heard the voice of the Sunbird. Slowly I raised my lantern, eyes straining, but the flame barely touched the glutinous darkness and I was not sure where to look until a gurgling cough drew me.

Although it seemed impossible that my fear could grow, it was with a shudder that I saw the Sunbird crawling towards me.

"Don't go." His voice cracked and foolishly I stopped. Immediately his hand closed around my ankle. His grip was iron, unbreakably strong and I pulled backwards to no avail. Like a determined child the overseer climbed my leg, broken limbs jiggling as they dragged across the floor. Then he gripped my hand.

Pain racked me and cold drove into my skin as if hammered there by a pick. Then the Sunbird rose to his knees, no longer forcing his hold on me. I stumbled back as he released my hand. "You must avenge us," he said.

Finally I saw the extent of his injuries. "How did you survive?" My words dropped from numb lips.

The sunbird stared through a clotted-crimson mask. "What makes you think I did?"

Justin stopped. "Are you sure you want me to carry on?"
   I nodded, sleepily.

"If this doesn't give you nightmares ..." Justin frowned. "Well, I warned you." He rubbed his head as I turned the page.

Almost insensible with terror, I still remembered to tighten my hand around the sack of treasure before I ran. As I reached the border of dark and light I threw the lantern and hurled myself up the final steps, blinking and half blind.

The smells of the dig site assaulted my nose: sweat, food and camel dung. On my knees I gratefully dug my hands into the shifting sand, celebrating the feel of the hot grains pouring through my fingers after the cold dark below.

I forced my eyes to open. The invading sunshine forced tears onto my cheeks, but I vowed never again to allow full darkness to wrap me in its embrace.

Then my precious sunlight was blocked and I looked up. The Professor stood over me, hands on hips. Titus crouched at his feet; a tiny warped reflection of the beast in the tomb. I struggled to my feet. No hand was offered in aid.

"What the devil happened? Where are the others?" The Professor clenched his fists with wild impatience but I had to clear my throat before I could speak.

"All gone." I looked at the sack in my shaking hand then frowned. In the centre of my right palm, where the Sunbird had clutched

*me, there was a stain, like an ink blot. The
hand tingled as if I had been stung.*

"Look at me, man. What do you mean, gone?"

"Dead," I responded in a low voice. "All dead."

"But you survived? How? Is it still in there?"

*Slowly I raised my head. "It?" The Professor
had known about the beast.*

*He responded to the accusation in my eyes with
measured deliberation. "I assume some sort of
wild animal was living down there."*

"You knew."

*The Professor removed his glasses and his face
assumed an expression both cynical and sly. "I
assumed one of the overseers would deal with the
tomb's protection. Now you'll have to do the job.
Take my gun and get back down there."*

*With a laugh of disbelief, I tucked my hands
beneath my arms, as staunch a refusal as I could
make. As I pulled back I saw the Professor's eyes light
on the sack. Immediately he pulled the gun from its
holster and directed the muzzle at my chest. "With
the treasure in that tomb I will be master of the most
powerful society in England. Return, or I will shoot."*

*That was when I ran for my tent. I don't know
how much time I have before the man forces me
back into the dark. I do know my sanity will not
bear it. I have condemned my children's children to
lives of servitude to a foreign god, I have sold my
own soul. I have seen the Lord of Death and lived.*

I would rather die than face him again.

Justin's voice faded and his palm landed on my forehead. Slowly he stroked my eyes closed. "There's more, but you need to rest. I'll watch over you, OK? I'll keep the Darkness at bay, just for tonight."

I yawned. "You can't keep the Darkness at bay."

"Watch me," he growled.

And I did. I opened my eyes and watched him guard me until lead filled my lids and I fell into a dreamless sleep.

23

You're in the club now

"Taylor, you'll be late for the bus." Dad's voice drifted up the stairs and I clenched my fists.

"And suddenly you're the school police," I muttered, kicking my heels against the bed post.

"What's the matter?" Justin leaned against the wall by the mirror, apparently his preferred spot. "Don't want to go to school?"

"Shut up." I tried to make myself rise, knowing Dad would soon come up to chivvy me along, but my body wouldn't obey me. I picked at a spot on my bedspread. "If you must know, Hannah isn't speaking to me."

"She'll get over it."

"What if she doesn't?"

Justin caught my eye. "Then she doesn't." He cleared his throat as if embarrassed. "You're the strongest person I know, you'll go on without her."

I swallowed and returned my stare to the loose thread on my coverlet. "I don't think I am strong without

Hannah. I'm not sure I can face the dogs on my own."

After a moment a cool hand covered mine and I jumped. Justin had moved to sit beside me on the bed.

"You are and you can." He spoke without meeting my eye. "You've dealt with this," he fingered the edge of my glove, "on your own for how long now? Three years? You put up with all our crap for longer than that. You just faced an oncoming train. You can do anything."

I swallowed again. "I just can't deal with it right now."

Justin sighed. "Everyone feels that way sometimes; at least you haven't run away to the Science Museum."

A snort made me cover my nose and before I could think about it I was asking, "Will you come with me?"

"To school? Are you kidding?"

"Just for today." I finally met his eyes and knew mine were pleading.

"One of the only good things about being dead is *not* having to sit through double French." He pulled his hand away from mine.

"What else are you going to do with your day?"

He hissed through his teeth. "Taylor, I–"

"It's your fault, the fight I had with Hannah. OK, I guess it's been coming for a while, but it wouldn't have been this week."

"I don't want to see Tamsin," he finally blurted.

I stared at him. "Right, I forgot." It would hurt Justin to see Tamsin all over James; a knife in the heart on top of the fall from the scaffold.

I stood up and forced a smile. "Don't worry about it. I'll manage."

Justin twisted his fingers together awkwardly.

"Seriously, I'll cope." I flicked my hair over my shoulders and straightened. "What's the worst they can do?"

Justin suddenly looked up with a grin. "Taylor, you've forgotten something."

"What?" I frowned.

"You're in the V Club now, you're popular."

The common room was crowded when I arrived and habit made me look for Hannah. I spotted her crown of bright hair over on a table by the window and automatically my feet started in her direction. As if she'd sensed me come in, she stopped her conversation and turned. Her warm eyes met mine and instantly cooled. My feet faltered as she, very deliberately, shoved her bag on the empty seat next to her and turned her back.

The air in the room fled and I stood in between tables, struggling to breathe, hurting and humiliated.

"What're you doing, Oh?" Harley shoved me in the small of the back and I stumbled. Anger swung me round like a top and my fists clenched at my waist.

He stepped back, hands raised. "Easy 'eye of the tiger'. I was just coming to get you. You looked lost."

I felt like an anime version of myself, as if I should have a huge question-mark blinking above my head.

"Come on, we've saved you a seat."

"You've what?"

Harley leaned in. "You're in the club now. You sit with us."

"You want me to sit with you?" I tested the words out, but they still felt foreign and wrong.

Harley shrugged. "'Want' is a strong word, but you're in V and you rocked the dare last night. I can't wait to see what you do next." He grinned. "Anyway, the rule is, V sticks together. You're with us now."

Moving like an automaton and half wondering if I was still asleep I followed Harley over to the "popular table". As I approached I expected the usual raft of insults to fly at me, but nothing happened. Tentatively I put my hand on the back of a chair. Still no one prevented me. Like an addict, unable to stop myself, I glanced over at Hannah. She was watching me with her jaw slack and her hands clutched to her chest.

One of her new friends nudged her and she closed her mouth and looked away.

Fine then. I swung into my new chair and dumped my bag at my feet.

Tamsin sat opposite me filing her nails. James was next to her, lounging cross-armed. His eyes fell on me and didn't shift, not even when it became uncomfortable. I looked away first, to find Pete looking at Hannah with sadness in his eyes.

"You were right," I muttered. "She's had enough of me."

Pete rubbed his head. "It's probably for the best. She won't ask questions now."

Tamsin glanced up. "What do you care? You're with us now, sweetie."

I nodded. But if I was popular, why did I feel like my guts had been scooped out with a spoon?

Just before bell a hand landed on my shoulder. I would have flown out of my chair if the weight of it wasn't preventing me.

"Well, well, well, Taylor Oh." Mr Barnes' voice confirmed the owner of the hand. "It seems you've 'dared' to become a bit more sociable." He laughed with forced joviality and for some reason my mind flashed up an image of the dead clown. "Didn't I tell you there were opportunities in this school, that the unpopular could rise?"

At the edge of my vision his meaty fingers twitched on my shoulder. "Yes, Mr Barnes."

"Yes, Mr Barnes," he falsettoed and his shirt sleeve rode up. On his wrist, mostly hidden by his cuffs was the edge of a tattoo.

As he patted my shoulder and stepped back I whipped around to look from James to the headmaster. James was grinning with a sly and superior air. Mr Barnes nodded at him, tugged his shirt back into place and strode away, already growling at someone for leaving their bag in the walkway between tables.

I rubbed my shoulder, as if I could remove the taint of his touch.

"I wish you wouldn't wear that dorky glove," Tamsin sighed. "It's so... gawd I don't know, emo."

I glowered at her. "Trust me, you want me to keep the glove."

24

Still got time

"So, how was it?" Justin was lounging on my bed when I got home.

"Really strange." I dropped my bag and pushed his legs so I could sit down. "Everyone's freaked out about what happened to you. And Tamsin was actually…"

"Nice?" Justin sat up.

"God no, but she wasn't like before either." I stretched and groaned as my shoulders cracked. Then I went still. "Hannah's still not talking to me."

Justin winced sympathetically. "I'm sorry, that sucks."

"At least I don't have to deal with all the bitchiness and I don't have to lie to her about V."

"See, silver linings everywhere." Justin spread his arms and I couldn't withhold a smile.

"Yes, this is just one big happy silver lining."

My hand had been throbbing all day. I fingered the glove for a moment, then with trepidation, pulled it back to reveal my hand.

Justin leaned closer. "It's darker."

My pulse thumped as I nodded. The Mark was so black I could no longer see the faint outlines of the veins beneath my skin. I ran my palm over the top of it then covered it over once more.

"We've still got time," I murmured

Justin's fingertips hovered over mine. "If you believe that, Oh, why are your hands shaking?"

I dreamed again that night and woke up with my mother's voice ringing in my ears and Justin's arms around my shoulders.

"He's hungry for the world," I muttered.

"What does that mean?" Carefully, as if he thought I'd bite him, Justin smoothed my hair out of my eyes.

"I don't know." I shuddered and gripped his arm. "But if someone in the V club wasn't involved in your death, I'll be an appetiser."

"What's going on?" I clutched my Oyster Card, unwilling to commit to swiping it. The bus was packed with more than double the usual number of commuters.

The driver glared at me, obviously harassed and impatient to be moving. "Central Line's down."

I glanced at the door, wondering whether to jump back off again, but a crowd had gathered behind me, anxious to get to work. I'd have to shove my way through them and there could be ghosts anywhere. I hugged my chest and my pulse pounded. My hand felt as if it was bleeding, as though the Mark were a real injury, worsening with every hour. I had told Justin we had plenty of time but I didn't believe it. I couldn't take another Mark.

But was it safer to stay on the crowded bus, or try and get to school another way?

My breath shortened and a sharp pain in my chest made me drop my bag. I felt as if I was being buried alive, as if grains of sand filled my mouth and nose, and pressed down on suddenly aching limbs. I gasped for air.

"Get a move on." Angry voices shouted from outside and the people began to press in on me. I couldn't stay on the bus, it was too crowded: I'd suffocate.

Wobbling, I scooped up my bag and backed out of the vehicle, earning myself an angry tut from the driver and furious grunts from the commuters I shoved aside in my rush to escape.

I could barely see, but I had to watch every face, I had to see who wasn't carrying a briefcase when they ought to be, who was reaching for me through the mass of heaving shoulders.

It was too much, how could I check every single face?

A pointed heel came down on my foot and I cried out. Tears worsened the situation even more. Finally I burst through the crowd and yanked my bag out behind me. It came free with a suddenness that knocked me off my feet, but I still scrabbled backwards in the pavement grime, desperate to be away from the crowd and find clear air.

But the air didn't clear, my chest continued to thump with the panicked hammer of my heart and I couldn't take a breath without feeling as if I was stabbing myself in the lungs. The world started to go grey, but I couldn't let it. I had to keep watching, had to keep away from the ghosts.

I gripped my chest, as if that would free me from the weight that bore down on me. It didn't help. Was I having a heart attack? What happened if I died and I was still carrying a Mark?

"Taylor, what's going on?" The voice was familiar and I focused on it gratefully. I couldn't answer. All I could do was keep trying to breathe and forcing my heart to keep beating.

"I think I've seen this before, OK, my aunt used to do this."

I shook my head, still unable to see past the grey veil that had covered the world. "My heart," I rasped.

"You're having a panic attack, Tay. You have to keep breathing."

"Trying," I gasped.

"You need a paper bag or something. But I can't get you anything, you have to do this yourself."

"Too many people." I was blind and I could be surrounded by ghosts with no way to know and no way to run. My pulse fluttered like a hummingbird in flight and in the distance a dog barked angrily.

"Tay, listen to me, I'm not going to let anything happen to you. There aren't any ghosts right now, I'm watching. You just have to concentrate on breathing."

"J-Justin?" I inhaled desperately. It had to be him; he was the only one who knew about the ghosts.

"It's me. Come on, Tay, in and out, in and out." He grabbed my hand and squeezed it as he took over responsibility for making me breathe. He was going to keep the ghosts away. I was safe.

Gradually my pulse slowed and my heart started to beat more ponderously. As the sand receded from my mouth and nose, my vision cleared and I saw him watching me with concerned eyes.

"Freak."

As the world came back into focus I saw that I was blocking part of the path, businessmen were stepping over me to get to the bus queue. Muttered insults propelled me to my feet. I grabbed my bag and staggered to a bench. Justin followed, his eyes darting, taking seriously his promise to keep the ghosts at bay.

I sagged onto the sun-warmed slats. "What are you doing here?" I rubbed my eyes, ashamed that he'd seen my breakdown.

Justin took one final look around then sat beside me. "I've been walking you to school, alright. Just, you know, making sure you were OK. Keeping the others back."

I blinked. "Others?"

He nodded. "There've been one or two like me. I ran them off."

"I didn't know."

"I didn't want you to."

We sat side by side in the sunshine.

"I guess I'd better get to school. I'll miss first period even if I walk fast." I hoisted my bag on my shoulder. "Are you coming with?"

Justin grinned and his hair caught the light, like black gold. "I'll take you to the gates."

As we walked, the final entry in Oh-Fa's journal kept pace with us. I heard it in a blend of Justin's voice and my mother's and knew for certain that it would not be much longer before I had my answers.

It is over.

I am alone in the camp with no map to show me the way back to civilisation. I will finish this journal. Then I will pack my treasure with what provisions I can and attempt to make it home. Although I do not deserve to see my daughter I will owe her an explanation when the time comes.

As I finished my last journal entry the Professor entered the tent and forced me outside.

"Murderer." I spoke with fervour.

The Professor gestured with the gun. "I don't care about that. As for you, die out here, or take your chances in there. And don't even think about turning on me, unless you think you can find the way back to civilisation alone."

Left with no choice I reluctantly took the gun. Then, half in a daze, I pressed my right palm to the back of the Professor's hand. An unnatural effervescence seethed beneath my skin and when I pulled my hand free, the Mark imprinted by the Sunbird's touch was gone. Now it lay over the Professor's tendons like a spider pressed in a natural scientist's book.

The Professor gestured impatiently. "Get on with it."

Fearfully I looked into the shadow coating the fourth step. Then I frowned at the mathematics of the situation; hadn't I been able to see five steps before?

And now there were only three. The shadows were advancing.

The Professor, determined to send me into the tomb, shoved me from behind. I wriggled sideways and pointed to draw his attention to the Darkness that now spilled into the camp.

Titus barked. He scampered towards the living shadow that blotted out a body length of sand and stopped at its edge, claws working furiously to keep him out of the boundary. He snarled continuously, a low sound of menace, and the Professor retreated. "What is it?"

I shook my head and watched the Darkness follow the Professor's movement.

For his part the Professor ran for his tent. "Make it stop." At his feet blackness reared like smoke, thicker and darker than the smog I had seen on my journey through London.

"Shoot it!" the Professor's scream rent the air.

I stood petrified as the Darkness struck. Titus howled and the Professor shrieked once then disappeared.

After a while the Darkness receded back into the tomb. The murderous Professor had been taken to Anubis, just as the beast had promised.

And now I understand my mission; the path my life will take.

Even now I see a shadowy figure approaching across the sand. Alone in this great desert he cannot possibly reside among the living. I hope he will at least lead me back to Giza.

I am so very sorry my children. Please forgive me.

25

The wheel keeps spinning

We stood outside the church, the last to arrive.

"Are you sure you want to do this?" Justin's anxiety was making him restless. "No." I wrapped my arms around my chest as if I could protect myself from what was to come. "After that last dare, James could set anything. What if I can't do it?"

Justin said nothing.

"Your last dare killed you. My initiation nearly killed me. This isn't a good idea."

He looked up at the stained glass window as if it held an answer and I rubbed my hand.

"I don't have a choice, do I?" I sighed and started forward.

"There has to be another way." Justin caught my arm. "Perhaps we could get hold of my police records or something."

I raised my eyebrows. "First of all, do I look like Nancy Drew? And second, if it was possible for me to hack into

245

Scotland Yard, or break in or whatever, I wouldn't find anything." I grimaced. "If your murderer wasn't going to get away with it, your touch wouldn't have transferred a Mark."

Justin held his hand to his face, as if he'd see something on it. "I'm sorry." He looked at me from the corner of his eye. "I didn't know. I would never have touched you otherwise."

I nodded and stood with one foot on the church steps. "Thanks for saying that and I know you didn't even know you were dead. But you would have come for me eventually. In the end they all do."

Justin opened his mouth and I stepped forward. "Come on, let's get this over with."

The room was laid out as before, with a large circle of chairs overseen by the Icarus poster. Only instead of a chair in the centre of the ring, there was a bicycle wheel mounted on an easel with a large circle of wood behind. The wooden circle had each of our photos on and the wheel had a pointer attached.

I stared at it, searching for the missing image: Justin's. Of course it wouldn't be there. My own face had probably taken his place.

James' picture was an old one; in it he was slimmer and his skin was bare of tattoos. The arrogant facial expression however, was the same. The image had a big pair of scarlet wings stuck on top with blu-tack. I figured that meant he was exempt from the wheel: the challenger.

"Nice of you to join us, Oh. Are you going to stand there all night?" James sneered.

The empty chair was between Pete and a boy I recognised from the year below. Alan fidgeted uncomfortably as I slipped into the circle and sat next to him. I shot him a glare, remembering the feel of sand in my clothes. It was obvious what he had done to get into the club. Justin took up a position at my back just as, with a death's head grin, James rose from his seat and put one hand on the black tyre. His eyes met mine as he whipped the wheel downwards.

I swallowed. Half of me; the sensible half, wanted the wheel to keep spinning, to land on any of the other fifteen smiling faces. The other part clenched my blackened hand and prayed for it to stop with the pointer covering my own image.

As the wheel spun, Justin stepped from behind my chair. Once inside the circle he raised his eyebrows. Feeling sick as a dog, I gave the smallest possible nod and he waited next to the wheel, like a compère, for the spinning to slow.

Tension thickened the air as the wheel started to clack less and less quickly and faces around the ring tensed and paled. I could hear Alan breathing through his nose, hard on the inhale, as if he couldn't get enough air.

I glanced around. Even Harley was leaning forward. His curls were a greasy tangle around his eyes as he waited for the outcome with gritted teeth.

Yet Pete seemed fairly relaxed. He sat on my left, arms dangling by his sides, legs crossed at the ankle. Then, there it was; the little muscle on his jaw that twitched when he was stressed. He was pretending not to care, but he did. No one wanted the wheel to land on them, not even Pete.

Today, they didn't have to worry.

Now I could see the individual spokes as the wheel turned. It wouldn't be long. Finally the wheel was barely moving. It was coming to a halt, stopping a full half turn away from my image.

The little pointer brushed Alan's cheerful face and he winced as if it had actually touched his skin. But it was still moving on past Harley whose exhalation made his curls shiver, past Tamsin who blinked and dabbed at her mascara, past a younger girl called Ella who sagged into her chair, past Pete. No, not past Pete. It was going to stop on his picture. I couldn't help myself, I turned with everyone else to look at him, see how he was taking it. James raised his arm, but then…

Then Justin gripped the wheel.

Sweat stood out on his forehead as if the tyre was resisting him. He only had to get it going again, just enough to move it past three more pictures.

My breath stopped as the wheel moved fractionally.

Pete groaned audibly as it moved past him, turning on, past one then two, images. Mine was next.

Then James reached out and touched the easel and Justin's hands slipped through the tyre as if it had turned to air. He could no longer touch it.

No.

My eyes widened as I stared at the wheel, willing it to keep moving. It trembled and then, thank God, momentum moved it a tiny bit more and the pointer sat directly over my face.

I was going to be challenged after all.

Pete frowned. "She's only just done a dare." He leaned back in his chair, acting as if he didn't really care. "Should we spin again?"

A chorus of negatives filled the space; voices tense with the fear that their reprieve might be snatched away.

"It's alright, Pete." I smiled tightly. "It can't be worse than the last one and I managed that OK, didn't I?"

Pete's eyes skidded from mine. "*Dying* to be popular, are we?" He shrugged and rose from his chair. "Your funeral." He leaned against the wall again.

I swallowed and turned to face James.

"Now we've got *that* out of the way…" James smirked and his hair glittered bronze in a shaft of dusty light. "Time for the challenge, Oh."

I nodded.

"Come on then. On your feet."

"Up, up, up." The refrain propelled me onto my toes. The temptation to take Justin's hand was so great I had to fold my arms.

"You know the rules now." James' voice was bloated with satisfaction. "I set the challenge but you can *double dare* if you want to send it back my way. If you do you have to double up, that is make the dare twice as hard, according to the moderators Harley and Tamsin here." He gestured and the light falling on his wrist made a shadow like a snake moving over the floor. "If you can't make the challenge doubly hard, it goes back to you. If I turn down the double dare, someone else is allowed to take it on, for points. If you would rather take a truth than the dare, you can enter the confessional." His smile widened like a sharks. "This week in the confessional we'll be testing the truth about your personality: how much pain can you stand? Of course, you can choose to swap your place in the confessional with someone else, your best friend in the group, the guy who proposed you. So what's it going to be, Oh? Truth or dare?"

"Just to clarify," I rasped. "I can go into the confessional and you'll hurt me until I can't stand it any more. Or I can make Pete go inside instead, which makes me look like a bitch and means Pete'll probably do the same to me next time he's challenged. Or I can take your dare, but I don't know what it is yet?"

"That's right." James nodded. "Fun, isn't it?"

"But I can double dare you?"

"Only if you can double up and not make the dare impossible."

"And if I win the dare I get to set the challenge next time?"

"That's right."

"And if I refuse the dare altogether?"

James glanced at Tamsin for a second. Her crimson lips curled. "Remember Derek?"

My mouth went dry. "But what if I lose the dare, if I just can't do it?" That was the only thing I wasn't clear about.

"Why, nothing," she answered.

"Nothing?"

"Nothing," James parroted. "If you genuinely try but still fail the dare, you go back on the wheel and I get to set another challenge next week.

"That's it?" I wrinkled my nose.

James leaned forward. "So what'll it be? Truth or dare?"

I met his gaze with a steely one of my own. "Dare."

Excitement made James literally dance on the spot. "Everyone listening? Here's the dare for this week. Remember what Hargreaves had to do the other week, and how he *failed*? Well that dare is still up. Oh, you have to go to the building site where he died, climb the scaffolding and walk across the part that hasn't got a handrail."

Gasps rent the air as the shock hit the rest of the V club. Justin literally growled and as I turned he launched past me, fists swinging. His right arm powered through James' cheek and came out the side of his head without moving a single carefully styled hair.

He landed on his side, spitting and furious.

"You can't be serious?" Pete rubbed his stubble-specked head.

I met James' smug gaze and blinked. My breath sat in my chest like an undigested wad. "Are you allowed to set a challenge that isn't possible?"

"Moderators?" James glanced over at Tamsin and Harley.

Slowly Tamsin nodded, but her face was now white. "W-we already decided it was possible."

Pete leaped back into the circle. "Come *on*, there'll be security now. Maybe even police. If we get caught they'll look harder at Justin's death."

James shook his head. "We have friends in high places, Petrol Pete, remember? The Met won't be looking into the V club."

"Fine, but wake up, Justin *died*. *Clearly* it isn't possible."

Harley's lips twisted under his acne scars. "I dunno, dude, it should be do-able. Justin was just unlucky."

"Unlucky?" This time Justin hurled himself at Harley, grabbing for his lapels. In the end he had to settle for screaming into his ear. "You *dick*, I'm *dead*. You call that unlucky?"

Tamsin sniffed. "Pete has a point, Justin did prove it impossible."

I forced myself to breathe past the obstruction in my throat. This dare was beyond crazy. The V club was out of control. But now I had a way to get the challenge on my own terms.

"I'll do it." I silenced the objections with a stab of my gloved hand. "But on one condition: if I make it, I get to set a challenge."

"Yeah, yeah, that's how it works." James waved airily.

"No, I get to set my challenge straight after. No waiting a week. I get to set a truth or dare right after I do this thing."

James sucked air in through his teeth. "Haven't we bent enough rules for you?"

I shrugged. "The moderators said the challenge was impossible, didn't they? So either you agree to bend that rule for me, or I don't have to do the dare and you lose your chance to set a challenge."

I heard Tamsin's inhalation from where I stood. Pete shook his head and stepped backwards, leaving me to my insanity. Only Justin rolled to his feet.

"Do *not* do this, Tay." His earnest face was centimetres from mine. "There has to be another way, I just haven't thought of it yet. Maybe I can haunt James until he cracks, or hang around these guys until someone talks about what happened." He looked hopeful, but I shook my head slightly and showed him my hand.

"It could take forever," I murmured into my gloved palm.

"What was that, Oh?" James jerked forward, but I stepped back.

"Just wondering what your decision was."

He pursed his lips and his eyes glittered redly in the lowering evening light. Outside a dog howled. "Go on then." Blood-thirst made him hoarse. "You come out with us tomorrow night and do this dare. *If* you succeed, you can set your own right after."

26

My last thought

I nursed a coffee in the kitchen and tried not to check the time every two minutes. Every bulb was blazing, even the ones under the cupboards, yet it still felt as if the shadows were closing in. Although it was a sunny day there was a quality to the light that suggested approaching night. The air was oppressive and I felt anxious and on edge, as if I was in the eye of a storm and it was about to break.

Justin watched me with solemn eyes. Finally he spoke. "I'm coming with you."

I tightened my hands around my mug. "I know how hard that will be for you."

I knew I should tell him to stay behind, but I couldn't bring myself to do it. I didn't want to do the dare alone. And if something went wrong I wanted someone with me. Someone I liked.

I caught my breath. I... liked Justin. I explored the sensation as if I was probing a broken tooth with my tongue.

Sure, he was good-looking, but he'd always been attractive; his attitude had made me immune. Somehow this last fortnight he'd become a friend and that had exposed my heart. I glanced at him then quickly away, afraid that he'd somehow be able to spot the change in me.

He knew about my curse and more than that, he was helping to keep the ghosts away. With Justin I felt safe and perhaps understood for the first time since my mum had died. With deepening depression I found myself wishing that there was a way that he could remain by my side, but when I found his killer he'd move on and leave me alone once more.

I thought of my mum's promise to me with a snigger. Was this the "love" that I was supposedly guaranteed? An unrequited crush on a dead teenager.

Hysterical laughter bubbled in my chest. At least if I was going to die tonight, I'd have had this feeling. Tainted with darkness as it was, it was better than the nothing that had filled me until now.

I swallowed it back. "I'd better find Dad and say goodbye."

Justin's fingers edged across the table until they touched my wrist. "Hey." He smiled gently as I looked up. "We're going to be alright."

We met the others at the bus stop so we could go together to the site of Justin's death. Before we left I had pulled the glove over my hand with shaking fingers. I'd never seen a Mark so black and I was pretty certain the

Darkness was coming for me, maybe even tonight. If I could just stay ahead of it for a few more hours I'd know who Justin's killer was and could pass the Mark on.

I wasn't even entertaining the thought that my plan wouldn't work.

I glanced along the back seat of the bus and my eyes skidded past Tamsin, Harley, Pete, and James: the group that had escorted Justin. One of them had to know what really happened that night.

Justin was sitting on an empty seat in front. He glanced back every so often, with an expression that said he was checking on me. And each time he turned his head I sensed the effort it took him not to look at Tamsin and James.

Biting my lip I looked out the window. Another ten minutes and we'd be getting off the bus. Apparently our stop was only a short walk from the building site. I fidgeted in my seat. I wasn't comfortable putting my toes on the bus floor. The shadows beneath the seat were definitely darker than they should be and they sucked at my heels when I put them down.

We stood outside the chippy on the high street. It was that odd witching hour in the suburbs of London between the shops closing down for the day and the bars opening up for the evening. A few doors remained open, a vendor selling sari silk, a Costcutter, a newsagent. These hopeful businesses spilled electric light and noise onto the pavement, but the street was fairly quiet and most shops were dead.

A man walked towards us with two huge dogs on leads. All three of them wore studded collars and I couldn't take my eyes off the hounds. They weren't friendly. As they drew level with us one of them sniffed towards the chip shop while the other drooled and looked at me with eyes so black they reminded me of the void imprinted on my hand. Inadvertently I took a step backwards and the dog growled.

Its owner glared at me as if I'd deliberately antagonised his animals and a flash of anger warmed me. Where did he get off?

I was sick of feeling hunted and being scared. I was going to climb that scaffolding and then the idiots with me would have to tell me what really happened to Justin. Then I could get rid of the Mark and… and Justin would be gone.

I was trying to keep my glances at Justin to a minimum. He stood next to Pete and watched me with wary brown eyes, so different from those of my one-time friend. Justin was the only one of us wearing a uniform, the others had insisted on hoodies and jeans for this trip, and he looked a little lost. His skin was still pale, his face pinched and nervous. Of course, when he was last here, he'd died. I should be checking on him, not the other way around. I gave him an encouraging smile.

"What're you gurning at?" Tamsin peered around James, seeing nothing but the Costcutter on the other side of the road.

I spread my gloved hand. "Nothing. Just thinking about stuff."

"Freak."

We stood a hundred metres down from the building site and I wondered if they'd stopped here last time too. Pete's hands were wrapped around the portion of chips he'd just bought. Grease and vinegar dripped from the paper onto the gum-stained pavement. Tamsin curled her lip and my own stomach rolled at the smell.

James nodded at the security insignia that hung on the link fence that surrounded the building site. "We need another diversion. You ready?"

Pete nodded and tilted his head. "I'll need Tamsin this time."

Arm-in-arm the couple walked down the street towards the building site. Suddenly the girl pulled away. "You can't talk to me like that!"

"I was only kidding." The boy thought he could talk his way out of whatever he'd said.

"What about the other day? What about the party? I've had enough."

"Where did that come from?" It was the boy's turn to pull back.

"You're a total waster. It's over."

"What?" He was shouting now. "You can't just dump me!"

"Get over yourself, I just did. Anyway, why would you care, you want someone with some 'junk in their trunk', right?"

"I was *joking*!" The girl was stalking away now, leaving the boy outside the building site. His eyes glittered above his dark jumper as he thumped the chain link fence. "Dammit."

"Hey." The guard's voice reached us. "What're you doing?"

"Didn't you see? She just dumped me." The boy rubbed his bald head. "I can't believe it." He looked at his right hand as if he'd forgotten he was clutching a bag of chips. "I don't feel like these any more. You want them?"

The guard glanced left and right, then shrugged. "Go on then."

The boy leaned on the fence. "Did you see her? She was fit. Out of my league really…"

"Come on." James pulled on my sleeve. "We've got a minute or two. Let's get round the back."

Tamsin rejoined us and fluffed up her hair. "Did you see Pete try and make me eat those greasy carbs?"

"It worked." James put his arm around her shoulder and led us down a side road to the rear of the site. "Pull up your hoods, girls. There's CCTV everywhere." Harley was already donning his and now James too covered his hair and pulled the cowl low over his eyes. Instantly he seemed even more menacing.

I shivered and tweaked my own hood over my eyes, narrowing the world to a tunnel.

The fence was at least six foot, but there was no barbed wire or anything. I was about to set my hands and feet on it when Harley grabbed my shoulder. I turned, mouth opening, and saw a couple hurrying past us with their heads down.

"Boo," he shouted and they crossed quickly to the other side of the road.

Tamsin smacked him as he snickered. "Way to call attention to us."

Harley just grinned and James gestured towards the fence.

Justin gave my fingers a quick squeeze, then phased through the chain link right beneath the "No Access" sign. I shivered as I watched him go. It was so easy to forget what he was.

Suddenly he reappeared. "Start climbing here, there's some stuff piled up on the other side. You can jump down."

I nodded and moved to the spot he indicated. Then I took one last look around. It was almost dark and the streetlights cast orange circles onto the grey pavement.

We were overlooked only by the rears of buildings. Bulging rubbish bags sat outside one scratched door; probably the back of a bar. A rustling sound made me jump and my eyes jerked back to the bins. A sudden glittering made me inhale as a fox raised its muzzle from the rubbish. It regarded us coldly then gave a short yip and disappeared down the street, slipping from light pool to light pool, then melting into an abandoned lot.

I licked dry lips and turned back to the fence.

Time to climb.

We were all inside.

Tamsin had made a bit of a production about it, but even she had managed to scale the fence. And I judged by Justin's disgusted expression that she would have been fine even without the help James had given her.

I looked away from her drama. I had to focus.

The scaffolding rose into the sky in front of me, like the skeleton of a decomposed building. Long metal bones, held together with bolts like sinews, were boarded with wood that looked black in the dim light.

I stepped forward and a light blazed white. It picked me out like a prisoner and threw my shadow against the fence.

I yipped as loudly as the fox and took a jump back.

"Freeze." Harley gripped my arm. "It's movement sensitive."

After a moment the light went out. There was no sign of the security guard; Pete must still have him talking.

"Now what?" I shook my arm free.

Harley shook his head. "There's no way you'll be able to do this, China. Time to leave."

Justin nodded agreement, but I ignored him and bit my lip. "Where's the light? Can we cover it with something?"

James draped his arm over Tamsin and pointed. The spotlight was fixed to a pole at the edge of the scaffold. "Cover it with what?"

"My hoodie. I could try and throw it over."

"Throw it?" Tamsin sneered and her nails peeped out from the sleeves of her sweatshirt as she stretched. "Who do you think you are?"

"I can't think of anything else, can you?" I looked meaningfully at Justin and pulled my jumper off. It tugged at my hair which fell back against my shoulders in a heavy curtain as I whipped it in front of me.

I made a show of judging the direction and distance to the light; then I threw. It shouldn't have made it, but Justin snagged the sleeve and ran. For the others it must have looked as though it had been caught by the wind. Finally Justin tossed the shirt over the spotlight. It caught by the hood.

"Wow." James stared at me, his lips pursed in surprise.

"Awright, China." Harley punched the air.

Under her own hood Tamsin's perfect eyebrows were raised. "Lucky," she muttered.

"Yeah." I checked on Justin, but he wasn't looking at me. Instead his eyes were trained on the far side of the site. At first I thought the guard was coming; then I saw the old woman. She was wearing a hospital gown and leaning on a crutch. No way had she just climbed the fence.

Justin whipped round to face me as the old lady started to limp forward. He could either help me climb the scaffold or keep the other ghost from giving me a Mark.

"Oh no," I whispered. "Not now."

"'Not now' what?" Tamsin leaned forward, her face feral in the dim light.

"Just a headache coming on."

"I don't want to hear excuses." James slicked a stray hair beneath his hood with the palm of one hand. "Are you doing this, Oh? I'm expecting great things."

I wrapped my arms around my chest. The ghost was still coming. Justin looked from me to the scaffold to the old lady, his eyes darting from one to the other.

Finally I pointed at the ghost. Like a beacon my white glove shone with the message: *Just keep her away from me.*

Miserably, Justin moved towards the spectre while I strode towards the scaffolding. Immediately the floodlight came on, but it was shining through my black top and the light was muted.

At the bottom of the structure I looked up. Justin had said it didn't look that bad from the bottom; that it was much higher looking down from the top. From where I stood, it seemed to tower above me so how high would it seem when I got up there?

I shivered and closed my bare hand around the first pole.

It was chilly; not as bitter as the touch of the hounding dead, but cold. Flakes peeled off and jabbed at my bare skin. I inhaled and smelled rust, like blood, on the shaft.

I looked back. Tamsin relaxed in James' embrace, watching me with her cat-like eyes. Harley held his phone in front of his face, recording me with impersonal precision.

I hadn't intended to do this climb alone. Automatically I tortured myself by looking for Justin. He was holding his arms wide in front of the intruding ghost, talking intently and making himself into a barrier.

My back straightened. I would take this in stages; the first thing to do was get to the top of the scaffolding.

It was just like a climbing frame, only higher. I forced my limbs to stop shaking and started my journey.

••••

Six feet up, I looked down and gasped. Beneath me, lit by the muted spotlight, tendrils of blackness were tangling together. They gathered like snakes to form an abyss that dragged at my feet like a black hole inhaling the air.

My heart thudded and my trainer slipped as my focus shifted from the scaffolding to the ground. I yelped breathlessly and threw my arms around a timber crosspiece.

"You're hardly off the ground, Oh, you're never going to make it." James and Tamsin were laughing.

I pressed my lips together, twined my legs around a brace and forced my shaking arms to unclench. Then I looked up. I hadn't even reached the top of the first floor.

Quickly I checked on the new ghost. One more Mark and the Darkness would ascend for sure. As my eyes met hers she grimaced at me toothlessly. Without having to think about it, I had a good idea what her story would be. An old woman in a hospital gown; she'd have me looking for her own Doctor Death. I frowned, feeling an unfamiliar wave of sympathy and reached for the spar above my head. I had to concentrate on the climb.

I was glad I was wearing Mum's glove because my hands were sweating furiously. It wasn't so bad walking along the girders, but every so often I had to swing myself from floor to floor and my palms were as slippery as if I'd soaped them.

The white glove glowed red in the dim light, stained with rust and oil. The odour of sweaty metal hung about my other palm as I climbed higher and higher above the street. Soon I was over the level of the fence and able to look out on the road below. The alley remained quiet, but I could hear the bars starting to fill.

A loud creak made me freeze and a pole shifted under my hand. Once my heart had started up again I gripped the crosspiece with my legs and gave the pillar a shake. A bolt rattled. It was loose, but should bear my weight.

I had to keep going. Unable to stop myself I looked down. Now Tamsin's face was only a white circle, her features erased by darkness and distance. I let my eyes shift further. The void below my feet remained, pulsating, waiting, but no longer moving.

And Justin? He was nowhere to be seen. The old woman was standing by herself, leaning on the fence. She saw my glance and waved. What had Justin said to make the ghost stay back? And where the hell was he?

My panicked gaze strayed back to the leering void. Had Justin tried to climb after me? Had the Darkness taken him? My chest tightened until I could barely breathe.

"We don't have all night." James' voice floated up to me. I swallowed, nodded and continued to climb.

Now when I looked up I could see stars. The building must be four stories. Not the highest in the borough, but high enough so that I could see over rooftops and into backlit windows.

I paused on a platform to take a breath, stepped backwards and knocked into a bucket, half-hidden by a coil of dangling rope. I jumped as it skidded off the edge and leaned forward to watch it crash onto the foundations and scatter bricks.

Tamsin shrieked. The bricks that bounced into the patch of boiling Darkness simply disappeared. The others rolled on the concrete and lay still.

Only then did it really hit me: Justin had fallen and scattered on the concrete right there. They found his body on that exact patch of ground.

I clutched my collar. What had gone through his head on the way down? Did he have time to think? Had the fall seemed eternal, or was it fast, one moment a slip, the next blackness?

"Oh God," I whispered. And I looked up again. The shaft I was expected to cross was right above me. I could still see a police marker on the pole; presumably where Justin's foot had slipped. He fell right past the spot I was standing on.

My legs started to tremble. "I can't do this."

"Yes, you can." Justin came up behind me and his hand steadied my elbow. "I thought I should come up round the back, there's something not right down there." He indicated the Dark with a tilt of his tousled head.

I swallowed with a dry throat. "It's the Darkness."

He nodded slowly. "Right where I landed?"

"Yes. Are you OK?" My eyes met his as he shuddered.

"I'll live." Then he snorted. "You know what I mean."

I nodded again. "Why isn't the old girl following?"

Justin licked his lips. "I explained to her about the Darkness. I told her if she waited and let you finish with me, you'd come back for her."

"You did what?" I clamped my mouth shut and breathed deeply. "You did the right thing." I rolled my shoulders; since Justin had returned it felt as if a medicine ball had been lifted from them.

I didn't want to think about what would happen after I got rid of the Mark. Justin would leave and I'd be, well not exactly alone, because the hounding dead made sure I'd never be by myself, but I would be lonely.

"Let's get this over with."

Justin gave my arm a squeeze and together we finished the climb.

At the top of the scaffolding there was a heady breeze. A floor below I'd been sheltered by the brickwork, but now I was completely exposed. The wind tugged at my hair like an old enemy, whipped it back behind my neck and slapped my cheeks with cold hands.

My grip on the final piece of pole was so tight my knuckles almost burst through the glove. My fingers ached and my knees felt like stiffened bolts holding my trembling legs against the prodding of the wind.

"Don't look down," Justin whispered.

I looked down.

He'd told me it looked terrifying and it did. Vertigo gripped me and I swayed. Nausea filled me with a hot stew that roiled in my gut and tried to bend me double.

I remembered the hall of mirrors, the one I'd entered during my first day living with the curse. Now my trainers protruded above a drop that stretched and dwindled, just like an image in that funhouse mirror, but it was real. "Oh help."

"It's going to be alright. I'll be holding you all the way."

"I can't let go. M-my fingers won't work." I stared at him, standing on the pole one over from mine, his arm spanning the distance between us. "H-how did you do it?"

His mouth twisted and his hand spasmed, pinching my skin almost painfully. Maybe it was meant to be a reassuring squeeze. "I didn't, remember?"

"Oh." I closed my eyes.

"I've got you." Justin released my arm and I opened my eyes to see him renew his grip on the strut above his head. Then he held his hand out. "Walk as if you're on a tightrope, hold my hand. It'll be four little steps then you can hold on again."

"Four little steps."

"Less than ten seconds if you do it fast."

My knees started to shake. There was no way I was going to be able to take even *one* little step. My legs would betray me, buckle and send me cartwheeling through the insubstantial sky, just like Justin.

Far off in the distance I could hear Tamsin and James. They were shouting at me, trying to make me move.

They could stick it.

"It's the only way you'll find out the truth," Justin murmured. "If you still think I was murdered, if you still think someone down there, one of my friends, had something to do with it. This is the only way you'll ever get to know."

"Four little steps," I choked.

"Holding my hand all the way. You won't be alone."

My arm was clamped to my side, but I forced it out like the wing of a bird preparing to glide. My shirt fluttered and the breeze tickled my empty fingers, almost pulled them back, tried to overbalance me. Then Justin's long fingers curled around my wrist and I clutched his.

I was still holding onto the pole with one hand, so tightly I thought I might leave behind an imprint on the metal. Panting I bullied my cramping fingers open.

I felt my balance shift towards Justin, panic compressed my chest and I quickly threw my arm out to the other side until I was standing still.

My toes itched inside my trainers, desperate to curl around the cylindrical bar. Thank God it hadn't been raining.

"Ready?" Justin murmured. He knew better than to surprise me by raising his voice.

I gave the barest nod of my head, terrified of altering my position in any way, and he took a tiny step forward.

With a moan of terror, I shuffled my right foot forward no more than a single inch.

"You can do it." Justin stepped again, leading me by the arm.

Whimpering steadily I forced my foot forward some more, then brought my left one to meet it.

The wind decided to play and jerked my hair in front of my eyes. "Stop," I cried and felt Justin wobble as he caught his balance and waited for me.

I tossed my head, trying to free my eyes; I didn't dare brush it aside properly. Finally the wind cooperated and tugged it back again.

I looked. One more step and I'd be in reach of the pole on the other side.

My whimpers turned into tears. I could feel them wetting my numb cheeks and a distant part of myself shouted that I'd never cried in front of Justin when he was alive, so why would I start now?

"Shut the hell up," I shouted at myself and took that last step, throwing my left arm forward at the very last second and grabbing the pole.

"I did it." I hugged the cold metal with my eyes closed. The other hand I left in Justin's.

"Yes, you did." Justin's tone made me look up. His voice was pleased, but his eyes were tortured. "Well done." I had succeeded where he had not. It must hurt.

"Don't let go." Alarm entered my tone as he loosened his grip.

"It's OK." He released my wrist and immediately weaved his long fingers through mine. "You did great."

There was a crossbar just in front of my pole and Justin carefully stepped across and stood in front of me.

Impulsively I released my hold on the pole and threw my arms around him. I could feel my heart thudding against his hollow chest, my cheeks wet against his cold throat.

"I thought I was going to die."

"I know." He ran his palms along my spine. Somehow, even up in the sky his touch calmed me.

I clenched my fists in his blazer and raised my head.

His face was right above mine. His lips were wet as if he'd just licked them and his eyes blazed with dark fire. Suddenly he bent his head and touched his mouth to mine. Gently at first, then hard, as if my kiss was the only thing he'd ever wanted.

I froze, surprise turning my lips into ice.

It wasn't my first kiss. Years ago I'd had a moment with Pete, but it hadn't felt like this. My limbs tingled and my blood sang in my ears.

Justin's lips were soft and slightly chill. After an eternity his mouth opened. I breathed past his lips softly but no breath came back to twine with mine. My nose pressed into his cheek and I inhaled the fading scent that was all him.

There was a hint of roughness on his skin, it wasn't yet stubble, but one day it would have been. I moved one hand to his face and breathed harder. Justin's lips seemed to grow warmer as if his skin was absorbing my heat. He groaned into my mouth as I felt his fists on my back.

Then I wobbled.

Off-balance we broke apart and gripped the poles on either side of us, gasping as we remembered where we were.

My knees were shaking and I felt a hundred years old. I guessed exhaustion had caught up with me as adrenaline poured out and was replaced by... something else.

I let my hair blow over my face and looked at Justin through the curtain. I opened my mouth to ask if he was alright, or maybe if he'd meant the kiss, but the whole world tilted and my knees buckled.

As unconsciousness took me, I sensed my fingers relax on the metal brace and felt myself begin to fall. My last impression was Justin's horror-struck face and my last thought: at least I wouldn't know about it when I hit the Darkness.

27

From the first moment

"Tay, you have to wake up. I don't know how long I can hold you."

I didn't want to wake up. I was comfortable, my hands were relaxed at my sides, dangling in a cool breeze, and someone had their arms around me.

"Tay, can you hear me?"

"Go away," I murmured.

"You *really* don't want me to do that."

"Justin?" I frowned and opened my eyes.

Then I remembered. I jerked and clutched at him, scrambling for a safe foothold as well.

"Y-you caught me."

He nodded and helped me move until I could sit carefully on a plank.

"Wait a minute, you're on the same pole I am."

His brow furrowed. "I thought it was because you were unconscious."

I pursed my lips. "I'm awake now."

I was gripping a crossbar with white knuckles. He knocked on the metal, sending some rust flaking off into the breeze.

Then the blood drained from my face as I realised: there was only one explanation. "I died."

"You didn't." Justin pressed his hand against my forehead. "You're burning up and you're completely crazy, but you aren't dead."

"It's the only way you could possibly be doing this." I knocked on the same bar and it shivered.

"I caught you, Tay. You really are alive. Why don't you wave at Tamsin, see if she waves back?"

I nodded, grateful for his suggestion. "You're right." I scooted carefully to the edge of the platform and waved.

After a moment James and Tamsin both raised their hands. James gave me a fist pump and Harley waggled his phone. They could see me. I wasn't dead.

Relief flooded me and I slumped onto the boards, inhaling brick dust and letting the splinters prick my cheek.

Then I rolled. Justin was watching me.

"You kissed me," I said and even I could hear my accusatory tone. He flushed but didn't move. I rose onto my knees. "I know you're in love with Tamsin, I see the way you look at her."

He cleared his throat. "Is now the best time for this conversation?"

There was a gap between two of the boards I was resting on. If I put my eye to it I could see straight down through all the floors to the leering Darkness. "It might be the only time," I whispered.

"OK." Justin touched my hand, gently. "Tamsin's hot. Who wouldn't look at her? And I can't believe she's with James already. But, I'm dead, so I might as well tell you the truth." He exhaled slowly. "The thing is I fancied you from the first moment you bitched at me about being in your chair. But that whole first year you barely said a single word to me. You only knew I existed when I pissed you off. Wiped your name off the whiteboard, nicked your pencil case, stuff like that."

I blinked at him. "You were trying to make me *notice* you?"

"Guess I had to die to do it." He shrugged.

"The others started to harass me and Hannah because they were copying you." My mind took me back over our fall from grace, the big fight I'd had with Pete after I wouldn't date him, the day he left me and Hannah to the dogs.

Justin winced. "When Tamsin showed an interest I gave up. If I could change things, I would. I didn't know what was going on with you."

I pressed my lips together. "No one did. If I hadn't been so wrapped up..."

"It wasn't your fault. The reason Tamsin hates you so much, it's because she knew how much I liked you back then."

I snorted. "Tamsin's *jealous* of me?"

Justin spread his hands. "At least a little." He picked at his nails. "We're together because of the club, you know? In the confessional she said she was in love with me." He peered at her distant figure with sadness greying his eyes.

I gnawed on my lip as the wind whistled around our platform, tired of our intrusion into its domain. "Do you think Tamsin was involved?"

"No chance." Justin touched my hand. "Things weren't that great recently, but we've meant too much to each other over the last couple of years."

I rocked onto my knees. "I guess we'll find out soon enough. Are you sure they'll tell the truth if I ask?"

Justin nodded. "This game is crazy. Look at what we do. Look at what you're doing. You don't break the rules, you just don't. Plus they've got something on you now. If you try and break the silence of the confessional, you'll be in trouble too."

"Not as much as them." I had to shout to be heard over the wind and I realised that the platform was creaking ominously. "We have to get back down." I pressed my palm against his, throat welling up; he'd liked me all this time. If I hadn't been blind, we could have had years. Instead, I got one kiss.

"Do... do you want to kiss me again?" My voice was hoarse. Some part of me still waited for him to push me away and laugh.

He didn't; with shining eyes he pulled me close and pressed his lips once more to mine.

When my knees started to feel weak I pulled away. "It's not safe doing this up here." I gave a half laugh, but my head was spinning.

Justin stretched like a cat with a tin of tuna. "I feel great." He grinned. "We should have done this before."

"Sure." I turned and started my careful descent. "But if we do it again, I'm going to be lying down."

"Oh yeah?" He swung down to my level like Tarzan and I shoved him away, before tentatively toeing the next bar.

"I feel a bit woozy. Just watch me, will you?"

His smile was gentle and he put one hand on my back as I descended. "You can trust me."

The nearer I got to the ground, the louder I could hear James and Harley whooping. Tamsin was quiet and her fists were clenched so tightly I imagined her nails were drawing blood.

"She does hate me," I whispered. Justin, sitting next to me on a pole, nodded.

Then I saw Tamsin clutch James' arm. Even in the semi-dark I could see her face whiten and she pointed with a trembling arm... right at Justin.

"She can see me." Justin straightened.

"That's impossible." I patted his knee and swung myself down to the final platform. I was below the level of the fence now and the void was sucking at my soles like quicksand.

Justin jumped like a leopard to land next to me. "Look."

He turned me to face Tamsin and yes, it did look as if she could see her ex. Her mouth was slack and the whites of her cat-like eyes were showing.

"She's just pissed that I did the dare, that's all. That I made it down in one piece."

"That's not it." Justin leaned towards Tamsin. James had his arm around her, talking intently, his hood bobbing under the light. "Tamsin." Justin shouted and waved and James had to catch her as she squealed and collapsed.

"She can see me," he insisted.

"She can't." I frowned. "The only other people in the world who'd be able to see you are related to me. And I promise you Tamsin Harper and I are not even distantly related." As I spoke she calmed down, peering blindly into the spot that Justin still occupied. "See?"

Abruptly Justin yelped. He'd been standing on the pole right next to me, but now it was as if it had turned into water. He fell through the metal, toes first and I screamed. Like a diver being dumped into the ocean, he was heading right for the Darkness below.

There was no way I could reach him. There was only one thing I could do: get off the bar so he could touch it again. I threw myself off the platform, as far out away from the patch of boiling Dark as I could.

As I flew I spun in the air, frantic to see what happened to Justin. As soon as my feet left the pole, his arms smacked into it and he was able to hold on, dangling above the pit with terror etched on his face. "Tay!"

Then it hit me: *I* was falling. My body went rigid. I knew tensing up was the worst thing to do but, damn, this was going to hurt. My hair lashed my face and the wind laughed in my ears as I tried to tuck in my arms and legs. What if I broke something?

The ground smacked into me like a sheet of rubberised lead and my breath flew ahead of me as I rolled.

I barely had time to register my bruised side before the Darkness reached for me, filaments like vines snaking from the pit to drag me back. I barrelled frantically, continuing to roll as far away as I could.

Finally I stopped and twisted. My ears strained. I could hear James and Harley laughing. The collection of blackness was palpitating, but something was holding it back. I looked up. I had landed right beneath the spotlight. Although my sweatshirt was covering the bulb it was casting enough of a glare to keep the shadows at bay.

I rubbed my face with shaking hands then tuned my ears into Tamsin's whine. "You saw him, didn't you? That's why you jumped." She sprinted to my side and grabbed me by my shoulders. "James wasn't looking and Harley was messing with his phone, but you were right there. You must have seen him."

I winced. I'd be black and blue tomorrow. "Let go, will you?" I rolled painfully to my feet. Justin had been right; Tamsin had seen him.

I opened my mouth and the fence rattled. Abruptly Pete's face appeared. "Taylor, thank God you're OK." He was gasping. "The guard's seen the light; he's on his way round."

"Time to go." Harley tucked his phone back in his jeans and leaped for the chain link.

Tamsin was still standing next to me, her face pale under her thick make-up. I grabbed her elbow and shoved her towards her new boyfriend.

My legs protested as I ran, muscles quivering, but I pushed myself to jump at the fence and groaned as I tried to scramble upwards.

"Taylor!" A voice called from above and I looked up. Pete was offering me his hand. I stretched, and my fingertips touched his. The security guard shouted and next to me Tamsin scaled the fence like a monkey.

Hands grabbed my waist and crumpled my shirt as they propelled me upwards. My palm slapped Pete's and he dragged me to the top of the fence.

I swung my legs over the link and my eyes met those of the angry guard. "Stupid bloody kids," he shouted. "You think you're clever? You want to get killed?"

I pressed my lips together, resisting the impulse to apologise and was about to drop to the ground when movement caught my eye. Justin was scrambling down from the scaffolding, staying as far from the Darkness as he could get.

Who had boosted me up?

My heart thudded as I looked down. The ghost of the old woman touched her cane to her forehead in a kind of salute and moved backwards.

I tightened my gloved hand on the fence. She could have Marked me easily; simple contact with the skin on my waist would have done it.

"I'll come back." My dry lips formed the words and she nodded as Pete tugged on my jeans. My ankles complained as I dropped to the ground and staggered back. A stray dog barked at us and scuttled away amongst the bin-bags. Then we all ran down the alleyway in a tight group as shadows boiled at the edges of buildings.

The street was busy. The others slowed to a walk, pulled off their hoods and blended. But when they headed towards the tube, I tugged at Pete's arm.

"I'm owed a challenge, remember?"

He raised his eyebrows. "You want to do that *now*?"

My eyes strayed to the shadows that bayed at the edges of the pooled streetlights. "Definitely."

"Where do you want to go?"

"Just somewhere quiet… and well lit."

"A bar?"

"Quiet." I reminded him.

"This time of night we'll be able to find a table." He rubbed his bald head and raised his voice. "James, alright if we go in here?"

We were passing a *Slug and Lettuce*. I peered through the doors at the pale wood and the long bar crammed with men and women still in their office-wear. Then I shrugged, Pete was right; the tables at the back appeared quiet.

As I made the decision my mind turned to Justin. I wasn't sure whether he should be with us for this. But while I considered ducking into the bar after the others, he appeared at a run, ignoring the bodies thronging the street and swishing through arms, torsos and legs, like a swimmer.

When he saw me, he slowed. "Did she Mark you?" He grabbed my arm.

I shook my head and my lips twitched; he was worried about me.

"I saw her touch you and I couldn't get there in time." Justin rubbed his hand up and down my arm and his eyes were nowhere near Tamsin. "Are you OK?"

I nodded, trying to show him I was pleased to see him without seemingly speaking to thin air. Then I leaned into him, just slightly and Pete pushed the doors open from the inside. "I thought you wanted to go in here," he snapped.

"Right." I let Justin put his arm around me and together we walked through the doors into the bustle and music.

There were three tables left at the back of the room. We took the one furthest from the bar and sat. "I'm getting some wedges." Harley grabbed the menu. "I'm starving."

Justin hesitated at the chairs. A few weeks ago it would have been the most natural thing in the world for him to have slouched down with the others. Instead he stood behind me and put his hands on my shoulders.

Immediately my eyes went to Tamsin, but she didn't even look in his direction. She may have seen him before, but she couldn't now.

Our table leaned against a window. The Darkness outside pressed against the glass, but didn't spill in. I slid our candle closer to my seat. I only had to defend myself against it for a short while longer; the truth was about to come out.

"I get to set a challenge now, right?" I turned to James. "That's what we agreed."

James blinked. "Don't you want to chill for a bit? I'll admit you were amazing up there."

I shook my head. "I want a truth. And I want it now."

28
What do you want to know?

"You want a truth," James sniggered. "That's a bit tame, isn't it? What do you want to know?"

I looked into his eyes, then past, into Tamsin's. She was still pale under her make-up, still rattled. If anyone was going to tell the truth at this moment, it was her. "I'm challenging Tamsin."

Tamsin blinked owlishly. "Me?"

I touched Justin's hand where it had tightened on my shoulder and nodded firmly.

She echoed her new boyfriend. "What do you want to know?"

I took a deep breath. "I want to know what really happened to Justin."

Pete gasped, Harley's eyes widened and Tamsin opened her mouth to deny all knowledge – I could see it on her face – but James' hand trapped hers. "Respect the rules, Tam." He glared at me from beneath his sculpted brow. "Oh's one of us now and we've got videos of her we can send to the police if we have to." He gave me a smile that didn't reach his eyes. "Isn't that right?"

I stared steadily back at him. "I have no intention of going to the police, whatever I hear."

"You won't talk to anyone at all." He still leaned back, but his tone was threatening.

"No one," I promised.

James released Tamsin's hand and straightaway she reached for her napkin and began twisting it in her fingers.

"Tell her."

Tamsin looked at James through her hair. "Can't you do it?"

He shrugged. "She challenged you."

Tamsin shook her head. "I wish I'd never seconded you, bitch," she muttered.

"Tamsin." Pete's voice contained a warning, but James was grinning.

"That's my girl."

After a moment Tamsin stiffened her shoulders and brushed her hair back. "You're not one of us, Oh. You might be in the club, but you'll always be a freak."

"So Justin's death wasn't an accident?"

Her fingers still moved, restlessly shredding paper. She glanced around us, checking that the waitress was nowhere near then she leaned forward. "Are you ready for this? Sure you want to hear our dirty little secrets?"

Under the table I slipped my glove from my hand and opened and closed my fist like I was cocking a weapon. "I'm ready."

"Fine." She leaned back. "Justin wanted out of the club." She looked at James and he gave a slight nod so she carried on. "He was worried about how *'dangerous things were getting'*." Her voice spiralled up until she imitated a whine: her impression of Justin. He grunted as if she'd sucker punched him and his hand vanished from my shoulder. I checked and saw him slump at the nearest table to ours, still listening.

"Can you believe it?" Tamsin exhaled. "After all you did to get in, can you imagine anyone wanting to leave?"

I shook my head.

"I warned him. I asked if he'd considered how it would affect me?"

"You?" I frowned.

"Hello, suddenly I'd be going out with the biggest loser in school." She tossed her hair and the peroxide strands caught the light like a fibre optic web.

I glanced at Justin. His own fists were curled on his knees and I couldn't see his eyes.

"I begged him not to leave the club. He said if I was so worried about my social life he'd tell someone, get the club shut down."

"He'd never have told." I leaned forward. "You guys have videos, don't you, proof of the stuff he'd done? He was going to Cambridge. It would have ruined his chances."

Tamsin shook her head. "He was so bloody... honourable."

My eyes went to the "honourable" ghost. He was pressing his fists into his thighs, shaking his head.

"He wouldn't have told," I reiterated.

"I couldn't take that risk. None of us could. You think he was the only one applying to a good university?"

"So you were worried about a future bagging prawn crackers?" I sneered.

Tamsin curled her crimson lips. "Why not? V is our ticket. You've already worked out that we're not the first generation. There's a whole network. People in V work for people in V. Members get the good jobs, the chances. How do you think Mr Barnes got to be a head in such a short time? He's useless."

I looked at James and he nodded slowly.

"So, if you were afraid you'd lose this network and your chance of a good degree, what did you do?"

Tamsin's fingers moved faster through the paper. "I spoke to James. He said he'd sort it."

"Sort it?" My words emerged through gritted teeth and my gaze slid to James. He felt my eyes on him and actually winked at me.

Immediately I returned my focus to Tamsin's drawl. "James told Justin he could leave without penalty on condition that he did a really serious dare. Then if he tried to go to the authorities about the club, we could grass him up."

Justin didn't move.

"So it *was* an accident?" I frowned.

Tamsin stared at her hands as if she had only just noticed what she was doing. "James asked me to make sure Justin agreed to his conditions. He had to take on a double dare when James gave him the nod. Harley was the one to find the scaffolding." She dropped the ragged remains of the napkin on the floor. "Pete had to paint a mark on the highest pole, but James gave him oil."

"*My God,*" Justin whispered.

My gaze went to Pete. *Petrol Pete* they'd been calling him. His feet were still stretched out under the table and his arms were crossed. But his knuckles strained like tombstones against his skin. "You made me do *what*?" His voice was low and strained, verging on an explosion. Slowly he folded his legs under him and sat straight.

"You knew," James sneered. "Why would I have wanted a paint stripe on the pole?"

Pete swore low and vicious. Tamsin's eyes widened.

"Language," James snorted and he straightened up too, a threat in his posture. "Part of you knew exactly what you were doing, Pete. And remember, if you do anything to me or if you decide to tell. Well, I've got the brush with your fingerprints."

Pete swallowed. His fists shook on the table, but he made no move towards James.

I leaned forward, prompting Tamsin. "What next?"

She inhaled. "Pete challenged James to climb the scaffolding." She ran trembling fingers through her hair. "James double-dared him to cross the part without a handrail. Pete refused – you can refuse a double if someone else will take it on – I gave Justin the nod and he took it."

Horror squirmed like scarabs in my chest. "So you were *all* involved."

She shook her head. "Justin shouldn't have tried to leave the club. Anyway, it was *James'* idea, his plan."

I nodded. "Maybe that'll be enough." Then I spun in my seat, reached across the table and slapped James hard.

"You bitch." James lurched to his feet. The black Mark glowed on his cheek for a moment; then settled in, as if something had taken a bite from his face.

Harley blinked as if he'd never seen James take a hit before and Tamsin jumped backwards, knocking her chair to the floor. "What're you doing, you psycho?"

"*I'm* the psycho?" I cried. "You effing killed your boyfriend so you wouldn't have to be like me and Hannah, for what, a year? Because you were worried you wouldn't get a great university place or a top job if the club was closed down?"

Justin was literally *growling* behind her. "Mark her," he snarled.

I raised my hand to show him that the Mark was gone, transferred to James. "Oh no," I whispered. The Mark remained, oozing over the tendons of my wrist like treacle. "It wasn't enough."

"What wasn't enough?" Tamsin towered over me, the glare from her eyes like a blowtorch. "What've you done to my boyfriend's face, you skank?"

My stomach felt full of rocks and they jumbled around as I moved towards her, making me feel old and ill. Sure, I'd threatened to Mark Tamsin more than once, but I hadn't really meant it. Justin was going to get his justice, but did she really deserve what was going to happen to her? Did any of them?

Outside the Darkness swelled, reminding me that I had no choice.

"You want to know what I did to James?" I grabbed her arm. I shoved her sleeve up as she jerked back, then pressed my bare hand to the unblemished skin of her forearm. My touch left a Mark.

She shrieked and grabbed my napkin, tried to rub it off.

Briefly I closed my eyes, *please, oh please*, but I knew what I'd see when I looked at my hand.

The Mark wasn't gone.

I turned to Harley.

"I am actually sorry, Harley." He wasn't in the same league as his mates. But the Mark wanted him.

He raised his hands, palms up. "Easy, China." I shook my head and slapped him in a gross mockery of a high five.

Frantically I checked my hand but the Darkness still wasn't satisfied. I had one more person to Mark. So James was right, on some level Pete must have known what was going on.

My eyes went to my oldest friend. He was sitting upright now, but he hadn't moved. "What're you doing, Tay?" he whispered.

Tears choked me. "You always wanted to know why I act the way I do. Why I seem so nuts."

He nodded. Behind him the Darkness had gathered at the window leaving the rest of the street in grey twilight. "Tay?"

James lunged for me, his face murderous. Pete's arm shot out and blocked him. "Tay?" he repeated.

If I didn't Mark Pete, the Darkness would take me. It was me or Pete.

My eyes stung as the tears welled from my throat. "Why did you do it? Why did you get involved in this craziness?" I spat the last word.

He didn't take his eyes from me. "After you," he finally said, "it was all I had."

James grinned horribly. "And don't forget the videos we've got of *you*, mate."

"Shit." I punched the table. "Shit, shit, shit."

"Tay?" Justin grabbed my elbows. "What're you waiting for? You have to Mark him."

"You helped kill someone, Pete." I spun back to him. "You and Harley, James and Tamsin."

"Keep your voice down, you stupid slut." James' brows were so low I couldn't see the expression in his eyes. "V's all about what we've got on *each other*. You promised you wouldn't tell, but if you forget and open your mouth, remember we could get you locked up for that little stunt on the underground."

I spoke only to Pete. "Justin was your friend."

Pete nodded, his face miserable. "It didn't seem so bad doing little things. It was surreal, like I wasn't involved at all." He shook his head. "If I could tell him how sorry I am…" He looked at me. "I didn't want you involved in this, Tay. I tried to tell you to stay out."

"I-I know. I couldn't." I showed him my hand. "I'm supposed to touch you with this."

"Do it." Justin pushed me and I lurched forward, just missing Pete's elbow.

"Stop it," I hissed. "Just stop it." I was finally crying. "It's Pete, I'm not going to *Mark* Pete."

I ran out of the restaurant. Behind me I heard James shout. "After her."

Chairs clattered and a waitress yelled as they sprinted after me. Where did they think I was going?

I crashed through the double doors, out into the street and a bubble of silence.

It's here.

I spun to find the Darkness rising in front of me like a pillar. I stared into its black heart and my shoulders drooped. I'd chosen this when I'd let Pete go clean.

Around me the street was silent. At the edge of my vision people walked on the other side of the road, eyes turned from me. They didn't see the Darkness, but they instinctively chose to avoid its presence.

My lip trembled but I raised my hand, showing the Mark almost defiantly.

The world seemed to draw breath and I knew the pillar was about to crash over me.

"Don't just stand there." Justin barrelled into me, grabbed my arm before I could hit the ground and pulled me into a stumbling run.

"Justin, it's over," I gasped.

"No." He shoved me in front of him. I saw him look back then he pushed me harder. "You aren't going with that thing."

Behind me there was a muffled thud. I dug my heels in and turned. The bar door had slammed into the wall. Harley, James and Tamsin were lined up on the pavement. Pete was hanging back.

"There she is." James pointed. "Get her."

I had time only to blink before the Darkness struck. Tamsin didn't even have time to scream. I met Pete's horror-filled eyes as his friends vanished, swallowed as if they had never been.

"It'll come for you now." Justin shoved me again. "Run."

Sure enough the Darkness, like a beast unsated, seemed to be seeking a scent. I hesitated one more second and it spread out on the pavement like it had turned to liquid, then started to flow towards me.

I caught my breath, looked briefly at Justin and ran.

I'd never seen anyone outrace the Darkness before, but it was worth a try.

29

There has to be a cure

"It's gaining." Terror bleached Justin's voice and even though he was right at my side, his words sounded like a distant cry.

Fireworks flashed in my vision. I dug my fist into my aching side as we sprinted through a silent world and ahead, people parted like a biblical sea, unknowingly moving for the Darkness.

As we turned the corner a Routemaster pulled away from the bus stop.

Justin propelled me forward. "Get on." He literally threw me toward the back of the bus. With my last ounce of strength I grabbed the bar; then moved out of Justin's way. He leaped on after me and gripped my hand as we turned to see if the bus was going to be able to outpace the spreading tide of black.

Shadowy fingers reached for the wheels and crept up the sides of the vehicle.

I retreated into the glowing interior.

The bus was full but the noise inside was muffled. A couple of kids pressed their fists against their ears as if they had just popped.

"It's here," I whispered.

"I know." Justin pushed me ahead of him to the stairs and I ran up two at a time. The top floor was empty, but we'd trapped ourselves; there was nowhere else to go.

For a couple of seconds, at the top of the bus, sound rushed back into the world and my ears pounded with the roar of the engine, horns from outside, a lone siren and a bus of chatting Londoners.

I allowed myself to inhale, then the void came crashing back down and everything was muffled once more. I wheeled. The steps behind me were black; as I watched, the last one vanished under a dark blanket.

I looked at Justin, focusing on his chocolate eyes. "I'm sorry I couldn't help you."

He squeezed my hand and I had to strain to hear his reply. "I wasn't sure about this moving on thing anyway." He fingers crushed mine. "We need more *time*."

I trained my eyes back on the Darkness, clinging onto a childish feeling that the thing in the dark couldn't get you if you watched it.

The bus shuddered to a halt and I staggered. The lights that glared into the window were red. The Darkness advanced more quickly.

"I wish you hadn't had to hear that back there, about your friends."

"They weren't my friends."

The seeping shadows seemed to be taunting us, surrounding us on all sides, but not yet closing in.

Suddenly the bus lurched and sped up. I glanced out of the window. We were finally on the Westway, able to move much faster.

I held my breath and the Darkness slid back as if it were a blanket being yanked off a bed.

"We're beating it." Justin punched the air.

We stood beneath the fluorescent lights in the centre of the aisle and when sound returned to the world I threw my head back, closed my eyes, bathed in the racket and tried to forget that it was impossible to outrun the Dark.

At the end of my road we leaped from the bus straight into a sprint and hurled ourselves directly towards my house.

"Nearly there." Justin pulled ahead and half dragged me behind him.

We ran through the pools of orange light cast by the streetlamps. Light-dark, light-dark. Each time we left a circle of brightness I caught my breath, fear clutching at my throat as my foot landed outside the glow and pitched me into the twilight of the spaces between.

I didn't know why I was running for home. The Darkness would find me there as easily as anywhere else. I only knew it was the only place I'd ever felt safe, and my Dad was there. Part of me needed to hide behind him, but really I wanted to say goodbye.

We pounded up the steps and I fumbled with my key as Justin watched the road behind us. "Tay." His voice contained a warning, but I knew what I'd see if I turned around: the shadows linking the streetlamps growing murky and starting to flow together.

"Quick." I grabbed his hand and dragged him through the door. Then I ran for the study. "Dad!" For the first time I burst inside without pausing at the threshold.

I staggered to a halt. It was bright in the study, electric lights blaring yellow as sunshine. Dad was bent over a microscope. As I entered he straightened and a smile cracked his face. "Taylor, what good timing."

"No more samples." Automatically I put my hand behind my back.

"Not that. I've got good news." He rolled back from the desk. "Look at this." He gestured towards the slide beneath the scope and I glanced at Justin then released his hand. I put my face to the eyepiece then blinked. "What am I looking at?"

"Now look at this." He slid another slide underneath. Red shapes blurred and curled under my vision.

"Are they meant to look the same?"

Dad grinned. "Yes. No. One is your blood and one is mine. Normally you'd be able to see a difference. But now you can't. Know why?"

I shook my head.

"I've successfully injected some of your mitochondrial DNA into this sample. Now my blood here is just like yours."

"What does that mean?" My heart thudded.

"*Your blood changed mine*. It *infected* it. It makes what you have communicable."

"We're back to this." I stepped away from the slide. "If you were going to catch this, you would have."

He grabbed my elbow. "You aren't hearing me. It's incredibly hard to catch, to do this I had to put your mitochondrial DNA straight into mine and that was hard enough even with medical equipment. That isn't the point." His eyes glowed. "Listen. If your so called 'curse' is communicable that means *it is a disease*. And that means there has to be a cure." His mouth opened on a happy grin. "Don't you see? I was right all the time."

"Dad…" My mouth emptied of words. How could I tell him he was too late?

"Taylor." Justin's voice in my ear was quiet, but it made me turn as if I was on a spit. Inside our room, light still reigned, but in the hallway the Darkness had arrived. It pressed against the door like a dammed tidal wave, a wall of blackness past which I could see nothing.

"What *is* that?" Dad started to roll towards the door.

"Don't." I pushed him back with my clean hand then I showed him the stain on my other one. "It's the Darkness, it's come for me."

The air itself inhaled and a familiar pressure began to build in my ears. Sounds that I hadn't even been aware of faded away: the hum of the fridge in the distant kitchen, the constant exhalation of the central heating, the mechanical whir of Dad's computer, the sound of our breathing.

"Taylor." Dad shook his head. "The Darkness is all in your head." But he didn't move any closer to the doorway and he kept shaking his head as if his ears had filled with water.

"Justin," I whispered. He threw his arm around me and didn't even suggest running. He knew we'd come to the end of the line.

Abruptly he pressed his lips to mine. To Dad I must have looked crazy, but I didn't care. I threw my arms around Justin's neck and kissed him back for all I was worth.

Suddenly my knees went weak and I half collapsed against his chest.

I was exhausted, I was terrified, but I'd never fainted in my life before today.

Finally my ears registered Dad's shouts. "Taylor, what are you doing? And who's that?"

I pulled free of Justin's lips and half turned in his arms. "Y-you can see him?"

"He wasn't there before." Dad wheeled slowly forward. "What are you?" He was speaking to Justin.

Justin looked at me, his brown eyes wide. "Your Dad can see me."

"Tamsin could too, after the last time we kissed." I looked at Dad. "Dad, he's a ghost. You can see him?"

Dad's chair lurched forward. "Get away from my daughter."

Justin half jumped back and I clutched at him with arms that felt like spaghetti. "Justin, I think I know what's happening. Kiss me again."

"Your Dad–"

"Do it," I hissed with one eye on the door.

Justin kissed me. I opened my mouth against his and the room swum. My legs went altogether and Justin had to hold me to stop me from collapsing to the ground.

He pulled back. "Tay, you're too weak."

"You're taking my life force or something. Every time you kiss me, I get weaker and you get less ghostlike."

"More alive," he whispered.

"Get away from her." Dad rolled towards us, murder on his face.

"No, Dad." I grabbed Justin's face. "Keep kissing me. Take it all."

"What?" I wasn't sure who cried out the loudest, Justin or Dad.

"The Darkness is coming for me." I gripped Justin's biceps urgently. "I failed. Don't you understand? Without me you'll never be able to move on. I've seen ghosts stuck here for *decades* waiting for justice. They're trapped until their murderer actually *dies*. Pete could live till a hundred."

Justin's face paled.

"If you do this you've got a chance. It might not work, but it might, you could live again."

His chest rose and fell under mine. I knew he wasn't breathing, was he trying not to cry?

"Tay, I'm not going to kill you."

"I'm dead anyway, or near enough."

"Taylor, get away from him." Dad's chair banged into the back of my legs and his arms went around my waist. He started to drag me back, but I clung to Justin's shoulders.

"Do it Justin, kiss me one last time. I *have* to do this for you."

He hesitated, lips trembling then he kissed me. On the forehead. Light as a feather. With firm fingers he unlocked my hands from around his neck and pushed me away.

I didn't have the energy to do anything other than fall into Dad's lap. I struggled, trying to rise, but he held me in an iron grip. "He's doing the right thing, Taylor." Dad's voice was tinny and distant.

"Let me go," I insisted.

"No," he growled.

"It's OK, Dad, I can't *make* him kiss me. I just need to stand up." *I have to be away from you when the Darkness comes.*

I turned and pressed my lips to his cheek. "I wish Mum was here," I whispered. Despite the muffling effect of the Darkness he heard me.

"I know," he replied. Momentarily his arms relaxed and I staggered to my feet, moving quickly out of his reach. I looked from one beloved face to another then stepped to the centre of the room.

I opened my mouth to say goodbye, but it was too late.

The Darkness crashed past the door like a wave that had been too long held back and hit me like a hammer.

I threw my arms out and the pure blackness eclipsed my last sight: Justin diving towards me with tears streaming down his face.

30

So many had been sent into the dark

Silence surrounded me, as oppressive as snow. The feeling of being watched was intense enough to make my skin prickle, but I couldn't see a thing.

Heart hammering, I tried to haul in a breath, but the silence was suffocating as an avalanche and I couldn't raise my chest against it. I needed oxygen. Sparks burst in the blackness behind my eyes as my brain frantically fired off electrical impulses.

My last breath tinged the void with its tiny warmth and nothingness pressed on my eyelids like deep water.

So it *was* death that waited in the Darkness.

Abruptly I was in freefall. I spread my arms and dropped like Alice down the rabbit hole. There was no sound as I descended. No rushing of air around me, no breath from my own body.

Then I landed, with bone jarring force, on a hard floor.

••••

I opened my eyes to find that I was still shrouded in Darkness. I was no longer breathing, so I lay motionless, on my back, waiting fearfully for oblivion to take me.

Nothing happened.

After a while I rolled onto my front. I had no need to inhale and where there had always been a thudding in my chest, now there was nothing. Otherwise I felt like myself. The blackness was absolute but I patted myself down with trembling hands. Everything else felt normal. I just wished that I could see. Finally, skin tingling with anticipation, I groped around me.

The floor appeared to be made of stone. As I swept my arms in widening circles, my fingers sent something rattling. Immediately I pulled my arm in, waited for silence then reached out once more. My hand closed around a thin strip of metal and I pulled it towards me. A heavy object rasped along the stone floor. I took the shape onto my lap and frowned; it felt like something I'd seen before. Mum had once shown me pictures of our ancestor's expedition and I was certain this was an old lantern.

I had no way of igniting it, but it represented light so I clutched it to my chest, as if to remind me that there must be a way to banish the Darkness.

I don't know how long I crouched, there was no way to tell, not even breaths to count. Finally though, I stood and started to walk. Strange as it seemed, I held the lantern out in front of me and moved like a kid in sand, pushing my toes along the ground. As I progressed

I knocked *things* clattering across the ground. They sounded like dice in a box. Once I toed something large and solid, and carefully skirted around it.

Eventually though, the empty lantern knocked into a wall and I felt along it with my fingertips. Bumps and grooves told me the stone was carved, but with what? Again my mind went to Mum's old pictures and I thought about hieroglyphs, and wondered where I was.

There was no way to know but at least the wall gave me something to follow.

My calves started to ache and I realised I'd been walking downhill. Suddenly the wall I was tracing ended and I stumbled. I froze immediately, sensing the edge of a cavernous space. I hefted the lantern and wondered whether to enter. On the one hand I didn't know what was waiting for me but on the other, I had nowhere else to go.

A few paces into the space the blackness surrounding me started to turn grey. Half a dozen more steps and the light had grown stronger. I peered up to find the source of the illumination, but could see nothing. Puzzled, I looked down and shapes resolved themselves into a silent crowd.

I opened my mouth and stared. The word "crowd" wasn't sufficient to describe the horde massed in front of me. I couldn't count them but there had to be ten thousand men and women ranged in rows.

Barely perceptibly the darkness continued to lift. I strained my ears. With so many people ahead of me, surely I should be hearing something.

Pimples burred my skin but I took yet another step. Each face I could see was turned in my direction. The wordless regard of the horde chilled me and although the cavern was blanketed with quiet, animosity pressed upon me like a rock-fall.

All were differently dressed yet there was something indefinably uniform about the stances and facial expressions. Another word for the throng occurred to me: army.My eyes flicked around the cavern in search of an exit. Now I took the time to look I could see that the walls were riddled with black spots that could only be other tunnels. My fingers fell open and the lantern dropped to the floor with a clatter that sounded like the end of the world. I was standing in the entrance to one of what must be hundreds of tunnels.

I was at the centre of a labyrinth with no idea how to get out.

For an age I stood, trembling, in front of the army then I saw a face I recognised: James. I ran forward, kicking the lantern and sending it clattering. Then I stopped in front of him. He was posed like a Greek statue, not a hair out of place. Only his eyes burned with hatred deeper and stronger than a black hole. Abruptly I jumped back, almost afraid of being sucked inside.

He didn't chase after me. He was awake and I was certain he was aware, but something was holding him in place. I recalled the look on his face when I Marked him. His face was still red where I'd slapped his cheek, but the Mark was gone.

I raised my own hand and my eyes widened. It too, was clean. So passage through the Darkness cleansed the Mark which had called it; perhaps the Darkness absorbed the stain back into itself.

I shuddered with relief. If I got out of here, I wouldn't have to Mark Pete.

If I got out.

I searched automatically for other familiar faces. Tamsin was in the row behind James, highlighted by her blonde hair. Harley stood next to her. Tamsin's face was twisted with so much terror that it made her ugly. Whatever had happened to her in here, it hadn't been good.

I walked on until I saw the agoraphobic housewife, still in her nightclothes, her eye-mask askew on the top of her head. Her face was more confused and resigned than anything else. I wondered if she thought she was still dreaming, or if she'd somehow been waiting for retribution all the time.

Then I found the gang member, Jay, his gun still in his hand. Surely if anyone would have been able to escape it would have been him. Whatever was down here, he could have shot it.

My mouth felt dry as bone. Assuming these people had arrived as I had, still mobile and alert, what had turned them into living statues? And why hadn't Jay's gun been able to save him?

With increasing speed I searched through the rows, finding face after face. I didn't recognise every figure; there had to be others like me spread around the world. Who knew how many of us were sending murderers here day after day? But at last there he was – the killer of the clown – my first mission.

The man, Bill, still wore his money belt bulging with fairground ticket stubs and cash. His muscles bulged from his wife-beater vest. Appropriate. This man had beaten his girlfriend then killed her friend when he tried to help her. By sending him into the Darkness I'd prevented him from hunting down the girl and probably saved her life. I looked around at the overwhelming mass of humanity. How many lives had been saved by removing these people from the world? How many could I yet save? Suddenly I understood what my mother had meant when she said she was proud of what she did.

Thoughts of my mother turned to her book *The Tale of Oh-Fa*; that was where my story had really begun. A great need to find the first of all the murderers burned in me. Oh-Fa's first Mark had been given to him by his overseer. He and the rest of the workers had been killed by Anubis; but it was the leader of the expedition, the Professor, who had made them break through the image of the jackal-headed god of death and sent them inside, knowing what was trapped in the darkness, waiting for them.

My mind raced back over the passages containing the Professor's description:

> *Due to an excess of coffee and lack of hygiene, the Professor's incisors are dark yellow and the colour ensures that his giant tombstone teeth are the locus of his narrow face… The glare of the sun on his round spectacles erased his eyes.*

I had always imagined the Professor like the German baddie from *Raiders of the Lost Ark*, so that was who I searched for.

I was racing through the middle of the lines to the back of the room, expecting the Professor to be the first man in the first line, when I spotted a pattern: not in the formation of regimented lines, but the dress of the entombed killers.

Bands of fashion cut through the rows like the circles of a tree, growing more modern as they extended to the outer edge of the cavernous space. In fact, it felt as if I was running through a museum of evil waxworks demonstrating fashions through the ages. I followed the lengthening of skirts, the smattering of changing army uniforms, the rising collars, the roughening materials until I found him in the centre, the crowds having grown around him.

He was taller and thinner than I'd pictured, but it had to be him. He sported old-fashioned desert dress and a gold insignia on the third finger of his right hand. He was just as Oh-Fa had described. And he wore a bag across his chest.

Oh-Fa's tale was *true*.

As if following its own plan, my hand reached for the bag. It had to contain the Professor's book, with translations of the hieroglyphs and most importantly, maps showing the location of Nefertiti's tomb.

Dad had said he wanted to find the original vector and this could tell him where it was.

Perfectly preserved, the man stood completely unmoving, without life or breath. But I didn't take my eyes from his face as I pilfered his notes. He looked sadder than James, as if his anger had long ago burned out. I wondered if he felt the passage of time.

As I tucked the book under my shirt I hesitated. The people here were all alive, even those that should have naturally been long dead. The Darkness did not kill, it preserved; in some cases for over two hundred years.

So if Anubis did not want their lives, what were the killers being saved for?

I swallowed, wishing I had some way of moistening my dry lips. If this really was an army, what was it for? *And where was its General?*

Something else was down here, hidden by the Darkness; something that had caught these people, frozen them and placed them in their lines.

I started to run back through the terrifying multitude.

Then I heard my name.

31

The greatest of the Lords of Death

It was only a whisper but it sliced through the silence like a knife. My heart leaped into my throat and I froze.

"Taylor, are you in here?"

I swallowed. It didn't sound like the voice of a monster. Carefully I peered around the back of what appeared to be a butcher, complete with apron and cleaver in hand.

"*Justin*! What are you doing here?" Abandoning caution, I hurled myself past the ghastly regiments of creepily silent murderers and flung my aching body into his arms.

He wrapped himself around me and I felt his lips on my hair. When I looked up though, he was staring over my shoulder. "Is that James?" he murmured.

I nodded into his shoulder then turned. "Tamsin's there too."

He stiffened. "Did you know this would happen to them?"

"How could I?" I pushed my hair back with an impatient hand. "No one's ever come out of the

Darkness." I paused and looked back at him. "How are you here?"

"I followed you." Finally Justin tore his eyes from his old friend. "The thing that took you – the Darkness – it was disappearing, shrinking, just like a portal. I wasn't going to lose you." His fingers tightened on my arms. "So I jumped inside. I fell a long way then landed in some sort of room, alone. I've been looking for you since. I don't know how long, it felt like days. There's no way to tell time."

"I can't believe you followed me. That was crazy."

"I told you, I don't want to lose you. Anyway, it was my fault you were Marked and ended up here. You think I'd let you face this, whatever it is, alone?"

I shook my head. "How is it your fault?"

His eyes flickered to James once more. "I should never have done that dare. I should have gone to the police, or told Dad about V, instead I thought I could get out with my reputation intact and they killed me. Then I touched you. So it's my fault."

I turned his chin until our eyes met. "It isn't your fault, it's theirs." I tilted my head towards his murderers. "You can't blame yourself for this."

Justin's face twisted with pain. "I don't know how you can forgive me, but I'm glad." He closed his eyes. "I just wish I had managed to close the club down."

I squeezed him tightly. "James won't be in charge anymore; that's something."

"Someone else will be."

"Think about it, maybe the old network could cover up your death, write it up as an accident, but what about

James, Tamsin and Harley? Their disappearances won't look good."

"They'll have them down as runaways."

"Perhaps. Or someone might look a bit more closely at things in the school."

Justin nodded. "It might be enough."

"And Pete's still out there. He might shut it down."

Justin stepped away from me. "*Why* didn't you just Mark him? You wouldn't be here."

"He's my oldest friend." I hung my head. "I couldn't."

"You're not close any more." Justin frowned.

"That's not the point. He said he joined V because he had nothing left, because I'd been a bad friend. If I'd been more honest with him and told him about our curse, he might have stayed out of it. I've lost Hannah now too, because I didn't trust her to believe me. I mean, *Hannah*, who is convinced that vampires and aliens exist. She'd have believed me if anyone would. I was so determined to suffer alone, and my friends paid for it. So maybe I deserve to be here." I shuddered as I looked around again.

Justin clenched his fists. "That's bull, Tay. You don't deserve to be here." He followed my gaze around the room. "Do you have any idea where we are?"

I nodded. "I've been thinking about it. I know it sounds mad, but I believe this is Nefertiti's tomb. After my ancestor returned to his family, it was swallowed up by the desert and has never been found. I think I landed in the room where Anubis destroyed the expedition." I pointed at the lantern I had discarded. "That might even be the lantern they fought over."

Justin closed his hand over my whitened knuckles. "Are you OK?"

I tried on a half smile. It felt uncomfortably tight. "It's selfish, but I'm better now you're here. I didn't even know you could jump into the Darkness, I thought it had to take you."

"I don't suppose anyone has ever tried before. I'm the only one stupid enough." His smile matched mine. Then he turned back to James. "They haven't moved. They look like zombies."

I licked my lips. "Something's happened to them all, they're frozen."

"Can we help them?" Justin took a half step towards Tamsin.

I shook my head. "I've already examined James; if he'd have been able to move, he would have."

Justin nodded. "Alright. But whatever it is could still happen to you. We have to get out of here."

I gripped the lantern tighter. "No one has ever come out of the Darkness. You'd think they'd have tried before they got stuck." I pointed to the figures of James, Harley and Tamsin and my mouth was dry as bone. "I don't even know if there's a way out through these tunnels."

"There has to be." His eyes raked the tunnels. "Your power brought us here, maybe it'll get us home. Which way do you want to go?"

"It isn't a power; it's a curse."

"Which way, Tay?"

I stared round at the hundreds of tunnels that spilled their darkness into the massive cavern. Some of them

The Weight of Souls

were above our heads, some below ground level and cut off by rough stone. They looked like laughing mouths, mocking our desire to escape with baying humour. I prayed one of the tunnels would leap out at me, that there would be a sign of some sort.

There wasn't.

"There are so many. They all look the same."

"Except that one." Justin pointed to a round hole at knee level just off to my right.

I squinted at it. "I don't see anything different." I frowned up at him. "What do you mean?"

"Are you serious?" His eyebrows climbed into his tangled fringe. "You can't see the light?"

"Light?" I clutched him tighter. "You can see a light?"

"Well, yeah. I wondered why you didn't want to go that way."

"You can see a light, but I can't?"

He shuffled his feet.

"Alright." I gave him some room. "You lead."

Justin took a single step towards the hole and, as if switched on, the entire army moved: every head, all ten thousand, turned with a susurration that made me clap my hands over my ears.

A small cry escaped my lips and Justin leaped back to my side. But the army weren't looking at us. Every one of them was gazing fixedly at a large passage on the other side of the cavern.

Carefully Justin pulled me towards him. "We shouldn't be here." He guided me sideways towards the hole. "We need to go."

He gave me a shove and I broke into a run. He was right. There was no way I wanted to see what was coming into the cavern.

The words of my ancestor came back to me. Oh-Fa thought he had faced the *greatest of the Lords of Death*. A jackal-headed monster who traded him treasure for his soul.

And now he was coming for mine.

Behind us there was a ten thousand-throated sigh but I didn't turn. Instead, I tossed the dead lantern to one side and, with Justin at my heels, hurled myself full length into a hole that glowed with a light I couldn't see.

The tunnel wasn't wide enough to stand, so we had to crawl, banging our knees and shoulders. A little way in the roof lifted from my head. Carefully I crouched then stood, all the time expecting a crack on the skull that never came.

Catching my hand in his, Justin took the lead. "You still can't see the light?"

"No," I gasped. As far as I was aware, we were standing in the pitch dark; this tunnel no different from the one I'd arrived through. "Keep going."

Justin drew ahead and I followed the drag of his hand, sprinting full out to keep up with his longer stride.

Then I heard a growl. It shivered through my skin and my veins trembled with the tenor of it. Immediately Justin dived left and almost wrenched my arm out of its socket. My gasp of pain cancelled my cry of fear and I fell quickly silent.

But the silence was eerie. The only noise we made
was the pounding of our feet against stone; my lungs
weren't heaving, no blood roared in my ears, I wasn't
even panting. Only the burning of my calves told me I
couldn't keep the pace up forever.

Then the silence broke inside my head.

Retribution, vengeance, justice, death.

I fingers tightened on Justin's. "Can you hear that?"

"Hear what?"

"Oh God." Inside my head the voice pounded,
replacing my vanished heartbeat with its own rhythm.

Retribution, vengeance, justice, death.

"It wasn't me, I didn't kill him," I cried out loud and
Justin swiftly pulled me into a new passage. Almost
before I could regain my balance, he turned again. Then
he shoved me against a wall, pressed the length of his
torso to mine and held his hand over my mouth. "What
are you doing?" he hissed.

"He's in my head." I sobbed. "He thinks I'm one of his
killers. He's coming to make me part of his army."

Retribution, vengeance, justice, death.

My body hummed with the beat and my legs
weakened. "That's how he does it. He gets in your head.
You really can't hear him?"

Justin shook his head. "Maybe it only works on the
living."

"But I've got no heartbeat." I pushed Justin's hand to
my chest. "No breath." I raised myself so he could feel
the lack of air on his cheek.

Justin nodded against my head. "So you're suspended

– like them." He nodded back towards the cavern. "Passage through the Darkness must have done it, maybe this is another dimension or something, a place where time moves differently. You're still alive, but one heartbeat could take a hundred years."

Retribution, vengeance, justice, death.

I wrapped my arms tightly around him. "That voice – I already feel like I can't run any more. If he catches me, I'll be just like James and the others."

I fell silent and listened desperately for the sound of clawed feet on stone.

Eventually I pressed my lips to Justin's ear. "Do you think he's gone? Can it work out where we're going?"

I felt him shake his head. "I don't know."

Retribution, vengeance, justice, death.

I leaned my head against his blazer. "Let's keep going, before I can't move at all."

"Sure?"

I tried to smile through the darkness, believing that he could see me. "We must have lost him. We've got to have some luck."

Justin touched my cheek then pulled away again. "This way."

It felt like we had been walking into blackness forever and the voice had grown faint, allowing the strength back into my limbs. That was when it struck me. "Justin, do you realise what this means?" I felt rather than saw his head turn towards me; his eyes touch my flesh with the lightest caress. "I can't see the light, but you can.

You're dead and you're going towards *the light*. You said you didn't see it. You were worried that it wouldn't be there for you, but here it is."

He said nothing in reply, but if he'd had a heartbeat I was sure it would have skipped.

My legs were aching when Justin pulled me to a stop one last time. "We're at the end."

I squinted. "I still can't see anything."

Justin squeezed my hand. "This is the exit." He caught my fingers and held them up pulling my hand forward.

"There's nothing there." I frowned.

"Feel with your toes."

I inched my feet forward and the ground disappeared. I leaped back. "I'm not stepping off that."

"You'll have to trust me." Justin's voice held a slight smile. "You did before."

My knees quivered. "Are you sure about this?"

"Course I am." He put his arm around my shoulders. "We'll step off together. Ready?"

"You're already dead."

"You'll be fine." He kissed me and this time his lips weren't cold. My fingers started to wind round his neck, but he ended the kiss before I could finish the embrace. "I-I think I might have loved you," he murmured.

With a gentle pressure he pushed me forward. I could have wriggled free and run back into the darkness. But I trusted him. I faced the front and let Justin propel me over the edge.

32

Hungry for the world

I opened my eyes and immediately had to close them again. Shards of light shattered my vision into a glittering mosaic.

I closed one hand over my chest to feel for my heartbeat. Once more my blood sprinted through my veins and rang rhythmically inside my ears. I inhaled and air flooded my lungs.

I'm alive.

I strained my ears to hear his voice – *Retribution, vengeance, justice, death* – but it was only a memory. The Lord of Death was gone.

"Justin?"

There was no answer.

I rolled onto my knees and sat back on my haunches. Then I shaded my eyes and squinted around. Familiar shapes, made strange by my odd vantage point, resolved out of the brightness. Dad's huge microscope was lying on its side on the floor and his fridge was open, the samples scattered. The wheels of his wheelchair were motionless by his desk.

"Dad?" I squinted up at him. His mouth was opening and closing soundlessly.

Finally he rolled towards me and grapnels of light caught in his spokes as he advanced. "T-Taylor? I didn't think you were coming back. I was… I didn't know what to do."

I rubbed the bright hooks from my eyes. "How long was I gone?"

"A-an hour, maybe." He fumbled with his sleeve and looked at his watch, stared back at my face. "I don't know, it seemed like forever."

As I lowered my hands to my knees I checked my palm. The Mark had not returned. The Darkness was no longer coming for me. "Thank God."

Dad's chair bumped my legs and he caught my shoulders. I hesitated for a moment, then launched upward and, for the first time in three years, permitted myself the comfort of his embrace.

"Where's the boy?" Dad peered behind me as though I was hiding Justin from him.

Cold flooded my chest. "I-I think he's gone." I swallowed and my throat felt as if it was filled with thorns. "He led us towards the light. He went into it with me. H-he must have moved on."

My heart shrunk: I hadn't even said goodbye.

Dad patted my shoulder and I decided not to look at his face as he did so.

Eventually I pulled back. Mum's book was open on Dad's desk, his glasses reflecting twin suns above the open pages. "You found Mum's book?" I murmured.

He offered me a weak smile. "In your room. I was hoping for a clue..."

I gestured towards the mess. "What happened to your microscope?"

Dad's jaw hardened. "I was wrong. All this time I should have been helping you. Escorting you." He exhaled. "You really have been looking for murderers." The thought made him whiten. "I thought there should be a rational scientific explanation for the Mark, t-the ghosts, but there isn't."

I frowned at the chaos. "You did this?"

He glared around the room. "Yes, I did."

I felt something hard against my waist and inhaled. "The notebook." I pulled it free. "Dad, *The Tale of Oh-Fa* is true. I found the Professor. This is his."

"We'll need to talk about this properly." Dad took the book in trembling fingers. "I know." I nodded and my head thumped with pain, I was dead tired. "Just not now."

"No, you're exhausted." Dad's fingers tightened on the book. "What should I do with this?" he muttered. "What use is it to us?"

"You said you'd be more likely to find a cure if you could find the vector. It could still be in the tomb, couldn't it? Nefertiti's tomb? And there should be a map, some instructions, something."

Dad dropped his eyes from mine. "Your mother was right, you can't cure a curse."

I grabbed his shoulders. "Since Mum's death you've been driven by your need to defeat the Darkness. You can't give up now. You said my blood infected yours. Where there's infection, there has to be a cure. So what if the Darkness is real? Now you have a *real* enemy." I hesitated, the idea of an enemy made me think of the army I'd helped create, the army waiting silently for... what? I stamped on the thought. "So things are more complicated than you thought." My eyes burned into his. "Who cares? It's still a genetic disease. And now you're even closer to curing it."

Dad placed his palm on my cheek. "You have no idea how like your mother you are."

I snorted gently and used his chair arm to get to my feet. "Do you mind if I...?"

He was already opening the Professor's notebook. "Go."

I hesitated at the stairs, then opened the front door and sat on the stoop instead. The sun had long departed and the air contained that breath of freshness that would be traded at dawn for the sunshine. I inhaled the scent of night blooming jasmine from next door and the tang of Mum's ivy. It was full dark, but not a hunting Dark. I was safe until the next ghost Marked me. I wrapped my arms round my knees and stared down the street. Tomorrow maybe I'd go and find the old lady at the building site. I owed it to her.

My knuckles whitened. Did I really want to continue swelling the ranks of Anubis' army?

Retribution, vengeance, justice, death.

The words were a distant whisper in the back of my mind, but I'd never forget them.

A dog barked in the distance and I groaned. I didn't have any choice. As long as the ghosts came to me I'd have to keep Marking their killers, or risk returning to that place myself.

With mild surprise I realised my cheeks were wet. I felt my face; I was crying. I put my head on my knees and let myself sob.

For just a little while I hadn't had to face the dead by myself.

Now I was alone again.

Suddenly my stomach cramped. My eyes widened at the pain and I cradled my gut with a whimper. The feeling grew in intensity until I thought I was going to burst.

I opened my mouth to call for Dad and the pain stopped as suddenly as it had started. I uncurled and wiped sweat from my forehead.

"Tay? Thank God."

"J-Justin?"

He stood on the bottom step, his school uniform crumpled for the first time I could remember. His hair flopped into his brown eyes and his hands were clutched across his abdomen. His face shone with pain to match my own.

I lurched to my feet and he smiled wryly. "I'm sorry that hurt, I had to follow the life force to get back to you. It's OK. I know where I'm going now. But the flow of life you gave me means I can't go yet. I have to wait for it to dry up."

I blinked. "How long will that take?"

Justin shrugged. "It could be any minute. I think it ran out before on the scaffolding. But you gave me a lot more last time. I don't know." He edged up the steps, his lips white. Was he nervous?

I held out a hand and he wrapped his fingers around mine. "So you could be sticking around for a while," I murmured.

His head tilted and his hair cleared his eyes. "I don't have to. I could go somewhere else, see the world."

I inhaled sharply. "You want to see the world?"

"I won't get another chance."

"True."

He sat beside me and together we listened to the distant hum of traffic.

Eventually I cleared my throat. "Still, London's pretty nice."

There was a grin in his voice when he replied. "You know, they say if you sit still long enough the whole world will come to you."

I raised my eyebrows. "Do they?"

"I heard it somewhere." His thumb started to trace patterns on the back of my hand and I shivered. Then I leaned against him.

"I'm going to speak to Mr Barnes and make sure the V Club is shut down." Justin nodded against my head and I sighed. "I can't believe I've got you back… at least for a little while."

Justin's arms tightened around me. "I've been thinking. If you don't have to spend the whole time watching for ghosts, you can get on with school, get decent grades and plan a life beyond all this."

I frowned up at him. "What do you mean?"

"I'm coming to school with you. While you're there I'll look out for the dead so you don't have to. I'll run interference, keep them away from you. You can spend some proper time with Hannah and sort things out. I can make up for everything I put you through."

I pressed my lips against his hand in a silent thank you then shook my head sadly. "Justin, you can't go back to school. They found your body, everyone knows you're dead. If someone sees you…"

Justin shook his head. "I won't come to class. No one will see me."

"You're solid now."

"I'm still a ghost. I have skills." He concentrated and his hand passed through the step beside us.

"Freaky." I blinked. "You can't be seen. Not at all."

Justin sighed. "I won't be."

"It'll be lonely." I squeezed him tighter.

"You can meet me in free periods. If you tell Hannah… and Pete… maybe they'll come with you."

"You'd be willing to see Pete?"

Justin fell silent. "Not straightaway. One day."

"You'll forgive him?"

Justin pulled me close and nodded. "It won't be easy, but he wasn't the worst, he was sorry. It helps."

"You're pretty amazing." I hugged him, my mind whirling with possibilities. If I could pay attention in class and do my homework instead of hunting for killers… I grinned. "I can't wait to prove Tamsin wrong."

"What do you mean?" Justin froze against me.

"She said I had a future bagging prawn crackers. This could really change things for me. Thank you."

"Tamsin was a bitch." Justin's voice was flat and I understood. Tamsin had hurt him in more ways than one.

"I ought to call Pete." I shuffled my feet. "I should see him before school, he'll have questions."

Justin's chin rubbed my head as he nodded. "Can I…" he hesitated. "Will I be allowed to come in the house with you?"

I looked at his face, taut with nerves. "You have to stay with us; you haven't anywhere else to go. I'll speak to Dad."

"He doesn't like me." Justin fidgeted.

"You saved my life, he'll love you."

"Maybe." Justin's eyes were tight with anxiety.

"We've got a spare room down the hall. Dad will read you the riot act, but he'll let you stay. If you're helping me with the ghosts he won't have a choice."

Justin relaxed. "Alright. Let's go and call Pete."

"There's something we need to do first."

"What?"

I kissed him.

Early morning mist clung to the grass verge and the sky remained grey with lingering dawn. I was the only one waiting at the bus stop; it was too soon even for the commuters to gather.

There was no sound, but instinctively I looked along the road. Pete was coming to meet me, just as he'd promised. I checked on Justin. He was standing a little way away, too far for Pete to identify him, but close enough to weigh in if the dead found us. As he caught sight of Pete, Justin's fists closed, but he made no further move. He was still looking out for me. I was safe. So instead of seeking ghosts, I was able to watch Pete approach.

He moved with a heavy tread. In the old days he'd walked as if there was a hip-hop tune bouncing around in his head, all energy and jigging rhythm. Now his music had been silenced. I wondered when that had happened, if it was only since he learned of his role in Justin's death, or if it had been long quieted. I hadn't been paying attention.

Pete's head was bowed, but a jerk of his shoulders told me he'd seen me. He shifted his bag higher and his step stuttered in hesitation, then he kept walking.

He didn't raise his head until he drew level with me. Then he dropped his bag at his feet and looked up. He wore a 5 o'clock shadow that said he hadn't shaved in a couple of days and his face was drawn and tired. His eyes were red, the skin around them grey from lack of sleep. Even the black stubble on his head had grown out enough to begin to curl once more. The bristles looked soft enough to touch. I tucked my fingers inside my coat.

"Hey, Pete."

"Taylor." He swallowed and kicked a stone that lay on the path. It skittered into the bus stop with a bang.

"Are you alright?" My eyes skimmed his face, seeking an answer.

"I-I'm not sure." Pete licked his lips. "What happened to James and the others, do you know?"

"I know." I looked up as the sound of an engine warned us the bus was on its way. "Let's talk on the bus."

He nodded and avoided my gaze until the behemoth pulled into the stop.

Once on I led him upstairs, giving Justin a chance to get on the bottom deck. I climbed the spiral steps, wobbling awkwardly as the bus moved off, then sat on the back seat, offering Pete plenty of room. He collapsed by the window, putting his bag between us.

"So what happened?" he said, finally.

I took a deep breath. "On my tenth birthday," I began, "I started to see ghosts."

"Oh, for the love of…" Pete leaned back. "I thought you were going to be honest."

"Just hear me out." I rubbed my hair out of my face. "This is what you always wanted to know, why I started acting strange. It's my family curse. I see dead people."

"Like the film?" Pete sneered.

"If you like. If a murder victim touches me they leave a Mark on my skin."

Pete regarded me carefully. "That glove you wear?"

I waved my unmarked hand. "I don't want to accidentally transfer the Mark to the wrong person."

"The wrong person being?"

"An innocent. Someone who didn't commit murder."

"And once the ghost touches you?" His voice trembled between mockery and curiosity.

I inhaled again. "I have to track down their murderer and pass the Mark on to them. Then the Darkness comes to take them away."

Pete's fingers tightened on his bag until the skin over his knuckles almost cracked. "Something took James, I saw it."

"It's why I joined the V club. I had to find out who killed Justin and send them into the Darkness."

"Are you telling me *Justin* is a ghost?"

I nodded. "He was in school that day the police came in. He put a Mark on my hand before I realised he was dead."

Pete swallowed. "You're telling me Justin knows who killed him."

"He knows about you, yes."

Pete's lips whitened and he shook his head. "I don't believe you."

I glanced out the window. "Justin's dead, you believe that, don't you?"

"Of course." Pete exhaled shakily.

"Alright then, wait here." I rose from my seat and, as the bus jerked and shook, I headed towards the stairs. Justin stood at the bottom, like a guard, with one hand on the rail.

"Pete doesn't believe me." I caught the rail myself as the bus rounded a corner. "I know it's a lot to ask, but–"

"You want me to go and see him."

I nodded.

"I'm not ready for that." Justin swayed in place and I watched the emotions war across his face. "Fine," he snapped. He edged past me and took the stairs two at a time. I followed more slowly.

When I reached the top I saw Pete lurch to his feet. Justin now stood in the middle of the aisle, holding the chairs on either side of him.

Pete panted frantically, almost choking on his own breath. "You're dead. I saw you–"

"You helped them kill me, you dick." Justin's tone was low and dangerous.

"God." Pete's knees hit the chair and he sank down. "How is this possible?"

"It's a lot to go into." I slipped under Justin's arm and placed my hand on his chest, holding him back. "For now, just accept that Justin's come back a ghost." I kept my eyes on Pete. His mouth was trembling as if he was going to cry. My own lungs tightened. "Is there anything you want to say to him?"

"God, yes." Pete raised his head. "I'm *so* sorry. I didn't know. I mean I knew something was way off, but I wasn't sure, and it was V, man, you just do what you do. You *know*."

Justin grunted.

"If I could take it back, I would. I'd do anything. When you fell – shit." Pete was trembling all over now. "I threw up, I've never been more scared. And James said this was the thing that would keep us all tied to V. We were lifers. No leaving the club. Ever." He rubbed a quivering hand over the bristles on his head. "And after that I really wanted to leave." He glanced at me. "When James disappeared into that darkness, the first thought I had was, *I can get out now*. Isn't that terrible?"

I had to leave Justin, but my fingers were reluctant, I trailed my hand along his arm as I went. Then I sat down next to Pete. "James is gone. I'm going to get this whole thing stopped so it can't happen to anyone else."

Pete shook his head. "You can't stop it, Tay, there're members everywhere. The head told us there's an old member in the police…"

"I know." I touched his hand and he flinched away. "If necessary I'll go to the papers."

Pete swallowed and rubbed his stubbled head.

"You don't believe I can fix this, that's fine, I don't need you to. But you do believe me about the ghosts?"

"Yes," Pete whispered.

"Alright." I looked at Justin. "The dead are why I behaved so strangely. And I couldn't hang out all those times because I really was doing family stuff with Mum, curse stuff."

"Why didn't you tell me?" Pete's eyes skidded over my face. "Don't answer that, I understand. I wouldn't have believed you."

"You had to see Justin with your own eyes."

The ghost in question was still in the middle of the aisle, but he had turned his back on us and was now guarding the stairs. My shoulders felt lighter than I could remember. I had been carrying the weight of enforced attention for so many years; the relief of letting someone else share the burden literally made me sit up straighter. I felt as though I was breathing for the first time.

I turned back to Pete. "I'm going to tell Hannah." I fiddled with my blazer. "She has to forgive me."

"If Justin speaks to her, she will." Pete stared at him once more. "She loves you, she'll come round."

"What about you?" I swallowed nervously. "Will you come round?"

The bus drew to a stop and Pete looked up as Justin stood to attention. "You know what I've done. You don't want to be friends with me anymore."

I grabbed for his hand and this time he let me hold it. His skin was drier than it used to be and his nails were cracked. I squeezed his knuckles under mine. "I'm your friend, Pete. I always was. Now you know about me we can both start over."

His hand twitched. "Tell me what happened to them – to James, Tamsin and Harley."

"They went to be judged." I decided to stay quiet about Anubis, I thought that might be one truth too far. "They won't be coming back."

"I should have been taken too, shouldn't I?" Pete's eyes burned into mine. "That Mark, you were meant to put it on me."

Justin spoke, his voice seemingly floating from his turned back. "She kept the Mark herself and the Darkness took her, like it did the others. She almost got trapped inside. For you."

Pete whitened further. "You did that for me?"

I said nothing.

"Why?"

"I told you, you're my oldest friend." I struggled to keep my voice steady. "Please say we're OK."

Pete forced a smile as the bus pulled into the school stop. "I'll never be able to repay you."

"That's alright," I grinned. "I take lunch money."

With an explosive laugh, Pete shoved me and I lurched to my feet. Together we followed Justin into the street. The school loomed in front of us, a promise of a difficult day ahead.

Justin caught my hands and pulled me close. "I'm going to patrol; it'll be better than just hanging in one place."

My heart rose as his head dropped and his lips hovered over mine. Pete cleared his throat and turned away. The faintest hint of breath touched my mouth and I opened my eyes in surprise as Justin kissed me. I pressed my lips against his and inhaled him in; the intensity of his scent, the suggestion of moisture on his skin, traces of life. My lungs tightened and my heart raced. I clenched my fingers in his blazer until I felt my knees begin to quake, then I pulled away with a tremulous sigh.

Justin stroked my cheek with his fingertips. "I'll be here at lunchtime if you want to see me."

I smiled. "I want to see you."

"Alright then." He stepped backward. "I'd better get on with it." He glanced at the school gate, as if he wished he was going in with me and I released his hand. He grinned and his hair flopped into his face. "Have a nice day." He jerked his head. "Get going."

"I'll miss you." I swung my backpack and headed for the entrance. "See you later."

Pete jogged until his stride matched mine. "So... you and Justin..."

"Yes." The smile crept back onto my cooling lips.

"He's dead." Pete shuddered.

"Yes." I raised my eyebrows.

"OK then." Pete stuck his arm through mine and I froze momentarily. Then I carried on walking as if nothing had happened, terrified of breaking this fragile new thing between us.

"This is going to take a bit of getting used to," he said and I nodded, looking for the first time in years at the flowers in the beds, the noticeboard by the main office and the mural on the outside of the sixth form centre.

Then I really did freeze. Hannah was walking from the direction of the library.

"What has she done to her hair?" My horror was focused so strongly on the travesty that I barely saw the two girls walking arm in arm with her.

Pete hissed through his teeth. "It doesn't suit her."

I blinked, blindsided, as the three came closer, all with matching alice-bands and brown shoulder-length bobs. Hannah's hair was still a mass of frizz, but she had tried to tame it with some product or other and it hung, lifelessly, along her face.

She was leaning into the girl on the left, giggling at something she said. Then she saw Pete with his arm in mine. Her feet tangled in one another and she would have tripped if she hadn't been held up by her new friends.

"We need to talk," I called.

"There's nothing to talk about."

Her new friends raised their heads and the trio started to march around us.

"Please, Han." I injected a note of pleading in my voice. Her chin jutted, she was hardening her heart against me.

"Just for a minute." Pete weighed in on my side and I suppressed a surprised gasp. "Hear her out and if you still aren't interested, I won't let her bother you again."

I bit my tongue. If Hannah didn't cave for Pete, then she wasn't going to.

"Come on, Hannah, we were going to the music room, remember." Her new friends tugged on her arm, but to my delight she pulled free.

"I'll meet you there." She waved them off. "I have a thing to do here. It won't take long."

I didn't take my eyes from her face, as the muttered complaints of her new friends grew more distant.

"I... like your hair," I started.

Her hand rose, as if to touch the alice-band, then stopped and dropped to her side. "What do you want?"

"I haven't been fair to you." I tried to move closer, but Hannah stepped back, out of my orbit, and I stopped. "I know I cancel arrangements at the last minute and blow you off with no explanation. I've been a lousy friend. But, things are going to change and I want to tell you what's been going on with me."

Hannah glared at Pete. "You were the one who told me not to bother with her any more and now look at you. Were you just trying to get me out of the way?"

Pete shook his head with a snort. "She's going to tell you what she told me, Han. It'll be hard to believe, but you should listen." He released my arm and backed off. "I'll save you a table in the common room."

I edged nearer to Hannah. "Can we sit? There's a bench." I gestured to the side and she nodded.

"I'm not staying," she snapped, but her knees folded and she sat.

"It started when I was ten," I began. "That's when I began seeing ghosts..."

Pete grinned widely as we entered the common room. Hannah's arm was tucked through my elbow and when we strode past the lockers her bag swung against my knees. He stood up when we drew close.

"You believe her?" He put his head near to Hannah's.

Hannah nodded. Her alice-band was at the bottom of her bag and her hair was beginning to defy the heavy product she had attacked it with, frothing out around her cheeks once more.

"You didn't need proof?" He looked at me for confirmation.

"I'm going to take her to see Justin at lunchtime. But she believes me anyway." I squeezed her tightly.

"I'm mad at her for not trusting me." Hannah fluffed out her hair and gave me a stern glare. "I can see why she thought *I'd* be cynical. Not."

I looked contrite. "I'm sorry. I am. But I wouldn't have believed someone who told me they saw ghosts, not before it happened to me. I didn't want to risk losing either of you."

Hannah pushed me onto the plastic chair and the curved edged bit into my thighs. She stood over me, hands on hips. "Honesty from now on." She turned to include Pete. "I mean it. No more secrets."

"No more secrets." I hid a smile.

She jiggled with excitement. "This is so cool, my best friend sees ghosts."

"What's going on here?" Mr Barnes loomed above me and automatically I leaped to my feet. He ignored Hannah and spoke to Pete and me. "In my office. Now."

Mr Barnes sat behind his desk, glowering from beneath lowered brows. Pete and I stood in front of him, like naughty children. His hand came down on his desk with a bang that made us jump.

"I've had parents on the phone. Tamsin's, Harley's and James' to be exact. Their brood didn't come home last night."

"Just like Justin," I muttered.

"What was that, Taylor?"

"Nothing." I looked him in the eye. He shifted uncomfortably.

"Peter, I want you to tell me straight up. Is this going to be another case like Justin Hargreaves?"

"Like Justin?" Pete's eyes widened.

"Don't play dumb with me, boy, is this something to do with the club? And if so, will it look like an accident?"

I staggered sideways, catching Pete's elbow to stop my legs from folding. "You don't care that they might be injured or dead?"

"I care very much." Mr Barnes rose to his feet. "But I'm not a paramedic. My job is not to save lives."

"Then what is your job?" I leaned forward. "You're our head teacher, you're meant to care."

"I care." He pushed his glasses up on his nose. "You're new, Taylor, so you have no idea yet what V can do for you in the coming years. Right now I have to do damage control. Your group has caused more problems than any other year group. I need to know what has happened to them, so I can tell our friend on the force."

"You mean so he can cover things up." Horror had blanched my face. My cheeks were cold as if I'd had water thrown on me.

"If necessary." He smiled, all crocodile-teeth. "If you were involved in what happened then you should be grateful to have an adult on your side. That's another advantage of V."

I slipped my arm out of Pete's and deliberately slowly I leaned on the desk. "Don't worry. James, Harley and Tamsin won't be found, not by the police, not by anybody."

Mr Barnes blinked. "You're certain about that?"

"Very. And I'm also certain that V is shutting down."

Mr Barnes guffawed, but his fingers were twisting nervously in his tie. "V shut down? You aren't thinking straight."

I curled my lip. "V is over. Four kids from one year-group are gone now. The authorities are going to have to start looking closely at the place. I'll speak to parents, newspapers, anyone who will listen. It won't be a secret society anymore. I imagine you'll lose your job."

Mr Barnes stood unmoving as though he'd been sent to Anubis. Then slowly his fingers uncurled from his tie. His mouth seized, eating invisible limes. Sour lines appeared on his face. "You're a nasty piece of work, Miss Oh." His small mustache twitched. "They should never have let you join V. I have no idea why they did. They were better kids than you could ever be."

"Wait a minute." Pete jerked, but I gestured him into quiet.

"All you want to do is destroy things for everybody else. I've seen your grades, when you get out of here you'll be a nobody. You won't be getting into university, I have no idea who'd employ a loser like you." Mr Barnes leaned forward. "But if you remain quiet and stay in V there is at least one university that will take you on, no questions. You'll walk into a good job when you leave. You'll have prospects. Imagine how proud your dad will be."

My breath stopped in my chest. Dad was losing hope. If I could go to university he'd be delighted. He would feel as if he'd beaten the curse. It would be a perfect gift.

Like a shark scenting blood in the water, Mr Barnes could feel me wavering. He smiled like a benevolent grandfather. "Think of what your poor, dead mother would have wanted for you."

My head snapped up. "You're right." I pictured her face. "I should think of Mum. She would never want this for me."

"Too true." He took off his glasses and rubbed them on the inside of his jacket. "So enough of this nonsense. Let's talk about your friends."

"No." I panted as if I'd run a marathon. "Mum wouldn't want me in *the V Club*, she was honourable."

I dug my nails into my palms. "She believed in justice."
I looked out of the window. There was a dark haired
boy in a school uniform standing outside the gates,
looking up at Mr Barnes' office as though he could see
me through the window. "Justin wouldn't want me to
stop either. I'm taking the V Club down, Mr Barnes. So
get ready."

I spun around and headed for the office door.

"Miss Oh," Mr Barnes voice was low and snarling.
"You don't want to make an enemy of me."

I grinned sourly. "Perhaps it's me who makes a bad
enemy."

"Are you threatening me?" He turned apoplectic
purple and I shook my head.

"You should think about what I said." I paused
with my hand on the door. "Pete and I have to get to
registration."

Pete caught up with me and his face was almost as
pale as Hannah's. "What have you *done*?" He shook
himself like a dog.

"I told you earlier, Pete. I'm taking down V. Now let's
go to class. I've got some work to catch up on."

33

The light seeker

Gabriel Oh rocked back and forth on his wheels, teeth on his bottom lip, pencil tapping the leather of his armrests. It didn't make sense.

He had both *The Tale of Oh-Fa* and the Professor's notebook open in front of him. *The Tale* described how Oh-Fa himself had found the image of Anubis carved into a stone tablet in the sand. He considered the text.

As I brushed sand aside, as I have done a million times before, the visage of a dog's head on a man's body resolved itself.

The Professor's translation of the tablet Oh-Fa had discovered was scribbled over three pages in his book. The first part of the translation was a fairly standard curse. Gabriel had seen other similar stanzas when Emma had sought the right words to carve on the house, to protect herself and Taylor from the ghosts. He swallowed; he had to re-evaluate every memory of his wife. Regret every harsh word he'd ever said about the illness. But not now. He turned back to the curse:

> *"This is a way, but not the true way.*
> *Death comes to he who enters the tomb*
> *through the Darkness on clawed feet.*
> *He will be nowhere and his house will be nowhere;*
> *he will be one proscribed, one who eats himself."*

In *The Tale* the beast was described as having clawed feet. He paged through until he found the passage. Then he muttered out loud. *A clawed foot slid towards me...*

So the threat was quite literal. Anyone who entered the tomb the wrong way would be killed by the clawed beast waiting inside. "And they entered the wrong way," he muttered. "They walked into the darkness, straight into a beast waiting to kill them."

That did make sense. But the second part of the translation did not.

> *"He who is in the place of embalming.*
> *Is hungry for the world.*
> *Bound to the queen's tomb by the priests of Horus.*
> *Until the coming of the light-seeker –*
> *Not living, not dead, not a child, not a man."*

As for him who shall destroy this inscription: He shall not reach his home. He shall not embrace his children. He shall not see success.

"*He who is in the place of embalming*" was another name for Anubis. Given that the first half of the curse appeared to have come true, could the rest of the inscription be taken seriously?

"*Bound to the queen's tomb by the priests of Horus.*"

Gabriel booted up his computer then nodded to himself; Horus had been Anubis' enemy.

The beast had named himself to Oh-Fa: "*If I kill you there will be no more death for Anubis.*"

So the priests of Horus had somehow bound the god Anubis to the tomb of the dead queen.

And he was stuck there until the coming of the light seeker.

Gabriel's mind span over Taylor's words when she had returned to him: "*He led us towards the light.*"

A chill numbed Gabriel until his whole body felt as dull as his useless legs. The pencil dropped from his frozen fingers.

"Not living, not dead. Justin was dead, but he had Taylor's life-force." His chair shuddered as he started to move, to shake. "Not a child, not a man – they wouldn't have had the word 'teenager' back then." His rubbed his face with his hands.

If the Professor's translation was correct, then Taylor and the ghost with her had just given Anubis what he needed to free himself.

Sick to the core he gripped the image of his wife, the one that always sat on his desk. "Can I believe this?" He looking into her eyes; caught on camera in a rare moment of light-hearted humour. "I didn't believe you. I must have made your life so much more difficult." Tears wet his stubbled chin. "I'm sorry."

He rubbed the picture like an aged Aladdin, somehow hoping she would speak back to him. "But this. Is it one step too far? Am I now being too credulous, believing the one thing I should not? Who would I even tell, what warning could I give?" The picture remained only that and he replaced it sadly next to the paired books.

"No." He shook his head. "This I don't believe."

He closed the books and headed for the door. Taylor and Justin were due home from school soon and he owed her some time and hot chocolate. For at least one day, the family curse could wait.

Acknowledgments

To my agent, the wonderful Juliet Mushens of The Agency Group, who believed in my writing and bashed it into shape with me. She is an inspiration.

To my editor, Amanda Rutter of Strange Chemistry, whose inciteful comments and hard work brought out the best in my manuscript.

To my family and friends, whose belief and support are invaluable, and to my in-laws Pat and Charles Pearce, whose practical help enabled the book to be completed.

To my existing readers, who have sent fantastic emails, messages and notes of support. Thank you.

And finally to my husband and children: Andy, Maisie and Riley. One day I trust that you will read and enjoy my work. In the meantime you inspire me and I love you more with every breath.

About the Author

Bryony Pearce completed an English Literature degree at Corpus Christi College, Cambridge in 1998 and afterwards worked in the research industry. After a while she moved to a village at the edge of the Peak District and went freelance so she could devote more time to writing.

She is now a full time mother to two children, writes as much as possible and enjoys doing school visits and events when she can fit them in.

Her first book, the award winning *Angel's Fury*, was published by Egmont in 2011.

For more information on Bryony, please visit her blog at

bryonypearce.wordpress.com

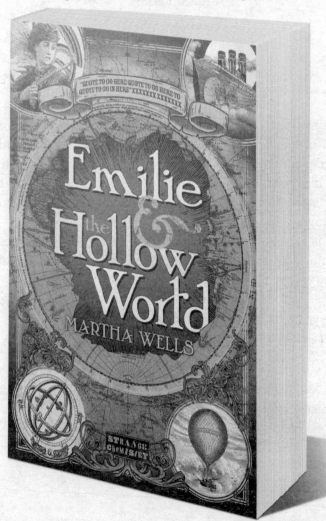

EXPERIMENTING WITH YOUR IMAGINATION

"An enjoying, compelling read
with a strong and competent
narrator ... a highly satisfying
adventure."
SFX Magazine

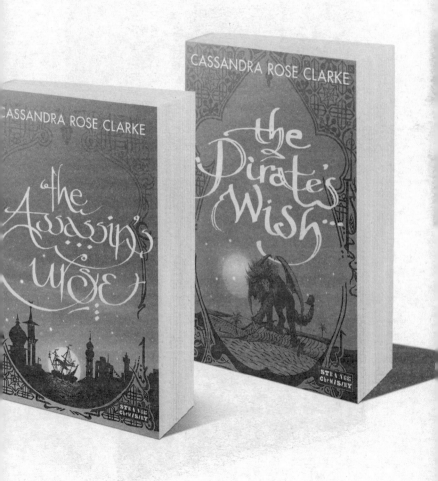

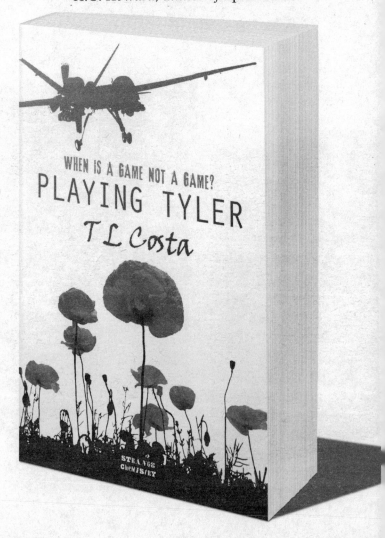

WHEN IS A GAME NOT A GAME?
PLAYING TYLER
T L Costa

STRANGE
CHEMISTRY

EXPERIMENTING WITH YOUR IMAGINATION

"Exciting, funny, clever, scary, captivating, and – most importantly – really, really awesome."
James Smythe, author of The Testimony